Cast of Characters

George Arrow. A bachelor of independent means  weak heart and so goes to Crane's Court to live out

John Burden. The odious new owner of Crane's Co. ing enemies of all its staff and guests. Well, almost a

Eleanor Keane. The ambitious officer manager, who ... to marry Burden.

Joe Flynn. The hotel porter, who scoffs at Eleanor's "notions."

Professor Daly. An elderly professor of English literature with a secret.

Barbara Henry. An attractive widow, the niece of the hotel's previous owner.

Mrs. Robinson. Dubbed the "Queen-bee," she knows how to get what she wants.

Mrs. Waters. Another old harridan, one of the Queen-bee's nastier disciples.

Colonel Waters. He was never really a colonel but he is certainly henpecked.

Major Dunlea. A convicted murder, but nobody can blame him for what he did.

Mr. Heaslip. A middle-aged birdwatcher who prefers to keep to himself.

Canon Poole, Mrs. Ryan, Mrs. Mullery, Mrs. Devlin. All quite old, and all ardent disciples of the Queen-bee.

Maggie. The housemaid at the hotel who objects to Burden's unwelcome advances.

Ned Conway. The chauffeur, who is betrothed to Maggie.

Esther. A middle-aged waitress who has a falling-out with the Queen-bee.

Mrs. Fennell. Very old and not quite right in the head, she's lives in a small cottage on the grounds where she keeps a dozen cats and tends to her luxuriant flower garden.

Bridget. Her faithful maid and caregiver.

Batt O'Reilly. The talented but volatile head chef, a hot-tempered Corkman.

Fitzpatrick. The long-suffering head waiter.

Inspector Mike Kenny, of the Irish Guard, and an old friend of Professor Daly's.

Sergeant Colm MacDonagh. An Aran Islander who could "make the stones talk."

Martin Hogan. A conniving reporter, ever a thorn in Kenny's side.

Horace Robinson. Mrs. Robinson's snakelike "literary" son, for whom she has plans.

Cooney. An amorous dentist who's besotted with Barbara, to George's disgust.

Dr. Morgan. An eminent cardiologist who is staying briefly at Crane's Court.

Mysteries by
Eilís Dillon

Death at Crane's Court (1953)
Sent to His Account (1954)
Death in the Quadrangle (1956)

Death at Crane's Court

By Eilís Dillon

Introduction by Cormac Ó Cuilleanáin

Rue Morgue Press
Boulder / Lyons

Death at Crane's Court
© 1953 by The Estate of Eilís Dillon
New material
© 2009 by The Rue Morgue Press
87 Lone Tree Lane
Lyons CO 80540

www.ruemorguepress.com
800-699-6214

ISBN:978-1-60187-040-7

Printed by
Johnson Printing

PRINTED IN THE UNITED STATES OF AMERICA

Introduction

My mother, Eilís Dillon, was the author of fifty books, ranging from children's stories to historical novels. She wrote and translated poetry, and had two plays produced by the Abbey Theatre company. Her books have been translated into fifteen languages. Fifteen years after her death, several are still in print.

She enjoyed working within the discipline of genres, while taking liberties with their conventions. Although her first forays into adult fiction were cast in the detective story mould, they are more concerned with character than with the intricacies of plot. The three mysteries from the 1950s, *Death at Crane's Court*, *Sent to His Account*, *Death in the Quadrangle*, enjoyed a good level of success and received extremely positive reviews. All three were reprinted in America; there were translations into Dutch, French and Italian. So why, given this promising start, do we not have a dozen Eilís Dillon detective stories?

A certain creative restlessness, visible at several points in her career, prompted her to move on, abandoning crime fiction in favour of ironic literary novels appealing to a sophisticated minority readership. In the 1970s, she changed again to write well-researched historical novels, dealing with patriotic themes in a style that combined elements of literary and popular fiction. That earned her a wide international readership, international critical acclaim, and the disapproval of some local book reviewers. Some of her later books tended to undermine or at least question the world-view of her first historical novels, and she also returned to other genres. Her last writing project was a novel which began to expose some of the tensions of her own early life. She fell ill while writing this novel, and instead of finishing it she devoted her last remaining energies to assembling and editing the academic essays that her second husband, Vivian Mercier, had left unfinished at his death in 1989. The resulting book, *Modern Irish Literature: Sources and Founders*, appeared from the Clarendon Press, Oxford in the year of her own death, 1994.

It is a pity that her last novel remained unfinished, as her early experiences had been interesting and formative. A non-fiction work, *Inside Ireland*, had touched on some of these matters, but without the dark irony that enlivened her fiction.

Even before her birth in 1920, Eilís's family had been deeply involved in the traumatic events of the Irish War of Independence. Her maternal uncle Joseph Mary Plunkett, a talented poet, was one of the seven signatories of the Proclamation of Independence, and was executed by firing squad following the rebellion of Easter Week 1916. The summary execution of the leaders of that rebellion proved to be a disastrous act of stupidity on the part of the British authorities, conferring the status of martyrs on a motley crew of amateur revolutionaries, and ensuring the secession of most of Ireland from the United Kingdom some years later. That secession provoked a formal split between Northern Ireland, with its Unionist majority wishing to retain British rule, and a mostly Catholic Irish Free State which promptly fell into a brief but bitter civil war followed by decades of economic and political stagnation. Both of Eilís's parents had spent time in jail. Her father, a professor of chemistry in Galway, left control of the household to her mother, Geraldine Plunkett Dillon, a woman of immense creative drive coupled with a powerful personality. Geraldine's vivid and opinionated memoirs, *All in the Blood*, were edited posthumously by my cousin Honor O Brolchain and published in 2006.

Geraldine loved some of her children unconditionally, but took every opportunity to marginalize Eilís, even in very old age. Back in the 1920s, another trauma struck the family when one of the six children died in early childhood. Also, there was rivalry between Eilís and her two older sisters. One did a law degree, one studied medicine. Despite a brilliant school career, Eilís was not channelled towards further study. This always bothered her, and left her with a tendency to marry professors (not such a bad choice, really).

When she reached the age when her sisters had gone to university, Eilís had been apprenticed to the hotel trade. Or so her mother described the arrangement. In reality, her duties as a trainee involved emptying chamberpots, collecting used condoms from tangled bedsheets, and having her handbag searched at the end of the working day to ensure that she was not stealing her employer's property. Finding this unsatisfactory, she got a summer job running the catering side of an Irish-language summer school, where she was spotted by a visiting academic, almost eighteen years her senior. This was my father, Cormac Ó Cuilleanáin, then a lecturer in Irish at University College Cork, whose curriculum vitae included a spell in jail during the Irish Civil War. They were married in 1940, shortly after her twentieth birthday. It was a quiet wedding because her uncle Jack Plunkett—the Plunketts were still capable of stirring up political trouble—was on hunger strike and expected to die. She went to live in Cork. In the midst of having three children, fitting into the patterns of respectable provincial life (which she found uncomfortable), and taking on the running of a large student hostel, she launched her writing career.

Still in her twenties, she started with books for small children, in the Irish language and published by a Government-owned company. On switching to English, she found London publishers more than willing to take her work. *Midsummer Magic*, a children's book, was published by Macmillan in 1950. Two years later Faber & Faber produced *The Lost Island*, first in a long series of beautifully written adventure stories for older children or adolescents; along with *The Island of Horses* (1956), *The Lost Island* remained in print more than half a century later, in the New York Review collection of children's classics. Faber were also the publishers of her three detective stories, and of her first three literary novels. By the time the last of these appeared she was living in Rome, returning to Dublin only when my father's rapidly declining health made life in Italy untenable. He died in 1970. With remarkable strength and courage she kept on working, publishing her biggest-selling book (the historical novel *Across the Bitter Sea*) in 1973. In 1975 she married the scholar and critic Vivian Mercier, Professor of English in Boulder, Colorado. When he moved to Santa Barbara she spent her winters there, returning in summertime to remark, irritatingly, that the Irish climate, as far as she could see, is not at all cold and rainy – is in fact far more pleasant than people say. She was very much involved in Irish cultural life, serving on the Arts Council and working within various writers' organizations. An increasingly free spirit and dispenser of wisdom both in public and in private, she remained an affectionate critic but also a sharp defender of Irish life. When she died, John Banville said: "Her books will be a lasting testament to her, as will her work for writers and writing in this country."

Apart from the occasional murder, there is little sense of personal, family or national trauma in the three early detective stories, which present an urbane, lightly comic view of life, sometimes poking gentle fun at the foibles and aspirations of Irish people from a seemingly external vewpoint. These amusing qualities were mentioned by several reviewers, who sprinkled their praise with words like *attractive, agreeable, civilized, lively, colourful, snug, beguiling, refreshing, delightful, entertaining, amiably relaxed.* "Miss Dillon writes with a charmingly light touch", said the *Irish Independent* reviewer of *Death in the Quadrangle*, while the Montreal Star commented, "They'll hate this in Dublin, but this is a fine example of the English detective novel." Strange praise for an Irish nationalist, and yet there is a long-established irony in writers' appropriation of a foreign viewpoint to "see ourselves as others see us". Besides, Eilís loved the English literary tradition and was extremely well read in it, back to Shakespeare. Our house was always full of contemporary international fiction—not particularly mystery books, although I remember G.K. Chesterton, Margery Allingham, Dorothy Sayers. Not Agatha Christie because despite her genius for puzzling, the quality of her writing ruled her out of consideration. Among English writers (by birth or adoption), Eilís particularly admired Evelyn Waugh and T.S. Eliot. From these names one might hazard a guess that a combination of high style, dry wit and Christian culture was the way to win her literary affections. British children's books were also our daily fare, from classic writers like John Buchan and Robert Louis Stevenson (her own children's books have been compared to RLS) to newer authors like William Mayne. She was also hugely though selectively fond of certain Irish writing: the poetry of Yeats, the fiction of James Stephens, the plays of Samuel Beckett and the astonishing flights of fancy of Flann O'Brien. There were Penguin classics, including racy dead foreigners like Maupassant and Apuleius, bought quickly before the Irish censorship board got to them and had them banned. She had whole collections of books by John Masefield, Baron Corvo, Willa Cather. She was well versed in folklore and fairy tales; she believed strongly that the bloodiness of traditional stories should not be airbrushed out of children's books. As time went by she read little crime fiction, possibly under the apprehension that it was not real literature. I completely failed to persuade her to read Ross Macdonald (whom she had actually met when she was living in Santa Barbara, California). With great difficulty I got her to try John le Carré's *A Perfect Spy*, and she was surprised to discover that it was a splendid novel. But she never felt the need to read another word of le Carré. Her sights were set on other things, and I suspect that her reading was largely a function of what she wanted to write.

In 1987, recovering from her first cancer operation, she did make one last foray into crime writing. The novel she drafted, *Journey to No End*, is set in an international conference centre, and introduces an intriguing cast of distinguished characters, one of whom gets murdered. Eilís herself had enjoyed a residency at Villa Serbelloni, the Rockefeller Center, beside Lake Como in northern Italy. By all accounts, staying there is like dying and going to heaven. But *Journey to No End*, most unusually for her, remains unpublished. Perhaps it was out of its time. Perhaps it needs a little revision. I might try doing that some day.

Her three detective stories from the 1950s, on the other hand, are very much of their time, not only in their subject matter but also in the sardonic style, the light touch, the slightly satirical stance adopted by the author. "Miss Dillon's eye is beautifully sharp, her skill impeccable, and her detachment absolute," wrote a reviewer in the *Belfast Newsletter*. Despite the arm's-length pose, however, some elements of the books are painfully close to her own experience. In *Death at Crane's Court*, her immersion in the lower reaches of the hotel trade may have provided models for the sleazy hotel proprietor ("a particularly revolting spivvish sadist", said the *Observer*), for the mad hotel guests, for the anxious intrigues of the hotel staff. Her husband's exalted position as Warden of the Honan Hostel at University College Cork had landed Eilís, as a young married woman, with responsibility for feeding forty people; she was well capable of taking charge, but the personnel management of her domestic staff was not the most agreeable part of the job. Yet the book also betrays a certain affection for the old-fashioned Irish country hotel. Crane's Court is partly based on a establishment called 'The Hydro' near Blarney in County Cork, where they did wonderful afternoon tea, with potato cakes. Like Crane's Court, it was full of old people. Eilís's beloved brother, Eoin Dillon, was a distinguished hotelier who managed iconic Irish hotels such as Renvyle House in Connemara, the Imperial in Cork, and the Shelbourne and Gresham Hotels in Dublin. Eoin always claimed that hotels are a subdivision of the theatre business.

Sent to His Account, the second novel, is perhaps the best plotted of the three, with some nice turns and puzzles. Atmospheric and poetic, it conveys a fine sense of life in a country house. Writing in *The Lady*, an august London weekly magazine whose readership is hinted at in its title, Edith Shackleton noted that "Miss Dillon presents modern Ireland realistically. She does not turn all the tenantry into Abbey Theatre characters and allows a Big House, for once in fiction, to be properly run." But behind the ample prose and comforting imagery lie some painful episodes from the author's life. The first remembered home of her childhood was Dangan, a beautiful country house outside Galway. As she writes in *Inside Ireland*, "A stream with kingfishers ran just beyond the gravel sweep before the door. On windy days the song of the pines made heavenly music. Distant dogs barked and were answered by ours." But her parents had taken on a debt to acquire this property. When they ran into financial difficulties the bank foreclosed, and the idyll was lost. This first home lends its name to the country house in *Sent to His Account*, which at the start of the book is suddenly inherited by what Maurice Richardson, writing in the *Observer*, called a "nice little rat-poor middle-aged person". And questions of inheritance were a live issue in Eilís's family. Her mother Geraldine Plunkett, whose grandfather had been a hugely successful builder in Victorian Dublin, eventually came to control valuable house property which she distributed to her favourite children, but not to Eilís. This did not cause particular economic hardship; Eilís's husbands earned good money, and over the years she built up a steady income from her literary work. It was not even that she lacked inherited property. Her grandmother Countess Plunkett (whom her mother passionately hated) gave Eilís a house on Dublin's Haddington Road when she got married, and an uncle left her another Georgian house in his will. So she was not, in the event, economically damaged by her mother's discrimination. What hurt was the emotional exclusion.

Death in the Quadrangle also deals with an environment that she knew well from family lore, and from her own experience: life and death in a small university. At the time she wrote it, she was living on the campus of University College Cork, under the hyperactive presidency of Alfred O'Rahilly. In the novel, the overbearing egotism of academics is used to fine comic effect. Some of her husband's colleagues in Cork suspected that episodes in the book referred to them, but she was reassured to learn that professors from foreign universities also wondered how she had come to know of the eccentric goings-on in their institutions. Clearly, she had tapped into an international pattern of bad behaviour. Her invention of King's College Dublin, situated in the splendour of the Phoenix Park, was echoed fifty years later by my own crime novel, *The Grounds* (2006), set in the same institution. This later novel echoes a sadder time when Irish academic life has been distorted by pea-brained bureaucratic interference and grand managerial fantasies; *Death in the Quandrangle* had presented a less constricted, more amusing world.

These three books are best read in sequence. They may be, as Anthony Boucher remarked of *Death at Crane's Court*, "long on charm and short on detection", but they are written with real literary skill and create a composite picture of the stagnant but beautiful Ireland of more than fifty years ago. An Irish reviewer praised the same book for its "County Galway background of such seductive peace as to make one wish to pack one's bags and take the next train to the West".

Cormac Ó Cuilleanáin, Dublin, 2009

Cormac Ó Cuilleanáin is Associate Professor of Italian at Trinity College Dublin. As Cormac Millar he is the author of two crime novels published by Penguin Ireland. For more information on Eilís Dillon and her works, see www.eilisdillon.com.

Death at Crane's Court

1

Although George Arrow was an experienced traveler, he began to flutter over his luggage quite soon after the train left the station. He took his overcoat off the rack, folded it and laid his hat on top, then unfolded the coat again to search futilely in its pockets for his gloves. He reached up to take down his suitcase, and then dropped his arms suddenly as he remembered. He sat down slowly, deliberately, and held his hands together on his knees. It seemed extraordinary that the recollection should each time send the same sick little shock through every part of him. He had not been warned about this, the worst aspect of his newfound disability. It was three months since he had sat opposite the doctor in his shiny room and heard that he was going to die.

His life had been easy until now. He had traveled through all the safest countries of Europe, pleased with everything he saw. At home in Dublin he had collected books and worked on charitable committees, and had given away part of his comfortable income every year to anyone who looked more in need of money than himself.

George was that mixture of caution and romanticism which is often the material of a predestined bachelor. For him, all the beautiful ladies floated above the ground, their feet on a soft pink cloud. Since they were so high up, they usually looked over his head. He never noticed the ugly ones, though most of them noticed him, for George was thin and fair and clean looking, and of a good height.

He might never have visited the doctor if he had not fainted in a bookshop one day. It had taken him a few minutes to recover, and though he insisted on walking home, the manager of the shop advised him to see a doctor. George knew no doctors, though he supposed that most of the Joycean medical students whom he remembered at the university had now become respectable, striped-trousered gentlemen with brass plates and motorcars. Especially he remembered Mick Moore, whose wondering admiration had flattered George's expositions on trends in modern philosophy. Back in his Merrion Square flat, his head swimming, he looked up the Moores in the telephone directory, and found that Mick was established across the Square. Without further deliberation, he arranged an appointment for the next afternoon.

Sitting opposite him, George was silently amused to observe how Mick had been, as it were, planed down to the shape and size of a successful doctor. Even his hair, though he was not yet thirty-five, had obligingly receded from his forehead, and had a discreet sprinkling of silver. He wore a look of mysterious solemnity as he tapped and listened and squeezed bulbs, and at last leaned back in his chair and announced his verdict. Then he suggested that George should go to live at Crane's Court.

"But isn't that a sort of nursing home?" George asked. "Surely there is no need to carry things to extremes."

Mick said:

"They call it a spa, though I never heard of any mineral springs there. It's just a good hotel, where old people and invalids are welcome. They do you very well there, I'm told."

And he had explained once more that George's heart was in such a precarious condition that he must never again exert himself, never travel, never lift heavy things, never stay up late, never get up early, never get excited, never argue. George tried to ask intelligent questions, to accustom himself to this extraordinary new way of life. Poor Mick was distressed. He sweated a little about the forehead and seemed about to burst into tears. George got up and said:

"All right, old man. Don't worry about me. I'll go to Crane's Court. It will be as easy to live there as anywhere else."

And he had gone home.

He meant, of course, that it would be as easy to die at Crane's Court as anywhere else.

He had no near relatives. He made his will in favor of a second cousin whom he had never seen, but who had a reputation for oddity, principally because he wore a two-foot beard and wrote savage but incomprehensible poems. George liked the sound of him. He put his house property into the hands of his solicitor. Then he gave up his flat in Dublin and put himself into the train for Galway, where Crane's Court was, in a state of immense loneliness.

He was by now obsessed with the idea that he was making his last journey. It was like something out of an old-fashioned play about dying peasants, he thought. "I'm afraid, Maggie, the time has come for me to make me last journey!" But even this reflection failed to cheer him, for more than a moment. He was so depressingly certain that it *was* his last journey.

He went on to think of Dublin's fair city that he would never see again. This reminded him to feel pleased that he had seen most of the capitals of Europe before Mick had found out about his heart. And Mick had said that Crane's Court was a good hotel, and that he wished he could go there himself to end his days. To end his days—his last journey—it was going to be difficult to live an ordinary life now, with these two phrases continually drumming in his ears. And still they fascinated him, so that he must return to them again and again, with a sort of pleasurable trepidation. He detected in himself too the sort of inner excitement that always goes with new places and new beginnings. And, after all, Mick had said that he would probably live for years, if he learned to look after himself. . . .

At this point in his reflections, George began to notice the only other occupant of the carriage. He was a man of about George's own age, which was thirty-six, dressed in a beige-colored gabardine suit, with white socks and suede shoes. He wore his hair rather long, and his mustache was so small that one had to look twice to see it at all. His eyelids drooped, as if they were always on the watch to hide the expression in his eyes. Even along the length of the carriage, he emanated mixed odors of scent and whiskey. He was occupied in reading a book with a brown-paper cover, turning the pages with sweaty hands and leering at the contents now and then.

As George watched him, he shut the book suddenly and looked up. He had very bright brown eyes that stared suspiciously for a moment before he said:

"They must have a damned donkey pulling this train."

"It picks up speed later on," said George, amused.

Glad of the diversion, he found himself chatting with the stranger, and presently accepting an invitation to visit the bar. They lurched along the corridor, and sat at one of the brown, baize-topped tables.

"My name is Burden," said the man. "John Burden." He jerked the ash off his cigarette nervously. "Your name is Arrow. I read it on your luggage labels. Rather an unusual name, if you don't mind my saying so."

"Yes," said George dryly.

Mr. Burden moved restlessly.

"You know Galway?"

"Not very well. I've been there several times, but I've never stayed long."

"What sort of place is it?"

"Very interesting old town. It has a thirteenth-century cathedral, and a variety of relics of the Twelve Tribes who set up in business there seven hundred years ago."

"Sounds sleepy," said Mr. Burden. "Any nice girls there?"

George almost said, "Not your sort."

But instead he laughed in what he hoped was an understanding way, and said, "I'm going to live in Galway now, for the first time."

He was surprised at himself for giving away this information. It was not his habit to confide in anyone, least of all to repulsive young men in railway carriages. Again he warned himself that no one, *no one* was to be told of his illness. He had not even told his solicitor, and he had warned Mick Moore not to inquire about his health if they should meet by chance.

"I'm going to live in Galway too," said Mr. Burden. "I've been left a business there. I can't say I'm looking forward to the prospect of living in a town with a cathedral and twelve tribes seven hundred years old."

"There are other things too," said George patiently. "There is the University College, and an art club, and an immense hinterland of the most beautiful scenery in the world."

"It doesn't sound my style. Still beggars can't be choosers."

When the waiter came, Mr. Burden ordered a double brandy. He raised his eyebrows at George's request for a cider, but George affected not to notice. Presently the drinks came, and Mr. Burden took a long draught with the accustomed aplomb of an old maid drinking tea. George said:

"But if you have a business to attend to in Galway, you won't find it dull. You'll make friends. . . ."

He broke off, because he could not imagine Mr. Burden making friends.

"Between ourselves," said Mr. Burden, "I was damned glad to hear that the old boy had left me the business. I thought he would leave it to a cousin of mine, a worthy widow with a child, who camped herself there on the spot to make sure she'd collect. Her plot didn't work, though."

He pulled hard at his cigarette.

"The old boy was our uncle. I can't think why he didn't leave it to her. Saw too much of her, I suppose. She was always about the place. Never went away for a holiday. And she's still there. That's the only snag. What would you do, if you were in my place?"

"I beg your pardon?" said George.

"I said, what would you do in that situation? Would you throw her out on her ear, child and all, or would you keep her there for the rest of her life, sucking your blood, managing your affairs, poisoning your girlfriends so that you'd never marry, making her child bring you your slippers so that you would leave him your money? What would you do?"

"I hardly know," said George faintly.

He thought that Mr. Burden felt well able to deal with his own problems, and that he was not really seeking advice. This conclusion was borne out by his next words.

"Of course it's no use deciding what to do until I've seen the lady in action. It might be rather fun to lead her on, let her crawl about licking my noble boots and so on, until we're both about ninety—well, she would be a bit younger—and then leave the whole shooting match to the Cats' Home. I'd enjoy that."

"But you would not be there to enjoy it," said George, pointing out the obvious flaw.

"I'd watch from heaven," said Mr. Burden with a guffaw.

George found nothing to say to fill the pause that followed. Mr. Burden was cogitating.

"I can think of various ways to annoy her," he said, with the expression of an unpleasant small boy.

George contented himself with saying mildly:

"Perhaps she will be as useful to you as she must have been to your uncle."

"That is true," said Mr. Burden. "I'll wait and see. I'm good at that. I usually find that it pays."

Again George was lost for a comment. Mr. Burden seemed not to notice. He went on after a moment:

"It's a queer thing suddenly to find oneself rich."

"I suppose so," said George, glad that the subject had changed a little.

"Very queer. It opens up so many possibilities. It gives one an immense feeling of power. Do you know, it almost makes one *feel* bigger!"

"Yes, people say that it does."

"I've found that out these last few weeks. A man's name is in the papers a lot, a man like Winston Churchill, or John D. Rockefeller. Then one day you see him, and you say, 'Is that all?' You find you have expected him to be twice the size of an ordinary man. Now I know that though he looks the same, he *feels* bigger. And that is the important thing, don't you think?"

"No doubt," said George.

"I've always wanted to have plenty of money," Mr. Burden went on after a pause. "I once tried to get some out of my uncle but it was no use. He was a peculiar man, my uncle."

George did not doubt that he was, since he was related to the man opposite. He found that he had become interested in Mr. Burden's strange mind and inconvenient relations. Mr. Burden was saying:

"Yes, I'm looking forward to having a business of my own. I'll be able to do what I like with it, change it all, make everyone do things my way."

"It's not always a good thing to abandon tradition," said George.

"Oh, I won't make any mistakes," said Mr. Burden confidently. "I used to be an accountant, you see."

"Yes," thought George, "adding up immense sums of other people's money, watching profits pile up, calculating dividends—it must have been an excruciating life for him. And with no opportunity of dipping his hand in the till."

George was surprised at this unbidden thought. He had had no indication that the man was not as honest as Socrates. But he certainly looked a scoundrel, and talked like one, and he seemed to have the forthright simplicity of an old-fashioned pirate. It occurred to George that it was strange how often he had found himself the recipient of the confidences of strangers. Perhaps it was because it was obvious that he would never interrupt with confidences of his own.

Presently Mr. Burden was pressing George to have another drink, but the cider was coldly sour, and George would not, though he did not wish to appear unfriendly. As he got up to go Mr. Burden said:

"I'll stay here for a while, if you don't mind."

Back in his carriage, George found that the companionship had done him good. He knew now that he could no longer be a solitary. He would play chess, perhaps, sitting silently opposite a silent fellow man, enjoying his proximity without the necessity for chatter. Or perhaps he could brush up his violin playing and join an amateur orchestra, where only the conductor need speak. Cheered by these prospects, he looked out of the window. Here the train ran along by the canal that connects the Liffey with the Shannon, and the smooth water reflected the green of its banks in a still pattern. A family of swans paddled along, the cygnets like long-necked brown ducks and the parents a fantastic perfection of white and black and orange. Farther on a tall blue-gray heron contemplated his shivering reflection among the reeds. George opened his book, which was called *Difficulties in Life*, and began to read.

It was a long time before Mr. Burden came back from the bar. They could see the sea now, and flat fields with limestone walls, and away off in the distance the high blue hills of Clare. Mr. Burden stared at the scene with a jaundiced eye, and made no further effort at conversation.

Presently the train crossed a crazy little bridge over an inlet of the sea, and now they could see the houses of the town ahead, dark gray stone and purple roofs. The late September sun made the windows of the houses blaze with gold. Inside the station it was dark like a cave.

Mr. Burden stood up and began to swing down his suitcases from the rack. George went to the window and signaled to a porter, hating his incapacity to look after himself, and hoping that Mr. Burden would not notice. Mr. Burden did. He said:

"I have some breakable stuff in one of my bags—I don't want those porter fellows to smash it up."

"Good God!" thought George. "The poor man thinks he has made a slip—a gentleman with money calls a porter!"

Amused, he followed his porter on to the platform. Mr. Burden was close behind, now provided with a porter of his own, whom he was instructing about the care of his suitcases. They all reached the outer steps of the station together, to find that the taxis were gone.

However, a tired-looking, middle-aged man in a chauffeur's uniform, who had been standing at ease beside an immensely long American car, came forward and said:

"Are you for Crane's Court, sir?"

"Yes," said both George and Mr. Burden together, and paused to look at each other with new interest.

The chauffeur turned to George.

"Are you Mr. Burden, sir?"

"My name is Arrow," said George.

"Oh, then you're Mr. Burden, sir," said the chauffeur, turning this time in the right direction, and with quickly controlled disappointment just showing in his face. "You're very welcome, sir."

George wondered why he was not welcome too. The chauffeur turned an agitated face to him.

"You'll excuse me, sir. I'm a bit confused."

He put them both into the car.

When they were moving silently through the narrow main street of the town, George experienced a feeling of uneasiness.

"Are you going to stay at Crane's Court while you look about for a place of your own?" he asked.

His fears were confirmed when Mr. Burden replied:

"I'm going to live at Crane's Court. It belongs to me now."

The chauffeur wriggled his shoulders and then sat up more straight than ever.

They drove through a wide marketplace on the quays, across a bridge over the swirling, rolling, white-waved river, through the settlement of new cottages that had replaced the unsanitary picturesqueness of the Claddagh, and so out along the windy road by the sea. Presently they passed hotels and boardinghouses, and the long promenade above the beaches at Salthill, and there was the whole blue bay, stretching away and away for thirty miles, with its fantastic back-cloth of blue mountains.

Mr. Burden brightened when they passed the golf links.

"Not that I'm much of a fresh-air man," he said unnecessarily. "But where there's golf links there's girls, and they don't always go for the fresh air either."

George rather thought he was going to be disappointed in the Galway girls. He wondered where Mr. Burden had been living up to now.

Some distance beyond the golf links, a gateway opened on the left on to a long winding driveway among trees. The gate-lodge was faked to resemble an English half-timbered cottage, and the blazing flower garden was fenced with wooden rails with the bark on. As the driveway descended towards the hotel, they passed various stone centaurs, sphinxes, nymphs and mermaids, who sprouted without any apparent order among the long grass. There were also two or three cottages opening on to the drive, all with the same coy air of fake and the same debauch of flowers in their little gardens. In one of the gardens an old lady was prodding the ground with a trowel. She straightened up to watch them pass and waved her hand amiably before going back to her gardening.

A moment later they rounded a corner and there before them was the hotel. It was an impressive sight. The central building, which was the original Crane's Court, had been built in the eighteenth century, with beautifully proportioned long windows and a wide graveled terrace. Later, when it became a hotel, long wings had been thrown out—how well the phrase suited them!—on either side, and other wings had been added to these at right angles, so that there was no logical plan that one could see. There was a wooden clock-tower, painted white and with its clock in good order, and a weather vane on top. The whole of the building, except the clock-tower, was covered in Virginia creeper, now turning red. The car pulled up at the front door, which was at the top of a shallow flight of steps. Beyond the door there was a glass-fronted veranda where a number of people could be seen sitting at small tables drinking tea. Their faces were all turned towards the front door, all the necks craned slightly forward, all the cups held in mid-air, as they watched.

From the terrace a flight of steps led to a croquet ground, which was neatly fenced around with a low white trellis. Below that there was another gravel path and then a smooth green park with occasional trees. And beyond there was the intensely blue water of the bay. For the first time in weeks, George felt complete peace flow through him. It was like a piece of music that begins so softly that you cannot tell at what moment you first heard it. There was protection here, the same feeling of security and order that he had not had since he had left the nursery. For a moment he wished he were old, old and sleepy, so that he could savor this return to the full.

His new mood persisted while he followed Mr. Burden into the hall. It was as if he had crossed an invisible boundary into a country where he could not be troubled, though his intelligence might clamor for a hearing. Or like a sedative injection, when one enjoys the relief from pain with the consciousness of having evaded something successfully. George wondered how long the sedative effect would last.

Inside the hall, Crane's Court began to look more like a hotel. There was an office, with a thin, big-boned girl in a black dress making up accounts. Here George and Mr. Burden parted company, but not before Mr. Burden had found time to say anxiously:

"I hope I can rely on you to forget my remarks in the train. I've never learned to keep my mouth shut."

"Of course," said George.

And Mr. Burden went off looking relieved. But George knew it was asking too much to expect him to forget what he had heard. He knew that his interest in Crane's Court had doubled since he had discovered that it belonged to Mr.

Burden. He hoped that by now he had achieved enough discretion to conceal his interest, and not to point like a gun-dog whenever the object of it came into the room.

The chauffeur had carried Mr. Burden's suitcases through the hall, and around the corner. When their owner had followed him out of sight the thin girl in the office leaned forward and offered George the hotel register to sign. She breathed into his ear until he had finished, and then she said:

"Were you on the train with Mr. Burden, sir? What's he like?"

She looked up at him through long black lashes, and then poked her head out through the little window of her office to look along the hall.

"To tell the truth, Mr. Arrow, I don't like the looks of him at all. I was as disappointed when I found out it was him and not you—"

She broke off, and George said hurriedly:

"I'm sure you'll find him all right."

"He hasn't the manners of a dog," said the girl. "Not as much as 'Good evening.' His uncle was a very different class of a man. Oh, Mr. Murray was lovely!"

Her eyes were turned up as she said this, but there was a sour snap in her voice. George regarded her more alertly now, and with considerably less pity. She was handsome in a hungry, big-boned way, and her smoke-blue eyes seemed to George to be full of restless discontent.

"He's dead three months already," the girl said mournfully, "and still I expect every minute to see him turn that corner and walk down the hall to me. Oh, it was the sorry day for us all that he died!"

"Oh, well," said George uncomfortably, "I'm sure you will be just as fond of Mr. Burden in no time."

She gave him a long look, and then leaned forward briskly and rang the bell on her desk. A young man in porter's uniform appeared. She said:

"Number forty-six, Joe."

"This way, sir," said Joe, lifting George's suitcases and starting up the hall.

George followed him, after an awkward salutation to the girl, who had turned back to her accounts.

His room was on the ground floor. Mick, who had booked it for him, had seen to that. Again he remembered his infirmity, with the familiar shudder. And still it was hard to remember it all the time. One cannot for long remain suspended in a state of horror.

Joe laid the suitcases on some racks between the long windows, and turned to go. George said:

"What is the name of the young lady in the office?"

Joe pulled an excruciatingly genteel face and said:

"That's Miss Keane, sir. Miss *Eleanor* Keane, sir."

He dropped a curtsey at her Christian name, and said in his normal voice, savagely:

"Ah, that one is daft. Full of high notions, sir, like the goats in Kerry. Don't mind that one at all. If you want to know anything, come to me."

"Thank you, Joe," said George gravely.

"You ought to go out now and have your tea on the veranda," Joe went on. "You saw it—that glassy place by the door coming in. I'll show you if you get lost." With his hand on the doorknob he paused. "Do you mind me asking, what kind is the new fellow?"

"He's all right," said George. "You'll get along with him."

"Thank you, sir," said Joe with an appreciative grin, and vanished.

George went over to the windows to look out. His room was on the graveled terrace facing the sea. He could see Black Head and the mouth of the bay, and on the horizon the faintest curving line where the Aran Islands were. Now it was all bland blue sea and pearly blue haze. Later it would be green and wild and terrible. But he must not let it excite him then. He must not fling up the window and go roaring out into the storm to wrestle with the wind and race the mad green waves. He turned back with a sigh.

His room was delightful. There was a moss-green carpet and green and gold curtains. There was an open fireplace with even now a fire of hard black turf on the hearth. There were two armchairs, and a good reading lamp, and an empty bookcase, waiting to receive whatever cargo he might wish. These things always seem more important, he thought, with the coming of winter. There is the instinct to gather in nuts, to wrap one's long feathery tail about one, and to hibernate.

George stood for a few minutes cogitating. He had just told two people that Mr. Burden was "all right." And if ever anyone was all wrong, surely it was he. Still, what could these simple souls expect him to say? That their new employer was vengeful, had a low taste in books, was not a gentleman, possessed, George suspected, a prying mind and a lust for power, destroyer of all the virtues? What did they expect? Convention allowed no reply but the one he had given. And they were all free. If they did not like Mr. Burden they could go somewhere else. But then George wondered if anyone who had ever come to live at Crane's Court willingly left it again. It enclosed one, it made one feel that no other part of the world was important. It would be interesting to find out if even hotel servants, who are migratory by instinct, folded their wings at Crane's Court. That would surely prove that its spell was as potent as it seemed to be.

He washed his hands meditatively at the basin, and then he left his room to look for the door into the glassy veranda, where Joe had said there was tea.

2

The veranda was still full of people when George reached the glass door and looked in. He was not a timid man, but he quailed a little before the barrage of eyes turned towards him. It was like looking into an aquarium full of ancient carp, he thought. For most of the people were old, and they all stared with the intense single-mindedness and lack of embarrassment of the aged.

He opened the door, marched in and looked about him, a little truculently, for a vacant table. There was dead silence. There was no vacant table. The old people were grinning fiendishly now, and one or two had begun to comment audibly, though favorably, on his appearance. His knees wavered. Then a voice beside him said, in an undertone:

"You had better sit here with me, Mr. Arrow, till the excitement dies down."

He looked sharply to his left and saw that the nearest table to him had only one occupant. He dropped into the other chair, got out his handkerchief and positively mopped his brow, though he tried to do it surreptitiously. The man opposite regarded him with amusement.

"You will be all right now," he said. "Once you are sitting down they will go on with their tea."

He was a round-faced, chubby little man, with snow-white hair standing up on top of his head as if it were blown by a perpetual wind. He wore a scarlet rosebud in the buttonhole of his perfectly pressed gray suit. His hands pouring out tea were soft and smooth, and they were continually lifting a little at the wrists as if to step back and admire their work. Gradually George began to recover and laugh at himself for his nervousness. His companion, who had introduced himself as Professor Daly, was sympathetic.

"The old are sometimes very terrifying," he said. "I know why, because I'm old myself. It's a return to the direct simplicity of childhood, but now they are free from childhood's discipline. They stare unrestricted, and gobble their food, and ask personal questions, and they make loud personal remarks. Just turn your chair a little and observe them."

But George laughingly refused to do this until he had been strengthened by his tea. Then, by pushing his chair in a half-turn, he found that he could look down the length of the room.

It was paneled in old oak along one wall, and the other long wall was composed entirely of glass, through which one could look out on the terrace and the bay. There was little furniture apart from the tables and chairs. The whole room was dominated by an immense marble bust of a man draped in what looked like the upper part of a Roman toga. This stood on a pedestal at the end of the room, between a pair of miniature brass cannon.

"That is Sir Rodney Crane," said Professor Daly. "He built the original house. He packed all the tenants off to America and made a deer park down there by the sea. But the deer all died, for some reason, and everyone said it was a judgment on him. He was a tough egg—just look at his frown and wrinkled lip and sneer of cold command. Author, please!"

"Shelley," said George automatically.

"Good boy," said Professor Daly. "English literature was my subject. Several eminent authors of today got their degrees from me. It saddens me sometimes when I hear how successful they are."

"You think good literature and success can't go together?" asked George.

"Not at all! Jealousy, young man. Plain, unvarnished, old-fashioned jealousy. You see, I was what you might call a carrier of literature. I inspired young men with zeal and industry, I showed them exactly how great literature is created, and then they just went and did it. I was amazed. I tried following my own directions, but it was no use. There was something missing."

"Perhaps you gave up too soon," George suggested.

"No," said the professor sadly. "After all, that was one of my first maxims. I covered acres of paper, quite expensive paper too. I have always hated cheap paper. But it was no use. Perhaps I enjoyed it all too much. I used to tell my students that the most successful writers agree that they would far prefer to break stones for a living. But I enjoyed every minute of it, the power especially, the power I had over my characters. If I made a man fire a gun, he didn't have to take lessons first, nor miss six times in succession. I just said he was a splendid shot, and that was that—he got the bull's-eye every time."

He nodded appreciatively.

"The power—that was it. I tried writing stories about myself, on the same principle. I described myself closely, and ended by saying, 'He was one of the world's great literary men.' But it wasn't the same thing. It gave only momentary satisfaction. Then I studied intensively the kind of novel that is really most successful. Am I boring you?"

"By no means," said George, who had not enjoyed himself so much for months.

"I went into the thing in great detail, and at last I thought I had it. But I was wrong. Though I made my young ladies leap in and out of strange beds with creditable agility, still one could see that their heart was not in it. I made them make lewd speeches, but they sounded like the things people say before their conversion, in a story in a pious monthly. Then I tried the stark stuff—you know, black-browed peasants brooding in grim valleys in the mountains, lunatic squires leaping stallions over cliffs for a wager—but that didn't work either. When I set a horse to jump a cliff, at the last moment the wretched animal always refused. Then I tried a religious novel—always a sure seller. I get indigestion every time I think of it."

"And were none of your novels published?" asked George.

"All of them," said the professor, "But my agent suggested that I write under a woman's name. I was quite glad to, in a way. You see, I know exactly how frightful they are." He leaned forward confidentially and whispered, "I am Rosemary Downes!"

George tried to look as if this meant something to him, but he knew he had failed when Professor Daly said:

"Ah, you never heard of me, I can see, Well, I should be grateful, I suppose. I don't know why I confided in you. It's a dangerous thing to have done, in many ways. I hope you won't tell anyone?"

"Of course not," said George.

"All these good ladies know the works of Rosemary Downes, and admire them very much, so much that I shudder at the prospect of being mobbed by them. I can see them gather round, like white ants round a carcase, to eat off my arms and legs and bring home my waistcoat buttons as souvenirs. For God's sake don't betray me!"

"I won't say a word," said George. "You can count on that."

The little man looked relieved. He went on:

"I try not to look like a university man here—though indeed, no one would connect Rosemary with the university. My fellow-guests think of a university degree as a disgraceful preliminary to the bloodsucking life of the bourgeoisie. A sign, moreover, that a man has to earn his own living. I sometimes wonder why I stay here. But it seems so difficult to go away."

"Yes, I've already felt that," said George.

Professor Daly pointed out an old lady who sat at the far end of the room, surrounded by a little coterie of clucking persons of both sexes, who sipped and cackled like hens.

"That is Mrs. Robinson," he said. "I call her the Queen-bee. She directs major operations, but she never takes part in a foray herself."

"A foray?" said George. "What are you talking about?"

"You'll see," said the professor, a trifle grimly. "Beside her, or rather a little behind her, you will always find Mrs. King. Then the small man with the Van Dyck beard is Colonel Waters (I don't believe he was ever a Colonel) and the thin nosey lady is his wife. She's a major."

"A major?"

"A very suitable description, applied by Maggie, the housemaid who does my room. Means a domineering female. The scraggy old lad beside her is a real major—Major Dunlea. Has some kind of a murky past, I've heard them say, but that might be wishful thinking. The clergyman is Canon Poole, a long-suffering poor fellow who rarely escapes from them. The other ladies are their followers: Mrs. Ryan, Mrs. Mullery, Mrs. Devlin—oh, you'll find out. They live here all the year round, have lived here for years, some of them. Mrs. Robinson and the Waters have been here ten or fifteen years."

"And who is the man in the tweed suit?"

George had taken particular notice of this man since he had come into the room. For one thing, his was the only head that had not turned to stare at George's entrance. He had gone on quietly reading a heavy book, with his back slightly turned towards the door. He was younger than the others, perhaps fifty or a little more, and he had an air of tranquility, and perhaps of self-sufficiency.

"That is Mr. Heaslip," said Professor Daly. "He has only lived here for a year. I enjoy a talk with him sometimes, though on the whole he likes a solitary life. He knows a lot about the bird-life hereabouts, especially seabirds. He goes for long rambles along the coast, and lies on the rocks waiting for birds to settle so that he can examine their beaks and their legs and their various other outcroppings. Then he writes papers about them for the journal of an international ornithological society to which he belongs, and sometimes he gives a lecture to one of the local clubs."

"One wouldn't think this would be a good place for a man who likes a solitary life," said George.

"There's a policy of live-and-let-live about it," said the professor. "We eat together, but apart from that one can usually be as peculiar as one likes in private without arousing any comment. That in itself is an unusual situation. And unlike most hotels, to live here all the year round is to be the most honored guest."

"Yes, I've heard that," said George. "But then I haven't seen anyone except permanent people about. Perhaps it's a bit late in the season for the others."

"Oh, there are plenty of them here still, mostly thin ladies in trousers who spend all day out of doors killing things." He waved a hand vaguely. "You'll see them at dinner. They're not allowed to have tea in here."

"Not allowed?"

Professor Daly chuckled.

"They have it in a back room, a very good room, to be sure, but it looks out on the stables. The Queen-bee said that that would be very nice for them, because they could keep an eye on their horses. They were very angry about it but of course they could do nothing."

"But does Mrs. Robinson have a say in that sort of thing?" asked George, bewildered.

"She certainly does, though she sometimes has to put up quite a fight. She waged war for months about the tea question, but she won in the end. It was

like this. There are several places in the house where you can have tea, but this
is the best of them—magnificent view and so on. But it's not big enough for
everyone, and naturally, being more active, the thin hunting ladies and gentlemen always got here first. By the time the old-timers would have hobbled
along, every chair was squarely filled by a saddle-galled fanny, and the old
people had to hobble off to one of the other rooms. So the Queen-bee complained to the management, but nothing was done. Then she held a meeting
and organized a plan of campaign, with the object of ensuring that the veranda
would be reserved for permanent guests for afternoon tea in saecula. It went
on for months, as I said, and it gradually wore down the opposition." He grinned
reminiscently. "It was most amusing to watch."

"But what did she do?"

"Lots of things. A notice on the door, to begin with, hand-painted by Mrs.
King, with lily-of-the-valley and illuminations, saying, 'Reserved for Permanent Residents.' Mrs. Henry took that down."

"Who is Mrs. Henry?"

"The old man's niece. Does all the dirty work. She'd be a cousin of Mr.
Burden, I suppose. Then there was a notice in every chair saying simply, 'Reserved.' That worked for a couple of days. Oh, I forget half the things. They all
worked for a few days and then broke down."

"And what was the scheme that did not break down?"

"Ah, that was masterly. Really, the woman is a genius. I believe she would
have stopped at nothing. Things developed gradually, until the issue became
the most important thing in the mind of everyone. The casuals were continually being insulted, and the hunters' blood was up. It was a fight to the death.
One day the Queen-bee marshaled her cohorts directly after lunch, and they
all marched in here and sat down. They took out their tatting, or whatever they
had, and chatted genteelly until teatime. When the hunters arrived, they just
looked up politely, and then went on with their tatting. I was here. I wouldn't
have missed it for the world. The hunters showed their teeth, but they were
foiled. It looked like the end."

"But it wasn't?" said George eagerly.

"By no means. Next day, the hunters ran from the dining room on their long
agile limbs and sat in the veranda with *their* tatting until teatime, and it was the
Queen-bee's turn to glare through the door. The hunters were bad at tatting. They
were out of practice. Next morning saw the master-stroke. After breakfast the
Queen-bee moved everyone in here, and here we all sat until teatime."

"You too?"

"Of course. I tell you, I wouldn't have missed it for the world. No one had
any lunch, except those who had been clever enough to bring some bread and
butter from breakfast. We had our tea—and what a tea!—at half-past four, and
then we were free.

"That was the end of the campaign. We had the upper hand because we were prepared to give the time to the thing. We did it for four days, and then the old ladies' doctors began to complain to the management. Their patients were getting no exercise, they said, and they were having no lunch. It was a disgrace. How would the management like to be censured at inquests, they said. The management was poor Mrs. Henry, and she gave in. There was no more to be said. The hunters were banished to the back of the house and the battle was over."

"But I saw no notice on the door as I came in," said George.

"No, there is nothing so pointed as a notice. But if you had been a mere fly-by-night, as we call the people who stay a mere matter of weeks, Esther would have ejected you so firmly that you would never think of trying to come again. Esther is the Queen-bee's man to the back teeth, if she has any."

Esther, George learned, was the middle-aged waitress who was serving tea. He looked at the Queen-bee with renewed respect. She was monumentally built, as are so many redoubtable women. Their girth and weight give them courage, he supposed. Her hair was pale blue, and sat in a dignified spiral on top of her head. Her mouth was firmly turned down at the corners. Her eyes, which darted about without rest, were those of a wicked old drake, brown and penetrating and deadly.

"She's somebody's mother, I suppose," he said distastefully.

"She is, in point of fact. I once pinned my faith on that too, as a reason for her existence, until I saw her son. He's like a weak-kneed cobra, if I make myself plain. He spends Christmas here. You'll see him then."

"I can hardly wait," said George faintly.

Just then the door opened and a young woman came in. All the old ladies said:

"Ah, Mrs. Henry! Come along, my dear, and have your tea. Come along!"

She moved forward slowly, until she came to the Queen-bee's table. George found himself thinking:

"She's afraid of them all. She's like a rabbit among foxes."

She was very tall and slender, with smooth pale gold hair in an intricate arrangement of plaits—just the physical type to appeal to the old ladies. Her regular, delicate features gave an impression of calm competence, but George had seen her frightened eyes for one moment as she stood inside the door. Now he watched her stand with a teacup in her hand, talking to Canon Poole, who was fluttering a little and calling her "Dear lady." She wore some kind of a soft, dark green dress which seemed to make her hair glow with a quiet light. Staring at her, George thought what an odd contrast she made with the human wrack scattered about the room. Perhaps they all felt it, perhaps that was the very reason why they all fussed over her, fed her with cake, forced her to drink tea she did not seem to want. So this was Burden's "widow with a child" that he knew so many ways of persecuting.

"Fine woman, isn't she?" said the professor's voice in his ear. "You'd never think she has an eight-year-old son. A snowy dove trooping with crows. All we old fellows make sheep's eyes at her. You're a bit young, perhaps, to do so with safety."

George found himself getting angry at this free comment, and also at the admission of himself to the fraternity of old crocks. After all, he was only thirty-six. She could be no more than thirty. But then he remembered Mick Moore's voice saying:

"It's not difficult, really. You just act like an old man."

That should be quite easy, George thought bitterly.

Now Mrs. Henry was at his elbow. He got up slowly and took her hand. She was welcoming him, asking about his room, his baggage, hoping he was going to like Crane Court's. Then she was gone.

The old ladies and gentlemen began to get up to go too. Mr. Heaslip closed his book and went out first, with a nod to the professor as he passed. He did not stop to be introduced to George.

"Some other time, when there are not so many people about, you'll meet him," said Professor Daly. "He's a shy man."

It took some time for the old people to disentangle themselves from their chairs. The first to leave, after Mr. Heaslip, were Colonel Waters and his wife. They moved in a sort of stately progress, he holding her elbow, both bowing to right and left until they reached the door. The bellboy in the hall leaped to open it, and they sailed through.

Next came an old lady who wove from side to side of the room, whispering earnestly to herself, and apparently searching the ground for some invisible object. George remembered her as the old lady with the trowel in the garden on the way up the drive.

"Mrs. Fennell," whispered the professor. "She has a sort of chalet in the grounds."

She was upon them, squeezing George's arm convulsively and fixing him with a mad blue eye.

"You must come to visit me. Yes, soon. I'll introduce you to Rodney."

She meandered out of the door, whispering.

"Quite harmless," said the professor. "She's been like that for years. Rodney is Sir Rodney Crane, of course. His ghost inhabits her sitting room."

Another old lady was pouring hot water into her teapot and transferring all the remains of her sandwiches and cakes on to one plate. Then she went out, carrying the plate and the teapot with her.

"Lots of them do that," said the professor, noting George's fascinated gaze. "It must affect the economy of the hotel—there is never anything left over. I suppose many people nibble a little in hotels, and these are either too poor or too parsimonious to buy extra rations."

A nurse came with a wheelchair and removed an old man from the next table. The Queen-bee and her retinue had stood up and were shaking their skirts and brushing the crumbs off their waistcoats according to sex. George and the professor got up to go. George felt glad that he would have time to digest his impressions of this party, and the remarkable saga of the afternoon tea, before he would have to meet them face to face. As they strolled out on to the terrace he said:

"Why are they all so friendly with Mrs. Henry, if she would not allow them to reserve the veranda for themselves? I'd have thought they'd tear her eyes out."

"It was touch and go, but they decided in her favor at last. They realized, of course, that she had to take her orders from the old man."

"Her uncle?"

"Yes, Mr. Murray. He lived here all his life; the place belonged to his father. He never mixed with us, but he used Mrs. Henry as a go-between. She's very good to old people—never talks to them as if they were imbeciles."

"Surely all that wrangling about the veranda was bad for trade?"

"I would have thought so," said Professor Daly. "I've seen irate fly-by-nights pack their bags and march out, swearing to blacken the name of Crane's Court from pole to pole. But presently they all come sneaking back again, trying to look like two other fellows, and trusting—rightly—to the hope that no one will remind them of their parting speeches. You see, there are not many hotels as comfortable as Crane's Court."

"What was this Mr. Murray like? His niece and nephew are so unlike each other—"

The Professor glanced sideways at George.

"I thought so," he said. "I got one glimpse of Mr. Burden. Not my style. Mr. Murray? We never saw him—well, hardly ever. Mrs. Henry used to visit him every morning and hear his views on hotel-keeping, and listen to his grumbles too, I suspect, though she never said so. He had a suite of rooms on the ground floor—I suppose Mr. Burden will have them now. Only one other person had the entree in there. A young woman who works in the office, a Miss Keane. She spent all her free time with him, drove about with him and so on. It used to make the old ladies hop about with fury."

George began to read new meaning into his recent conversation with Miss Keane.

"And when did Mr. Murray die?" he asked, to keep the professor going while his mind followed the possibilities of this new line of thought.

"Three months ago. Rather odd, that. He seemed quite well, and then he just went and died without warning. Miss Keane was somewhat taken aback, and made some wild statements at the time. But she soon shut up when she realized that a king's plaything has no power once the king passes on."

George wondered what the wild statements could have been, but he decided to put the question later.

They spent some time walking up and down the terrace, before turning down a path at one end which led through small trees to the shore. To the right of the path was a long flowerbed, and George recognized Mrs. Waters weeding with a trowel among the tall autumn plants. A white-painted notice said, "Private. Do not touch the flowers." As they passed by she raised her head and nodded distantly.

"Ah, you are honored!" said the professor. "She doesn't recognize everyone." He waved in the direction of the flowerbed. "There is another sample of the amenities of Crane's Court. As you know, a perfect lady is born with a silver spoon in her mouth and a trowel in her right hand. A lady who has not got a patch of mud to grub in is only half alive. So Mrs. Waters simply put up an intimidating notice, and bullied the gardeners until they made a flowerbed for her, and there she is."

They had to descend the path in single file, until they emerged on a grassy bank just above the shore. A fine curving strand stretched off before them, and on it a solitary figure was walking, kicking up the dry sand in a curiously clear gesture of bad temper.

"It's Burden," said George after a moment. "And he's coming this way."

"Shall we run? No—we'll stay and be introduced like a gentleman," said the professor. "Come along, young fellow. Look more cordial!"

"Well, I'm a little overwhelmed," said George lamely.

"My fault, I'm afraid," said the old man. "I always was a gasbag, I fear."

George made reassuring noises, and then Mr. Burden was upon them. This was almost literally true, for he was so intent on watching the toes of his shoes that he almost walked through them. At the last moment he looked up and growled:

"Oh, good evening."

It was very ungracious, but George introduced the professor as if he had not noticed. Mr. Burden shook hands with sour brevity. The Professor said affably:

"You're exploring your new domain, I see."

Mr. Burden guffawed nastily.

"I'm escaping from my new acquaintances," he said bitterly. "Do you know, I haven't been for a walk on a strand since I was a small boy. I've always hated sand." He kicked it savagely. "But I guessed that those doddering old witches wouldn't be likely to get down here after me. If I had my way I'd kill off everyone over the age of sixty-five."

He stared rudely at the professor, whose face reddened, George noticed, with real anger. He succeeded, however, in producing his usual tone as he said:

"Old people require a special technique. You'll get accustomed to us."

"Technique! A hatchet would be my technique for them!"

George said hastily:

"I think the whole place is charming, don't you?"

"Oh, the house is all right. Very well got up. And the gardens too. But the company! I'm only in the place an hour, and already three aged females have waylaid me to tell me how to run my own business. And each of them warned me against the others. There was no need to warn me—I wasn't born yesterday." His face took on an ugly expression. "When I had finished with the last one, she wasn't much inclined to stay and chat with me."

George and the professor were silent for want of a suitable reply.

"I was civil enough to the first ones. They were small, at least, though they whined, and one was as mad as a hatter. But the last one was a big battling cruiser with blue hair."

Professor Daly looked sideways at George and said:

"And what did you say to her?"

"I told her to skip off out of my way. I said it was my hotel, and if she didn't behave she could get out. She stayed there even then, trying to talk me down. In the end I had to tell her plainly to get out to hell before she'd go."

He grinned nastily. Professor Daly said:

"When did this happen?"

"A quarter of an hour ago. You were walking on the terrace. I saw you there as I came down through the field. Why do you ask?"

"Young man," said the professor. "I would suggest that a little more discretion would be in order." He held up his hand. "Now, don't interrupt. My profession has long ago made me impervious to rudeness."

George doubted this, but it silenced Mr. Burden for the moment. The old man went on:

"This hotel is unique of its kind. The old people have always been the mainstay of the business. You should not make any changes until you know the place better."

Mr. Burden stood regarding him malevolently.

"They were probably able to make my uncle do as they liked. I'm going to straighten out a lot of things here. I've made up my mind," he said. "If people don't do as I say, they can leave. I'm not going to have a procession of old harridans after me, whispering and clutching and spitting at me."

"I think people who live in hotels are protected by the law," said George mildly. "I doubt if you can just ask them to go."

"Perhaps not, but I can make life so unpleasant for them that they will be glad to go. I'm good at that."

"Good day to you," said the professor suddenly, and gripping George's arm, he walked on.

Mr. Burden stood for a moment grinning after them, and then, his good humor restored all at once, proceeded back towards the hotel on springy steps.

They had walked for several minutes before the professor slackened his pace. Then he let go of George's elbow and said:

"To be old—what a crime it is! *Old* freaks—*old* witches—*old* harridans—age is the real offense."

George said, trying not to sound too consolatory:

"I don't think Mr. Burden is a fair sample of public opinion."

"Sometimes I fail to see the use of his sort," said the old man. "And he's playing a dangerous game."

"A cruel, heartless game," said George.

"Dangerous, too. Old people have not much to lose, and they are therefore freer in a fight."

George found himself thinking how convenient it would have been if Mr. Burden had fallen out of the train window on the way from Dublin. It did not occur to him to pity himself for being so soon involved in such unpleasantness, nor to fear that his newfound peace would be shattered. There was no room in his mind for more than the most impersonal pity for all these people who seemed to be at Mr. Burden's mercy. Deep within himself, a little lamp glowed before the image of a tall, sad figure with pale gold hair.

The Professor was saying:

"Of course, Mr. Burden has a distinct advantage. Everyone here has lived in a state of tension since we heard that he had inherited the place. Now he can play on their nerves, make them put themselves in the wrong, even get them quarreling among themselves."

"I doubt if he is subtle enough to do that," said George.

"He looks a coarse-grained enough customer, in all conscience. I wonder where he has lived up to now?"

"He said he was an accountant," George remembered.

"Then perhaps he'll see by the books the advantages of keeping on the old people. In any case I think he's heading for trouble. Keeping even an ordinary hotel requires more tact than Mr. Burden can command."

They strolled along the grass bank for a while. Professor Daly's flow of talk was not at all diminished by their unpleasant encounter, and his accounts of university maneuvers and academic conspiracies kept George entertained.

"I was good at settling these things—I sometimes miss the excitement," said the professor regretfully. "I used to see into people's minds, to what I have come to believe was an unusual extent. I was almost an official peacemaker, in the end. When warring professors saw me approach, they knew the game was up, and they came quietly. Yes, sometimes I miss it all. It had the charm of the chase, as well as the sense of virtue for recompense."

George discovered that his undergraduate vision of the professor lost in scholarly dreams was not altogether correct.

"There was, for example, the case of my two eminent colleagues whose lecture-rooms were situated one above the other, and whose views had differed on some point relating to the glandular activities of the frog. The upper professor used to wait until the lower one had announced the text for his lecture, so to speak, and then he would flush the upstairs lavatory, which happened to be a very noisy one. The lower professor, who was hot-tempered, then became so angry that he would dance about in a manner most diverting to his students, but injurious to his own dignity. When he went so far as to pursue the upper professor with a dissecting knife, the college thought it was time to intervene, and I was called in."

Professor Daly coughed modestly, and flicked at his rosebud with a delicate finger. George held his breath.

"My remedy was simple. I ordained that the two gentlemen should alternate lecture-rooms week by week. Thus the man on top one week was underdog the next. They soon declared a truce."

"Perhaps you could exercise your talent for peacemaking on Mr. Burden," George suggested.

"No. I don't claim to be infallible. The technique for him is the one he suggested himself—the hatchet."

The smooth sea was dyed with a flame-colored sunset as they turned home. The tide was high, and the small, cold waves were whispering among the stones. Far off, the orange lights of the hotel were a comforting antidote to the heartbreaking flavor of autumn in the air. George found himself looking eagerly towards them, as if he had lived under their protection all his life.

3

Within a few days, George had dropped into the self-seeking invalid's routine of Crane's Court. It was so easy there to believe that his own comfort, the very angle of his chair and the temperature of his room, were important. Everyone took it for granted that he would be selfish, particular and critical of what was done for him. Maggie, the housemaid who brought his breakfast in the morning, drew his curtains with an anxious look towards him, as if in fear that she had not done it exactly right. He began to develop silly likes and fancies, to arrive for meals at the same moment every day, and to be impatient of the smallest delay in the service. He arranged his room with an old-womanish precision, and got a solemn satisfaction from Maggie's eager following of his instructions about the laying of his fire.

The curious thing was that one half of his consciousness had no time for these petty occupations. But the part of him that wanted to live vigorously, as he had always done, was constantly taking warning that the only protection for him now was this barrier of little meannesses. It was fortunate that Professor Daly had attached himself to him. On account of his age he classed himself with the invalids, but he could never take himself seriously enough to behave like them. His attitude was that he and George were in the privileged position of commentators. He announced his intention of preventing George from becoming an oddity, and he appeared to see nothing incongruous in the fact that he himself was going to be George's guardian in this respect.

One morning, when he had been several days at Crane's Court, George came out on the terrace after breakfast. It was a morning of rich September sun, deepened by the orange and gold-tipped trees in the park below. The sea was a smooth, cool blue, fading into a pink haze on the horizon. The old people, huddled in shawls and overcoats, were sitting on the seats along the terrace. Professor Daly was standing a little apart, talking to a middle-aged man in riding-boots. He came a pace or two towards George and said in a low voice:

"The leader of the opposition has arrived. He always comes for a few months at this time of the year. I want you to meet him."

As they reached the stranger he said:

"Mr. Arrow—Mr. Quinn."

Then he looked at them both expectantly.

Mr. Quinn seized George's hand, squeezed it as if he were wringing its neck, threw it from him, fixed an earnest brown eye on George's face and said fiercely:

"You hunt, sir?"

"Well, no," said George apologetically.

"Shoot, sir?"

"I'm afraid not."

"Ga!" said Mr. Quinn contemptuously and strode away.

"You see," said Professor Daly, looking after him delightedly. "We're all a trifle odd here."

"What a fine thing to be as rude as that with such conviction," said George enviously.

"He's gone to talk to his horse, I suppose," said the professor. "I've never seen him in bed, but I'm prepared to swear that he has his pajamas made like jodhpurs. Shall we go for a stroll?"

But before George could answer, the door on to the terrace burst open, and the stamping, raging, gesticulating figure of Colonel Waters shot out on to the terrace. He was waving a large piece of cardboard in his hand. He pointed to it and punched it and gibbered until Professor Daly stepped forward and took it from him. Then he drew a deep breath and seemed to swell up with the effort to hold himself still while the professor turned the card over in a leisurely way, pretending not to notice the craned necks of the old people on the seats. The farther off ones had begun to hobble towards him.

" 'This is not a private bathroom,' " the professor read aloud from the card. " 'Time limited to thirty minutes.' " He turned an inquiring eye on Colonel Waters. "Where did this come from?"

"Tacked on to my bathroom door—*my* bathroom door!" the Colonel spluttered. "I was inside when he did it—the impertinence! I heard the hammer go tap, tap, tap on the door, like a—like a blasted woodpecker! And I got out of the bath to—to tell the fellow to go to blazes and there was that beastly Burden outside. Laughed in my face, he did, and shoved *this* into my hand," he held up a crumpled piece of paper which he had been clutching, "and walked away making some smart remark about serving a summons. I'll have his blood for this!"

The old people made horrified sounds, though George thought he detected a note of encouragement too. Professor Daly reached out and took the crumpled paper neatly, smoothed it out and read aloud to the eager company:

" 'Private bathrooms—two guineas extra per week.' "

There was silence for a moment, and then the cackling began again. George and the professor moved away, leaving Colonel Waters in the center of an excited group on the terrace. When they looked back some time later, they could see them all shuffling in and out in a kind of war-dance.

"To tell the truth," said the professor as they walked along the terrace, "the Colonel's appropriation of that bathroom is outrageous. He ejects everyone who goes in, and spends hours there in the bath with the door unlocked so that all the ladies are afraid even to try the door."

"I know," said George. "He ejected me. He kicked the door until I opened it. It was such an obscene display that nothing would induce me to risk provoking a repetition of it."

"We had one lady, a Mrs. Fitzgerald," the professor went on, "who took one look at Colonel Waters and announced that he was small meat for her. She was a sort of female version—female by courtesy, that is—of Mr. Quinn. She hunted and shot and fished and ratted with unflagging fortitude. I am not much of a sporting man, but I must confess my interest is always aroused by a well-matched pair of contestants, to quote our local newspaper. I could hardly wait for the result of the contest."

"She was routed?"

"She was. Without a single shot fired. She had not looked far enough ahead. She opened the bathroom door intrepidly enough, but she had not seen that the next and only logical step was to lift the Colonel bodily out of the bath and deposit him, dripping, outside the door. She balked at that," said the professor regretfully, shaking his head. "She has not been here since. She had hunted with the Galway Blazers for forty-five years, but her failure broke her spirit."

George was conducted through the gardens that morning. The apple-trees were heavy with fruit, and Mrs. Henry was there, gathering windfalls. They stayed to help her, and she tactfully left the heavy basket to be carried in by the gardeners while she brought them to watch her cut dahlias. As usual, George found himself unable to speak to her. Furiously he envied the professor's easy use of her name.

"Barbara," he said, and "My dear Barbara."

Still he was glad the old man was there, for left alone with her he would surely have disappeared like a blown-out candle-flame.

At last she had to go away. George led the professor back to the garden where they had met her. He found another apple, and held it in his hand. Professor Daly coughed.

"I'm an old man, never noted for my reticence," he said. "Is it as bad as it looks?"

"Worse," said George shortly.

"Is there any future in it?"

"None."

"Heart?"

George nodded. Here was the first person to be told. He supposed it could not be kept a secret forever.

"Ha." Professor Daly cogitated. "Plenty of people with hearts get married."

"Not like mine," said George, and dropped the apple.

"If you'll forgive an apparent association of ideas," said the professor after a moment, "our Miss Keane seems not to have let the grass grow under her feet. She has become Mr. Burden's henchwoman and ally, not to say secret service agent. Every night after dinner she puts on a very tight garment and a string of imitation pearls, and goes to visit him in his rooms. There every chair brings forth a sigh for the departed Murray, and from the depths of her wounded soul arises distilled venom in the shape of warnings and informations and advice-for-his-own-good. It seems she's a girl after his own heart. I see her hand in the incident of Colonel Waters's bathroom. If she goes on at this rate, the place will soon be in an uproar."

"Mr. Burden did mention that he was on the lookout for a sympathetic girl," George remembered, glad to leave the subject of Mrs. Henry.

"Miss Keane's mother is the lodgekeeper here," said the professor delicately. "It would be something of a triumph for the girl to—shall we say— hook the owner of Crane's Court."

George suggested that the old people would not be pleased.

"There is open war between them and Miss Keane," said the professor. "She used to try to incite Mr. Murray to get rid of us, telling him that Crane's Court could be made the sort of hotel where the best people—and the thirstiest—would make a point of spending some time every year. She used to lament over the waste of fuel for our bedroom fires—which are free here, by the way. Of course the old people drew all this on themselves by being so snobbish to Miss Keane. They constantly look down their long noses at her, and make remarks about beggars on horseback, so that the poor girl has become overenthusiastic in the matter of bettering herself. She also wanted him to do away with various other little privileges one enjoys here, which cost the hotel nothing. But Murray always put her off—said the old people were the backbone of the business. I'm afraid she'll find a readier listener in Mr. Burden."

"How do you know all this?" George asked curiously.

"I have my sources of information," said the professor airily. "She had just become engaged to be married to Murray when he died."

"But I thought he was quite old!"

"All of seventy-eight," said the professor cheerfully. "That only served to make him more attractive. With any luck, the lady would not have had to wait more than a few years to haul in the returns of her work. The testimonial she brought here said she has a real head for business, and it's perfectly true."

"It seems a pity to have the old people in such a state of nervousness," said George.

"It's more than a pity, young man. For most of them it's sheer tragedy. I have a good pension and no responsibilities. Moreover, Rosemary Downes, good little girl, makes a lot of money for me. I can live where I like. But many of these people have been settled here by their exasperated relations. All the cousins subscribe to pay the hotel bills, but there is no margin, and they don't allow extras. Then there are those who could afford to live somewhere else, but who are so long here that they are afraid to move. It's no wonder that they all feel that the owner of the hotel is their owner too. Unfortunately they have let him see this, and the temptation to chivvy them seems to have become too much for him."

A few days later George received a letter from Mrs. Fennell, inviting him formally to drink tea with her at a quarter-past four. As he left the hotel by the front door, he saw Mr. Burden coming along the terrace. He was smiling like a small greasy Mephistopheles, and he came straight up to George and slapped him on the shoulder.

"You've just missed a bit of fun," he said gleefully. "Oh, it was the funniest thing I've seen for years."

He looked so innocently pleased that George found himself smiling too.

"What was the joke?" he asked.

"I've just had my nose to the veranda window," said Mr. Burden, "watching the old pussies being bested at their own game. I'll tell you what I did—I told Mr. Quinn to bring all his friends on to the veranda for tea, and when the old ones arrived, half of them had to go away again, including old Ma Robinson. Oh, it was funny!"

He positively doubled up with laughter. George stood regarding him uncertainly, wondering if there were any way of impressing him.

"Don't waste your time giving me advice, old man," said Mr. Burden, when he had stopped laughing. "I haven't enjoyed myself so well for years. Besides, I've had all the advice I need. I've had enough advice to keep me going for the rest of my life. That old Ma Robinson thinks she'll get the better of me, but I'll show her who's the owner here. I have several shots in my locker still, and when I begin to fire them off we'll have fun."

"Tell me," said George, "were you by any chance brought up by a cross old woman?"

"My grandaunt," said Mr. Burden. "Did you know her? Same name as myself."

"No, I didn't know her."

"Why do you ask that?"

"Curiosity," said George gently, smiling to himself.

Mr. Burden stared.

"You know, Arrow, I don't understand you. But I'd like to tell you that I don't mean any harm to you, nor to the professor. Nor to Heaslip. He's all right, too. It's these bullying old ones. I can't stand them at any price. Letting me see they think I'm not out of the top drawer. Telling Miss Keane I'm not a 'real gentleman.' "

He used a mincing tone of voice for the last words, but the bitterness under-lying them was very evident.

Miss Keane again, thought George. He said:

"Don't make the mistake of thinking you have a power of life and death over these people. Apart from the morality of it, their relations could make it hot for you if you—if you drove them too far."

"I won't. All I want is for them to give in and do as they're told, and then I'll let them alone."

"That's too much to expect of most of them," said George. "You can't change a person's nature, especially at the end of a long life."

"I can try," said Mr. Burden, and walked off jauntily.

George continued on his way to Mrs. Fennell thoughtfully. Halfway down the drive she had a sort of little cottage made of white-painted wood, with apple-green window-frames and door. There was a little front garden, where she had planted haphazard an extraordinary variety of flowers, all grown big-ger than life-size. He picked his steps through the flowers—for there was no path—and went to the door. Before he had time to knock, however, it was opened by a middle-aged woman in a white coat. At the same moment Mrs. Fennell herself came trotting into the little hall.

"I was watching you through the window," she said. "You were admiring my flowers."

Her voice was the soft, carefully taught lady's voice of fifty years ago. It was coolly restful. Standing in the doorway in her gray dress, with her soft white hair and soft mad eyes, she reminded George of one of those pointless, badly drawn Christmas cards of just such flowery gardens. She gripped his arm above the elbow and squeezed it agonizingly.

"I'm so glad you were able to come. We have a lovely tea ready for you. Haven't we, Bridget?"

The woman in the white coat smiled and nodded. Mrs. Fennell put her lips close to his ear and whispered:

"Of course it's really only our afternoon tea sent down from the hotel, but it feels as if I had got it all ready for you myself."

She squeezed his arm again, and trotted before him into a little sitting room off the hall. It was prettily furnished in the same Christmas-card style, and there was an open turf fire on the same lavish scale that was everywhere at Crane's Court. In front of the fire sat a row of cats, upright and silkily still, opening and shutting their eyes gently to emphasize their enjoyment of the warmth. There were eight of them, tortoiseshells, blacks, tabbies and one mag-nificent Siamese. George, who liked cats, fondled their ears as he sat by the fire.

"There are more outside," said Mrs. Fennell. "I usually have about a dozen, as well as the kittens. They're named after the Apostles. This is Peter." She pulled the Siamese on to her knee. "I have had him the longest. Andrew is the small tortoiseshell. James is out ratting, and John is nursing her kittens."

They talked about cats until Bridget brought in the tea. There were three cups on the tray.

"The third cup is for Rodney, in case he comes in," she explained seriously. "But he seldom takes tea."

"Do you find it lonely here away from the hotel?" George asked.

"By no means. There's Bridget, though one doesn't count a servant as company. And in any case, perhaps you noticed, she's a little bit odd. Not mad, of course—oh, no. But odd. And then there are the cats, and Rodney never leaves me for long." Every time she mentioned his name, she smiled a little to herself. "He's very faithful. He tells me such wonderful things about the people at the hotel—he spends a lot of time there—that I can hardly keep from laughing out loud when I meet them. We have many secret jokes, Rodney and I."

She certainly made him sound real, George thought. He commented that cats are good company.

"And *so* useful," said Mrs. Fennell. She cocked her head for a moment to listen, and then leaned forward to whisper: "I'll let you in on a secret that I don't tell to everyone. You admired my flowers as you came in. Now don't deny it. I saw you!"

"I certainly admired them," said George. "I have never seen such flowers."

"Well, I'll tell you how I do it. Rodney told me. It's the cats!"

"I see," said George faintly, wondering wildly if there was any further suitable comment he could make.

Mrs. Fennell was sitting back in her chair, smiling, rubbing Peter's fur and nodding.

"Yes, it's the cats. I would never have thought of it myself, but Rodney told me what to do. It's as easy as say it, he said. Just put a cat's body under each plant—Mr. Arrow, are you feeling ill?"

"I'm all right," said George weakly.

"I'm sure you're ill. Have some more tea."

She poured it solicitously, and waited until he had drunk some of it before she went on:

"Yes, Rodney thought of it. He's so clever. He can solve anything—anything!"

"But how do you—how do you—?"

"How do I kill them?" she said archly. "Ah, that is my secret—mine and Rodney's." She stroked the Siamese, Peter, lovingly. "I'm saving Peter for the new Maréchal Niel rose that I'm getting next month. Yes, I don't know what I would do without my cats."

George edged his chair gently away from the row of dignified little creatures in front of the fire. Mrs. Fennell said:

"Are you liking Crane's Court?"

"Very much," said George, relieved at the change of subject.

"Ah, but it's not what it was. Things are changing, Rodney tells me things are changing terribly. It all began when Mr. Murray was murdered."

"Murdered! Surely not!"

"No wonder you are surprised. Yes, Mr. Murray was murdered." She nodded slowly. "I know, but no one else seems to have thought of it. You see, Rodney told me."

George laid his head against the back of his chair and closed his eyes for a moment. He opened them again to ask:

"Did he tell you who did it?"

"No," she said slyly. "He would mention no names. He's very particular about that sort of thing."

"Did he know why Mr. Murray was killed?"

"He thought it was something to do with diamonds," she said vaguely. "I asked and asked what that meant, but he didn't know himself."

Suddenly she stopped and looked frightened.

"I said I wouldn't talk about it. I swore I wouldn't talk about it. Don't tell, don't tell, don't tell!"

Her voice rose to a scream.

"I won't tell anyone," said George. "It's all right, Mrs. Fennell. There's nothing to be afraid of."

Desperately he patted her shoulder and made soothing noises. He was relieved beyond measure when the door opened and Bridget came in. She went straight to Mrs. Fennell and put an arm around her.

"Come and lie down," she said. "You're frightening the cats."

"What a silly thing to say," said Mrs. Fennell in her normal tone of voice. "Cats never care about anyone but themselves."

But she agreed to go and lie down, and made a gracious little farewell speech to George before Bridget led her away. George sat moodily staring at the unconcerned cats, trying to accustom himself to the outrageous implications of the old lady's statement. Of course she was as crazy as a coot, poor old soul, and it would be foolish to believe everything she said. Still, according to Professor Daly, Mr. Murray's death had been unexpected. George found that he had become interested in the mysterious Mr. Murray, and he hoped that it might be possible to learn more about him, if his name cropped up in conversation again.

Bridget came into the room, saying:

"Excuse me, Mr. Arrow, for keeping you waiting. Mrs. Fennell sometimes gets a bit upset like that, but it passes off again. When she gets excited about anything, she's not so reliable, but she's quite all right the rest of the time. Do you mind telling me, sir, what she was talking about?"

George saw no harm in telling her that Mrs. Fennell had been talking about the late Mr. Murray.

"I guessed as much," said Bridget. "She's been worse since he died, and much harder to look after. When she's not wandering about the hotel, she sits here all alone, whispering—to Sir Rodney Crane, she says." Bridget smiled brightly. "I've had much worse to look after than her. She's a real lady, always. You'll excuse me, sir, for talking so much about her, but I thought you might be worrying about what you saw. She'll be all right with me."

She ushered him out into the garden, and he picked his way distastefully through the giant flowers. He could not help thinking of the graceful little skeleton lying under each, and as he walked he imagined that his feet crunched on tiny bones.

He walked up and down for some time on the drive to collect himself, and it was half-past five by the clock in the little wooden tower when he reached the hotel. As he approached he could see Professor Daly standing on the front steps, and a moment later Mr. Heaslip came out of the front door to join him.

"We're going for a walk," Daly called out to him. "Would you care to come with us?"

George accepted gladly, and they started for the winding path down to the strand. Both Daly and Heaslip were very concerned about Burden's behavior. The old man said:

"He's like a child who must look with his fingers, as we used to say in my nursery long ago. He has a passion for interfering. He even interfered with our good chef, O'Reilly, but was pursued from the kitchen up the back stairs with a carving-knife. Sorry I missed that," he sighed, "but I can't be everywhere."

"Why should he interfere with the chef?" asked George. "The cooking is first-rate."

"Excess of devotion to Miss Keane." The Professor shrugged. "She has ideas, that young woman. Bad ones, mostly. O'Reilly slighted her, she said."

"Miss Keane?" said Mr. Heaslip. "Curious how persistent she is. And how restful life would be without her."

George was surprised that Mr. Heaslip had taken note of her at all. He seemed so detached from all such human considerations. The Professor was saying:

"Burden gets all his information from Miss Keane. It's unfortunate that she bears a grudge against so many people. I can't think where it will all end. Mrs. Robinson has announced her intention of demanding Miss Keane's dismissal. She said she's going to do it before dinner tonight."

"Oh, I say! Couldn't she be stopped?" said George in distress. "She can do nothing but harm that way."

"I tried to stop her," said the professor, "but it only seemed to make her more determined."

"Perhaps it would have been better to encourage her," said Mr. Heaslip. "That might have produced the opposite effect."

"Major Dunlea says that Burden ought to be shot," said Daly. "He offered to do it himself."

As they passed by Mrs. Waters's flower garden, George saw that the notice had been removed. He said:

"Has he got around to this too?"

"He had the notice taken away several days ago," said Mr. Heaslip. "That was a double attack on the Waters family."

"This may be more serious than it looks," said Professor Daly thoughtfully. "I'm beginning to wonder about the effect on some of these people of such a determined campaign."

"You said that before," said George. "Do you mean that one of them might injure him?"

"I hadn't thought of that," said the professor. "I was referring to the possibility of his making one or more of them turn the corner from mild oddity to certifiable insanity."

There was silence for a moment. Then Mr. Heaslip said:

"I'll have a talk with him this evening. He seems to like me. Perhaps it's not too late yet to make him see reason."

At the end of the long strand, the professor and George turned home, leaving Mr. Heaslip to continue his way along the shore. They stood for a moment watching him climb over the rocks, looking like a huge heron in his blue-gray tweeds.

"He'll probably catch up with us on the way home," said Professor Daly. "I think one reason he elects to go farther is that he can enjoy a brisk walk home alone. We're too slow for him."

As they strolled back, George remarked that he had visited Mrs. Fennell. He kept her secret about the disposal of her cats, even when the professor said:

"It is remarkable how lunatics seem closer to nature than the sane. Did you notice the luxurious growth in Mrs. Fennell's garden? In this age of science, one feels that there should be a simple explanation for everything, but now, here at our doors, there is a phenomenon that defies explanation. The older I get," he sighed, "the more I distrust science, and the more eagerly I hope for the inexplicable. I could write an article on Mrs. Fennell's flowers that would shake our scientific agriculturalists."

George was almost unbearably tempted to break up this illusion and have a laugh at Professor Daly's expense, but he forced himself to make some neutral remark, which in any case was all that was expected. Neither did he tell of the curious end of his visit, nor of Mrs. Fennell's statement that Mr. Murray had been murdered. He wished to have time to consider it all at leisure. He was not at all sure that even if it were true, his conscience would oblige him to do anything decisive about it.

In the hall, George and the professor separated to dress for dinner. Dressing for dinner at Crane's Court was as important as not eating with one's knife. No one was exempted, not even the clerical staff who ate in a kind of limbo near the service door, pretending not to hear the outrageous language of Mr. O'Reilly, the chef, as he carved the joint at the hot-plate.

In George's room, Maggie, uniformed now in black and white with frills, had stoked up his fire, opened his window exactly as he liked it, and was even now laying his evening clothes on the bed. She gave him a look of embarrassing devotion.

"I mended the buttonhole in your cuff, Mr. Arrow, so the link won't be all the time coming through," she said.

George thanked her, but to his surprise she did not move towards the door. Instead, she came close to him and said:

"Mr. Arrow, sir, maybe—maybe you could tell me what I ought to do."

She stood looking down at her very elegant high-heeled shoes, and twisting the goffered edge of her apron hard between her fingers, ruining it completely.

"Why, of course, Maggie," said George. "What's the matter?"

To his horror, a slow tear fell on to her twitching hands. She looked up at him suddenly, and the anger and tears blazing in her eyes gave her a beauty he had never noticed before.

"It's Mr. Burden, sir," she said bitterly. "I could—I could poison him! 'Twould be easy enough to put something in his morning tea!"

She laughed venomously. George inquired gently again what was the matter.

Maggie's story left him once more aghast at the obviousness of Mr. Burden's villainy. It seemed that Maggie was betrothed to Ned, the chauffeur, who being much older than she was and convinced of her attraction for everyone, was insanely jealous. But Maggie was devoted to him, and more than that, convinced that she had received a special honor in his attentions. In fact, she said, she was the luckiest, proudest, happiest girl in the world. George congratulated her gravely and sincerely. Then, said Maggie, along had come Mr. Burden. She laughed angrily.

"It's—it's *old-fashioned*, Mr. Arrow, so it is! There's Ned, as decent a man as ever was born, and old enough to know better, threatening to shoot Mr. Burden. It's like one of them old songs they do be singing at weddings. I'm distracted with it all, so I am. It's no use talking to Ned. I told him Mr. Burden was a nasty greasy little yoke, and that I wouldn't be seen dead with him, but that didn't satisfy him at all. He wants his blood, he said. I said, joking him, like, that he wouldn't know what to do with it, and he just looked at me as if I wasn't there. And he's the quietest man! Mr. Burden is always trying to put his dirty paws on me, and the only time he managed to do it, Ned happened to come around the corner—"

"Would it be any use if I had a word with Ned?" George asked hastily, as she seemed about to break down again.

The prospect was not attractive, but it occurred to him that if he could explain to Ned that public opinion was almost unanimous against Mr. Burden, it might have the effect of lessening Ned's own grievance. In any case, he had to promise some solace to the distressed Maggie, and no other course occurred to him. She was obviously pleased with his offer. She thanked him repeatedly, and promised to put her mind at rest until after his proposed interview with Ned. Then she went away, probably to change her apron and do up her face, George thought, apparently quite confident that he would be able to put all her affairs in good order with a wave of the hand.

He dressed moodily, promising himself that his interview with Ned would contain a solemn lecture on the charms of Maggie, and the self-indulgence of Ned in causing her so much pain. He began to practice suitable phrases before the glass. He wondered as he tied his tie if Ned would give him a hearing.

The gong sounded for dinner before he was finished, but following his new habit he did not hurry. He brushed his hair and selected a handkerchief as if he had time in plenty. Then he left his room and walked in a leisurely way towards the dining room.

At Crane's Court, people were rarely late for meals. For most of the guests the meals were the only points of interest in the long slow days, and the sounding of the gong was superfluous, for they watched the last seconds tick away with as much excitement as if they were to be executed instead of fed at the appointed hour. Before the gong was heard, most of them were on their way to the dining room. Thus, George was not surprised to see through the glass doors that the company was already seated. As he opened the door, Miss Keane came from the direction of the stairs and she preceded him into the room.

Tonight she was dressed in the tight garment of which Professor Daly had spoken, and which she usually wore only after dinner. It was scarlet, instead of her usual black, and it fitted her like a bathing suit. There was a startled silence as the guests, idly waiting for their soup, became aware of her. With a little expressive chin-lifting gesture she walked up the room, not to join her colleagues in their limbo near the hotplate, but to Mr. Burden's own table at the top of the room. Mr. Burden had not yet arrived.

There was a little gasp. Mrs. Robinson said: "Well!" George hurriedly seated himself at the table he shared with Professor Daly.

"See that?" the old man asked superfluously. "Something has happened, I'll swear."

Sitting at Mr. Burden's table, Miss Keane was trying to look unconcerned with the stares directed at her. George was relieved when the arrival of the soup diverted attention from her.

First to come into the room was Fitzpatrick, the head waiter. He was followed by his little army of waiters and waitresses, bearing soup tureens. The Professor sniffed the air.

"Borscht," he said appreciatively, and unfolded his napkin.

Presently the diners were falling on their soup with little satisfied noises. As he laid his spoon down with a sigh, Professor Daly said:

"Ah, the Crane's Court borscht! As the Gentleman Poet so aptly puts it, there is none like it, none. Don't look up now," he added, "but there is a little unpleasantness attending on our Miss Keane."

When George did look up a moment later, he saw that she was the only person who had not been served with soup. She was looking angrily at Fitzpatrick, trying to compel his attention, and he was as busily avoiding her eye. As clearly as if he had shouted it across the room, his expression said, "Nothing will induce me to serve you while you sit at that table."

Anon Miss Keane looked hopefully towards the door, obviously hoping for help and protection from Mr. Burden. But he did not come.

The fish arrived, and still Miss Keane was ignored. George began to feel hot and uncomfortable, and full of real pity for her. All the guests were now aware that something was wrong, but their reactions were diverse. The old people were frankly pleased and talked loudly and heartily to show it. The hunting people, not being permanent residents, did not fully grasp the situation, though they understood more than did those who were on a late holiday at Crane's Court for a week or two. These last wore the miserably self-conscious expressions of guests who have found themselves in the midst of a family row, and who long violently and vainly to be miraculously transported somewhere else. Mr. Heaslip, who had a small table to himself by the wall, seemed buried in his book, but even he moved his shoulders a little uneasily from time to time, so that one could see the atmosphere had penetrated to him. George was appalled at the prospect of sitting through several further courses of this. He said:

"Shall I ask Miss Keane to sit with us?"

But before the professor could reply they became aware of a little excited group of people outside the door. Then the porter, Joe, came marching purposefully, though red-faced, down the room to confer with Fitzpatrick. Both of them marched on a sardonic-looking, white-haired man who sat with his wife in the middle of the room. The white-haired man raised his eyebrows, placed his napkin resignedly on the table and went out, and then Joe and Fitzpatrick were at Daly's elbow, still whispering.

"It's Mr. Burden, sir. Will you for the love of God come out and tell us what we're going to do. Maybe you'd come too, Mr. Arrow?"

"Of course," said George, as they both got up.

"What's happened, man?" said Daly.

"Mr. Burden is dead!" hissed Joe, and marched out of the door.

Professor Daly looked anxiously at George, but George's only thought, wildly irrational, was, "Now I won't have to have that difficult interview with Ned!"

Silently they followed Joe out of the room.

4

Joe was waiting outside the door with the white-haired man, who looked bored and impatient. Professor Daly, who never lost time in becoming acquainted with new arrivals, was able to introduce him to George as Dr. Morgan. He nodded ungraciously, and then as an afterthought shook hands. Then he turned to Joe and said testily:

"If Mr. Burden is dead I can't do much for him. Give us a look at him quickly so that I can get back to my dinner."

George admired this professional calm. His own appetite had quite vanished. Joe was hopping from one foot to the other with excitement, one could almost say with pleasure. His tight black trousers and white mess-jacket seemed to emphasize his agile enjoyment of the dramatic situation.

"There won't be much dinner eaten tonight," said Joe. "I'm telling you there won't!"

And a giggle escaped him.

"Joe!" said Daly sternly. "Stop that at once! Where is Mr. Burden? What has happened to him? Take us to him at once."

Joe sobered a little.

"Yes, sir. This way, sir," he said.

As if he had to control his dancing legs by force, he started towards the corridor that led to Mr. Burden's rooms. He turned his head once and said, unable to keep the note of delight out of his voice.

"Someone stuck a knife in Mr. Burden, sir!"

And then he fairly ran ahead of them. They looked at each other, shrugged and followed more slowly.

George had never been in Mr. Burden's rooms before. Joe paused now with his hand on the door handle, and then flung the door open with a flourish. Dr. Morgan walked straight in, and the others followed him.

They were in a pleasant sitting room, whose long windows, now curtained closely, looked out on the tree-bordered lawn at the back of the hotel. There was Sheraton furniture and soft gray carpet. There were several delicate Chinese prints on the walls, of sophisticated pale yellow persons calmly contemplating, and sepia-boughed trees laden with pink blossom. The electric light shone from pink shaded wall-brackets. The firelight gleamed rosily on perfectly polished brass fire-irons and fender. And in front of the fire, on the gray and rose hearthrug, lay Mr. Burden himself, with, as Joe had mentioned, a large knife inserted in his chest.

"Well, well, well," said Professor Daly. "As George Tesman would say, think of that!"

Dr. Morgan was down on one knee, with his fingers on Mr. Burden's out-flung wrist. George stood by the door wondering if his complexion now resembled that of the Chinese gentlemen on the walls. He felt distinctly ill, but he stood his ground and tried to think of something helpful to do. The doctor stood up and dusted his trouser knees.

"Dead as mutton," he said cheerfully.

There came a gasp from the open door. George turned and saw a group—the same group that had escorted Joe to the dining room—standing open-mouthed outside. He shut the door gently on them. He could hear them scuttling off, with little shrieks.

"Better call the police," said Dr. Morgan. "They'll want to know how this happened. He didn't fall on that knife."

"Poor fellow," said Professor Daly. "He didn't mean to be so nasty, I'm sure."

From George's memory of Burden's conversation, he thought that he had not had opportunity for more than half of his intended nastiness. The doctor looked sharply at Professor Daly.

"You know who did it?"

"Good God, no! How should I?"

"It's usually very obvious," said the doctor in a bored tone. "Old farmer found transfixed with a graip—the Guards simply arrest his son who breaks down and confesses that he was only assisting Providence, with the object of inheriting and getting married." He contemplated the body of Burden. "I only met him once. Didn't care for him, I must say."

Even now, when he had had his moment, Joe seemed to be bursting with a secret. He said eagerly, "You can call the Guards from here, sir. There's Mr. Burden's own telephone there behind you, on the table. That goes straight outside, sir—it doesn't go through the office at all."

"Don't let anyone in till they come," said the doctor. "I'll be getting back to my dinner."

He made for the door and then paused.

"Or perhaps I should wait. If anything gets moved they'll blame me, you may be sure."

"George, here, and Joe and I will stay," said Daly. "We'll watch each other, and we won't let anyone into the room until the police arrive. You can go and enjoy the rest of your dinner with a free mind."

As the door closed behind the grateful doctor, Professor Daly said, "A strong stomach, obviously."

They all turned to gaze at the mortal remnants of Mr. Burden. He lay sprawled on his back. He was dressed in a pale gray suit, silk socks and suede shoes. His waistcoat was dove-gray knitted wool, and from it, in the neighborhood of where one might expect to find his heart, protruded the long ivory handle of the knife.

"No blood, thank God," said George cautiously, after a moment.

"Internal bleeding. It's probably a very sharp knife," said Professor Daly. "I wonder where it came from? With that handle it could be a paperknife."

At his elbow, Joe snorted and emitted a knowing "Aha!"

Professor Daly turned to regard him distastefully.

"You're up to something, young Joe," he said. "I've known you since you were in short pants, long enough to know when you're up to something. Out with it!"

Joe backed away.

"No! No, sir! I won't say nothing till the Guards come. They'd have my life, so they would. I won't say nothing."

The Professor clutched his brow.

"Your grammar, Joe! It cuts me to the bone! You won't say *anything!*"

"That's right, sir. Not till the Guards come."

He pulled his handkerchief out of his pocket and covered his hand with it before lifting the receiver.

"Fingerprints—an elementary precaution," he said. Then when he had wound the old-fashioned handle vigorously he went on in sugary tones, "*Hello,* Miss Murphy." The telephone clucked like a doting hen. "Beautiful weather indeed, for the time of year. And may I ask how are the little dogs? Good! Excellent! Now could you connect me with the Guards in town, please? No, just a little private matter. Ask them to send Inspector Kenny to the telephone. . . . Thank *you,* Miss Murphy!"

He covered the mouthpiece with his hand and made a grimace. "Inquisitive old witch! Now she'll listen in on the line, and she'll probably hold up all my future calls for an hour in revenge. Oh, hello! Yes, I'm holding on."

A moment later he said briskly, "Is that you, Mike? Can you come out here at once? Yes, I'm at Crane's Court. Its owner is lying dead on the hearthrug a couple of feet away from me." He grinned fiendishly into the telephone. "I'm afraid poor Miss Murphy has had a shock. Yes, dead as a doornail, or as mutton, if you prefer the doctor's expression. . . . Dr. Morgan, a guest in the hotel. . . . Suspicious circumstance is right, Mike. Stabbed deep as a well with an ivory-handled knife. . . . Come on and have a look—nothing to pay. . . . What's that? Of course I haven't touched anything! . . . Well, how could I telephone you without handling the telephone? . . . Yes, it's here in the room. . . . Well, how sharper than a serpent's tooth is an ungrateful—what's that? . . . Come to think of it, I needn't have called you at all. Next time I'll let you find your own body. . . . Yes, yes, yes, we'll stay here until you come, three of us watching each other, watching the body, watching—oh, good-bye."

He turned to the fascinated George and said unnecessarily, "He has hung up, but he'll be along very soon. Seems interested."

"Don't you think we should tell Mrs. Henry about this before they come?" said George. "I suppose she'll have to take charge now."

"By Jove, you're right," said Daly. "I had quite forgotten her. Yes, of course we must tell her at once. Curious how a murdered man becomes public property."

He opened the door into the passage. Feet scuttled and he called out, "Hey, you! Lizzie! Come here a minute! I won't bite you."

A small redhaired girl appeared in the doorway, eyes shining, vainly trying to peer round the professor's bulk into the room. He said:

"Don't do that. You won't like what you will see. Now go and find Mrs. Henry and tell her I want her here. Just tell her Mr. Burden has had an accident. Yes, an accident. Now, off you go."

He shut the door thoughtfully. George said:

"Do you think it would be all right if I—if I intercept her before she comes here and break the news to her?"

"That's very clever of you, George. Yes, please do that. Joe and I will watch each other."

When George had gone Joe looked uneasily at Daly, no doubt expecting a further cross-questioning now that they were alone. But the old man did not even glance at him. He wandered around the room, parting the curtains to look behind them and returning to the fireplace to contemplate the body. He looked at his watch once or twice, but said nothing.

Presently George came back alone.

"She has gone to her room," he said. "I thought there was no need for her to come here and see—that."

He nodded towards the body. Professor Daly said:

"Quite right. The idea of a dead Burden can be forgotten, but once seen he might keep returning to the mind's eye, like an embarrassing photograph."

A few minutes later they heard the sound of heavy, purposeful boots. Professor Daly got up and opened the door.

"Our vigil is over," he said. "Come in, gentlemen."

With the instinctive bending of the head which big men are inclined to accord to strange doorways, the two Guards came into the room. They were in plain clothes, of course, but the second one might have been the model for whom the original uniform was designed. His massive head seemed built to carry a helmet, and his thick neck to stick uncompromisingly up out of the stiff blue numbered collar. His stomach would surely lend splendor to silver buttons, and at its widest point would have been aptly finished off with the glittering buckle. Not a wrinkle showed on his colossal boots, which bore him up as steadily as if he had been a carven stone monument in a city street. Only his innocent, questing, mild blue eye looked disconcertingly out of place. Following Daly's contagious habit of quotation, George remembered the comment that inside every fat man there is a thin man shrieking to be let out.

His companion was also very tall, but of an alarming thinness, from his finely drawn forehead to his long, light shoes. Professor Daly introduced him to George as Inspector Kenny.

"This is Sergeant MacDonagh," said Mr. Kenny.

"He's from the Aran Islands. He led a very sheltered life until he came into the Guards in Galway. But he's learning; aren't you, Colm?"

Sergeant MacDonagh grinned with simple pleasure and said, "I am, that!"

Daly indicated Joe.

"This young man has a guilty secret. I'd advise you not to let him get away. He wouldn't tell it to *no one* but your good selves."

"Good man," murmured Kenny.

"And this," said the old man with a flourish, "is the body, the reason we're all here. Mr. Burden!"

As if in some well-rehearsed dance, the sergeant went to stand with his back to the door, while Kenny bent down to examine the body. A moment later he stood up and said tersely to Joe, "Well, young man, what do you know about this?"

"I didn't to it," said Joe hotly. "That's the professor at his jokes, so it is!"

"I didn't say you did it," said Professor Daly. "Never shake your gory locks at me. Tell your story to the nice man, that's all."

"Will I tell it in front of him?" Joe appealed to the inspector.

"That's all right. You can go ahead."

Professor Daly preened himself, while Joe scowled at him for a moment before saying, sullenly, "I know where that knife came from."

"Do you indeed?" said Kenny easily. "And where did it come from?"

"From the kitchen."

"It doesn't look like a kitchen knife."

"It does not, sir," said Joe. "But it's a carving-knife, all right. It belongs to Mr. O'Reilly, the chef. It's his personal property, you might say."

"I see. Well, perhaps you would go and fetch Mr. O'Reilly for us."

Joe leaped for the door. Professor Daly said, "Please don't give him the impression that he's about to be arrested, Joe."

"Won't I?"

Joe was obviously crestfallen.

"Just tell him Inspector Kenny would like to see him, if he has quite finished serving dinner. I'm sure he has heard about this regrettable business by now."

"Yes, sir. All right, sir."

When the door had closed behind Joe, Daly said, "You should be grateful to me for frightening that lad for you. He was planning to keep you waiting half the night for his measly bit of information."

"I am grateful," said Kenny. "By the way, was Burden the owner of Crane's Court? I heard it changed hands lately."

"That's right," said Daly. "He's only been here a few weeks, but it's clear from the state in which you see him that he was not loved by all."

"I'll be relying on you to give me some information about the inmates of this place," said Kenny. "I've always heard that it's full of cracked old buzzards—"

He stopped suddenly.

"Present company excepted, to be sure, Mike," said Daly blandly.

There was a tap on the door, and the sergeant opened it to admit the chef, but he excluded Joe, who protested vigorously but fruitlessly before being shut outside.

Mr. O'Reilly was still in full chef's regalia, high bonnet, white overalls and immensely long apron. He was a large, glowering, middle-aged man, with a spreading figure acquired from perpetual food-tasting, and the savage brown eye of an artist. He gazed, fascinated, at the body of Mr. Burden, and at last dragged his eyes away to look from the inspector to the sergeant and back again. Then he said, hoarsely, "You're the Guards!"

"That's right," said Kenny amiably. "We just want to ask you a few questions."

He sat on the edge of an armchair and opened his notebook on his knee, saying, "Your name, please?"

"Bartholomew O'Reilly."

"Native of—?"

"Cork," said the chef truculently. "What have you to say to that?"

"Nothing," said Kenny conciliatingly, closing his notebook. He indicated the body. "Bit of nasty business here, as you see."

"That Burden was a nasty business," said the chef. "He's no loss."

Kenny coughed.

"Well, that's beside the point at the moment. We wanted to ask you—have you ever seen that knife before?"

"Of course I have. You wouldn't be asking me if you didn't know it's mine."

"Can you explain how it came to be in its present position?"

"Young fellow," said the chef menacingly, "are you asking me did I stick my good knife into that young caffler lying there on the floor?"

"Well, did you?" asked Professor Daly mildly.

"No!" roared the chef. "That knife will never be the same again. Ruined, that's what it is! Ruined!"

The sergeant grinned happily. Professor Daly said gravely, "It was very thoughtless of the murderer to use it. I suppose it was a good knife?"

"There wasn't another like it in the country, sir. I bought it in Italy six years ago. It was a darling knife. And that Burden took it from me. Came into the kitchen and took it away with him!"

"When did that happen?" asked Kenny quickly.

"This morning, sir. He came around asking what was for dinner. I told him, though it was Greek to him. But still I suppose he had a right to know, being the owner of the place. Next thing he opened the drawer where I keep all my knives, and pretended to be admiring them. Then he started talking about Miss Keane. She's a lassie that works in the office here. Very matey with the boss, she was. And with the old boss before him. And if there's a new boss now she'll be getting matey with him too, I've no doubt. Well, it seems she'd been complaining that I'd been giving her all the queer bits of meat for her dinner." He laughed sourly. "And it was true for her too. I used to pick out the little gristly bits, and the little queer-colored fatty bits that you find in every joint, and myself and Fitzpatrick used to see that my lady Keane got them."

"Who is Fitzpatrick?"

"The head waiter, sir. Can't stand Miss Keane either. Well, Mr. Burden told me I'd have to give her the best bits in future. I told him I would not. I said the guests get the best bits and the staff can have what's left, and that's the way in every decent hotel in the world. I know hotels where they don't even do that—they cook special low-class dinners for the staff. What's wrong with Miss Keane, I said, is that she has too much of a notion of herself. When a goat goes into the church, I said, he won't stop till he'll reach the altar!"

It was clear that this had been a triumphant moment.

"Well, he got real mad at that, and he said I'd have to take his orders. 'Orders!' said I. '*I'm* the one that gives orders in this kitchen, and out of it you're going now!' He was fiddling with that knife at the time. I had a big pointed one in my hand and I waved it and made a run at him. He took one look at me and ran for his life. I followed him up the stairs—just to give him a run for his money, like. It was only when I got back to the kitchen that I found he had gone away with my knife. I had no time to go after it then, but I said to myself that I'd come up after it tonight. And I'll take it now, sir, if it's all the same to you."

He started towards the body. Kenny said curiously, "Do you really think you can just take it away with you now?"

The chef paused and cogitated.

"Well, no," he said at last. "I suppose not. But I'll get it back sometime, won't I?"

Inspector Kenny sighed.

"No doubt. Now, tell me, do you often chase people out of your kitchen with carving-knives?"

"Not often. But I do get terrible cross sometimes. And a chef must get respect. Some people don't see that."

"And threats help?"

"They do," said O'Reilly simply.

Sergeant MacDonagh ushered him outside, and after a nod from Kenny, went with him. Kenny looked at Professor Daly and said, "Is that the artistic temperament?"

"A judicious mixture of cunning and temperament," said the old man. "As he puts it, violence is one of the ways for commanding respect. That story of his has the awful sound of truth. He made no attempt to conceal what happened—"

"Well, half the people who work in and around the kitchen must have heard about it," the inspector pointed out.

"Yes, but if O'Reilly had killed Burden later, he would hardly be gloating still over his success in routing him from the kitchen. The lesser deed would have given place in his mind to the greater one of doing him in."

"Probably," said Kenny.

"And another thing," said Daly. "O'Reilly is not the sort of man to come along here much later in the day and stab Burden in cold blood. If he had caught up with him on the stairs, with his long, pointed kitchen-knife, he would have been capable of anything. He would have stabbed him then—in the back, incidentally—and then had a fit of hysterics and been hauled off to jail in spectacular circumstances. But this hole-and-corner stuff—I don't see him doing it."

"There is nothing hole-and-corner about sticking a foot-long knife into a man's chest," said Kenny. "In fact, it must be one of the most direct actions one can perform." He stroked his jaw meditatively, with a scratching sound on bristling whiskers. "Of course, any man who admits to brandishing carving-knives as a habit is not quite balanced, in my opinion. And think of his child-like wish to have his knife back!"

The inspector got up and stretched his long legs.

"Well now, to work! Sergeant, see if the lads have arrived, and send them up at once if they have."

The big sergeant went out.

"And now, gentlemen," said Kenny blandly, "I won't delay you any longer. You have been most helpful."

And with soothing, congratulatory noises he ushered them both outside.

George had had quite enough by now, and was very glad to be released, but he could see that Professor Daly was sorely disappointed. The old man did his best to cover it. He said, "Nasty company, dead or alive, was our Burden." But he could not keep the note of longing out of his voice, and George was not deceived.

Left alone, Inspector Mike Kenny seated himself again on the arm of a chair and fumbled for his pipe. He contemplated the body of Mr. Burden and reminded himself that this was not going to be an easy case for him. Mike was a Galwayman, born and bred. He had a deep understanding of his people, which up to now, he believed, was the reason of his success as a detective officer. But at Crane's Court he was bewildered. Here were no simple Galway peasants, killing for land hunger, or for the possession of an old tarry boat. Why, even the chef was a Corkman. He hoped that the guests would not all prove to be like Professor Daly, whose agile tongue and air of righteousness had already persuaded Mike into doing something of which he would have thought himself incapable. Never before had he allowed a stranger in the room while someone was being questioned.

And the professor's friend, Mr. Arrow, who seldom spoke, and whose eyes were full of controlled fear—how would he ever come to an understanding of him? How could he even question people like this with an air of authority? He decided to begin with the people he knew.

He rang the bell by the fireside and Joe appeared with startling speed.

"Come in, Joe," said Mike easily. "Don't look at the body. I wouldn't bring you in here only that I must stay until the sergeant comes back."

"That's all right, sir," said Joe heartily. "I've got kind of used of the idea now."

"You're Joe Flynn, aren't you?"

"That's right, sir. I was wondering would you remember me."

"That's my trade," said Mike. "How long are you working here, Joe?"

"Nearly a year, sir. The mother thought that if I came here and learned something about hotels, I could help her to run the digs at home later on. But she's making a mistake if she thinks I'm going home after seeing a spot of this kind of life. You won't tell her I said that, sir?" he asked anxiously. "She'll never let me alone if she gets wind of it."

"I won't say a word," said Mike. "Now tell me, who found Mr. Burden like this?"

"I did," said Joe. "I was only waiting to get you alone to tell you. Mr. Arrow is all right, sir, but the old Professor does be always codding."

"Of course. It's no one's business but mine. Now tell me just what happened."

"Well, sir, Mr. Burden was a very vain little fellow. You can see that by his clothes, can't you? They're like what a woman would wear. And I think he wasn't used to much. He was always asking me questions about what clothes he should wear and things like that. Then he'd slip me an odd ten-bob note for myself. I needn't tell you I didn't mind teaching him if I was paid for it.

Every stitch of his clothes was new, too, sir. What do you make of that?"

"Well, what do you make of it?"

"I didn't need to be a detective to answer that one," said Joe complacently. "I knew it was because he was on his uppers until he came in for this place.

And he was mad anxious to be a real gentleman—wasn't that an old-fashioned sort of an idea? I could have told him that a worn-out old tweed suit was the thing for a gentleman, but sure, he used to love buying fancy socks and shirts and ties, and snazzy pullovers, and I hadn't the heart to say a word against them."

"You weren't earning your ten bob honestly," said Kenny.

"Well, sir, it would have been no use telling him something he didn't want to hear. I'd have lost my job for nothing. He was that sort of a man." Joe lowered his voice confidentially. "Between ourselves, sir, I thought it was the way O'Reilly had stuck the carver in him because he got fed up with the boss's bullying ways." He looked appraisingly at the body. "A great little bully he was, sir, but you could get around him if you knew how."

"Miss Keane got around him, I understand."

"That one? She was after him before he was a day in the house. She knew how to handle him too," said Joe with grudging admiration. "She had a knot tied in him in two shakes. I'd say he'd have married her, even, for she was just the sort for him. I've often seen a pair like that, staying in this very house—a small kind of a greasy fellow with long hair and a nasty face, and a big showy woman dressed like a haitch—"

"Like a what?" asked the startled Mike.

"It's a word for a bad woman, sir," said Joe, blushing. "It begins with a haitch. I don't like to say it out loud."

"I think I understand you," said Mike gravely, heroically controlling an almost irresistible chuckle. "You're quite a philosopher, Joe."

"Oh, I know my way around," said Joe, pleased.

"You were going to tell me how you came to find the body."

"Well, I wouldn't say I came to find the body, exactly, sir. But I came to find Mr. Burden, if you see what I mean, because he was late coming to his dinner and I wondered what would be keeping him. There was a bit of dirty work in the dining room, and I thought he should come along quick and put a stop to it."

"What sort of dirty work?"

"I only saw it through the door, sir, but it was something to do with Miss Keane. I can't stand her myself, but at the same time the public dining room is no place for showing off what we think of each other. The reason for it all was that she went to sit at Mr. Burden's table tonight instead of with the other office girls at their own table."

"Did she indeed?" Mike made a note. "Well, go on with your story about finding the body."

"I came up here, sir, because though he used to love dressing for dinner he was no good at it. I thought he might be having trouble with his tie, like he nearly always had. He wanted to get one of those made-up ones that you just clip on at the back, but I wouldn't let him. I told him no one but the lowest people wore them things."

"Your conscience does you credit."

"I was often sorry enough, though, for I was heart-scalded with that same tie, fixing it for him night after night. So up I come, and I opened the door. The light was on, just like now, and there he was, laid out on the hearthrug. He hadn't even begun to change his clothes. But I says to myself, he needn't bother now, and it looks as if O'Reilly got cross and finished him off. So I just went down and got Fitzer to call Dr. Morgan out from his dinner, and the professor and Mr. Arrow too, so that there would be plenty of people to take the responsibility."

"You did well. And now tell me why did you think O'Reilly did it?"

"Only because it was his knife, I suppose," said Joe uncomfortably. "And because he threatened him. Though indeed he wasn't the only one."

Mike's spirits rose. He asked softly, "Who else threatened him?"

"Maybe I shouldn't say, sir. Maybe they didn't mean any harm."

"Someone meant harm," said Mike, indicating the body.

"Well, sir, there was old Major Dunlea, and Colonel Waters, and old Mrs. Robinson for a start, and then there was Ned, the chauffeur, and O'Reilly, of course—"

"Did all these people threaten Mr. Burden?" asked Mike, appalled.

"They did, sir, and others too, though some of them weren't so noisy about it. But sure, people are always threatening to spill other people's blood," said Joe tolerantly, "and they don't mean the one-half of it."

"Fortunately," said Mike dryly. He wondered how to put his next question without causing Joe's ears to twitch. He said, "You'll be in a bit of a mess now, with no manager, I suppose."

"Not at all," said Joe. "We'll be back to normal, as you might say, with Mrs. Henry looking after the place. Not that Mr. Burden ever did any work. He just used to go round after Mrs. Henry and upset everything she had settled. Oh, he was a real little heart-scald. God rest him," added Joe piously.

The arrival of the police doctor with a couple of ambulance men put an end to the conversation at this point. After them came a photographer from the town, looking distinctly nervous. His eyes popped and he turned pale green when he saw the unusual pose of his customer. Leaving Sergeant MacDonagh to superintend affairs, Inspector Kenny left the room with Joe. It was clear that his next task, whether he liked it or not, would be that of approaching the hotel guests in search of information. He had decided to begin by interviewing Mrs. Henry and he hoped that she would help him to a clearer picture of the relationships at Crane's Court.

5

Joe established the inspector in the library, and went off to fetch Mrs. Henry. It was a well-shaped room, like all the Crane's Court rooms, and it opened off the main hall to the front of the house. There was a large fire here, too, and a great air of comfort and calm. It was furnished with deep leather chairs and leather-topped tables. There were several bookcases along the walls. While he waited Mike glanced at the titles. Most of the books dealt with the care and slaughter of animals. There were innumerable books about horses, including many novels of the Charles Lever sort. There were also books about foxes, dogs, otters, badgers, wild boar, deer, lions and tigers, hippopotami, even rats. Blood flowed copiously through them all. And there was a copy of Ape and Essence, which he thought must have been bought under a misapprehension, perhaps in the hope that it was a manual of monkey hunting. All the books, except this last, were obviously well read. Surely, thought Mike, people who were so familiar with blood would not be squeamish if it happened to be human blood for once. He made a mental note to compile statistics, someday, of the prevalence of murder among the hunting classes.

He was examining a work on pig-sticking when the door opened and Mrs. Henry came into the room. Mike put the book back into its place and turned round to introduce himself. He commiserated with her on the death of her cousin. She thanked him gravely. Mike said:

"Of course there must be an inquest and a police inquiry at once. We'll try to make it as easy for you as we can."

"You're very kind," she said. "It's the most shocking thing—I'm afraid I have no idea what I should do."

On her invitation he sat down by the fire, and while she sat opposite him, he fingered his notebook quietly in his pocket. But he withdrew his hand empty after a moment, for he was anxious not to intimidate her. He said: "What was your first thought when you heard how Mr. Burden had died?"

"That someone had followed him here from Dublin."

"Were you surprised?" Mike asked softly.

She looked at him sharply. It was clear that though she had had a severe shock, she was in full control of herself. She said acidly, "I imagine that one is always surprised to hear that a person one knows has been murdered." After a pause she went on, "You must have heard by now that my cousin was not—was not a very pleasant person."

"Yes, I had heard it," said Mike. "He seems to have made plenty of enemies here."

Mrs. Henry looked uncomfortable.

"That is true," she said. "But they were not serious enmities. People who live together often bicker."

Mike was not sure that the strains at Crane's Court could be dismissed as bickering. He had already sensed the closed-in cut-off atmosphere of the place, just the atmosphere to generate fierce, irrational, disproportionate hatreds.

"Can you tell me how Mr. Burden came to inherit Crane's Court?" he asked.

"Yes, you'll have to hear all about that, I suppose." She pressed her hands together on her knees. "When my husband died I was left rather badly off, and I had to think of making a home for my son. He was only two years old then. I was not qualified in any way to support myself. My uncle needed someone here to look after the housekeeping and I—I asked him to let me have the job. I was able to see more of my son than if I had had to go out to work. There are good schools in the town, too."

She stopped suddenly. Mike wondered what all this had to do with his question, but he only said quietly, "Yes?"

Mrs. Henry laughed nervously, and he noticed that she was slightly flushed. He thought that he had rarely seen such a handsome woman.

"My uncle got an idea that I wanted him to leave me the hotel in his will. In fact I had not thought of this at all, until he mentioned it. Then I realized, of course, that it must look as if I had brought my child to live with him so as to increase the impression that I was a poor, pathetic, deserving widow. At first I thought it might be better for me to look for another job, but I soon changed my mind. You see, I had my son to consider, and I thought it unlikely that I would find as good a place for him again. I decided to ignore my uncle's gibes, and give such good service to the hotel that he would realize that it would be as much to his own disadvantage as to mine if he asked me to leave. You see, I did not know then that someone was filling my uncle's head with lies about me."

"And who was it?" Mike asked.

"A girl called Eleanor Keane, who works in the office," said Mrs. Henry reluctantly.

Miss Keane again, thought Mike. He saw now why Mrs. Henry was telling him this painfully intimate story. No doubt he would hear another version of it from Miss Keane. He said:

"I'm afraid I'm a little confused about the date when all this happened. You came here six years ago?"

"Almost six years ago, yes."

"And when did your uncle begin to make these remarks to you?"

"Only a year ago—soon after Miss Keane—became friendly with him."

"And during the intervening five years had you not established yourself in your uncle's eyes as a person of independence?"

"I had very little to do with my uncle. I saw him once a day, to talk business, and that was almost all. He was out a good deal."

"But how did Miss Keane—?"

"She used to go for long drives with him."

"How did you discover that Miss Keane was injuring you with your uncle?"

"I didn't exactly discover it," said Mrs. Henry slowly. "I just put two and two together. She is the sort of girl who likes to make a scene now and then, and she used words to me which he had used only a few hours before."

"What were they?"

"Something about stepping into a dead person's shoes."

"That is a fairly common phrase," said Mike cautiously.

"Yes, but then it convinced me of what I had suspected before. I had been living under a great strain for a long time, and perhaps my judgment was not good. In any case, I made up my mind to put a stop to the whole affair. I went to my uncle and advised him to make a will in favor of his nephew, John Burden."

"What!"

"It seemed a good idea," said Mrs. Henry, leaning forward in her chair. "I have heard that when a man keeps on talking about who will inherit his property when he is dead, often the reason is that he has not made a proper will at all. You see, John Burden was not my uncle's real nephew. He was the son of his stepbrother. It was likely enough that if my uncle made no will, his property would come to me."

"And he took your advice?"

"Yes."

"Don't you think that was a strange thing to do?"

Mrs. Henry stirred uncomfortably. She looked appealingly at Mike.

"I see I must tell you the rest of the story," she said. "It would have been a strange thing to do, but for the fact that my uncle thought his life was in danger. You see," she went on rapidly, "if he left his money to someone who certainly did not expect to benefit by his will, he felt he would be safe."

"But safe from whom?"

"From me," said Mrs. Henry simply. "I think he thought I was going to poison him. Oh, Miss Keane will tell you," she said bitterly. "When I advised him to make his will in favor of John Burden, I think he almost believed I wished him no harm. But he took my advice, all the same, perhaps to make certain."

"How soon afterwards did he make his will?"

"The very next day, I think. He brought it to my room one evening, quite late, and showed it to me."

"That was an odd thing to do."

"I thought so too." She forced a smile. "You can imagine that I didn't expect to discuss the question with him again. I was surprised when I answered the knock on my door and saw him standing there." She looked into the fire and seemed almost to be talking to herself as she recalled the scene. "I asked him to come in. At first I thought he would not, he looked at me so uneasily. I got angry. I thought how ridiculous it was that he should be so afraid of me. Then I saw that it was not fear. It was a sort of mixture, of apology and—and appeal, as if he knew that he was in no danger from me but was still afraid to trust me completely. Then he came into the room. He showed me the will. I caught him looking at me anxiously to see how I was taking it. I congratulated him on its clarity, and told him he should not worry any more. Then he asked me not to tell anyone about it."

"Why?"

"I don't know. I was not likely to talk about it anyway. Perhaps he thought that if someone were really threatening his life it would be better if there was some doubt as to who would benefit by his death."

"Would it not have been better to have told everyone? Then no one except Burden would have reason to wish for his death."

"I was glad to promise him not to talk about it," said Mrs. Henry. "I did not want people to know that he did not trust me."

"Tell me," said Mike after a moment, "did you really think someone was trying to murder your uncle?"

"I didn't know what to think," said Mrs. Henry. "He was a very old man—he was seventy-eight when he died. I thought he might be imagining it all. But still he seemed so sure. And one thing he told me would be difficult to imagine. He had an Irish terrier that used to sleep in his room. My uncle always had a glass of milk put in his room in the evening, but if he didn't care to drink it he used to give it to the dog next morning. Then one morning, after it had drunk the milk, the dog died. He sent the body to be analyzed, and they said it was full of arsenic. He told me this story, but I had not seen the dog, and I thought it was all too like a story out of a book."

"And how did your uncle die eventually?"

"We went in one morning and found he had died quite naturally in his sleep."

"There was no inquest?"

Mike knew there could not have been, for he would have heard of it. Mrs. Henry said, "Of course not. His own doctor gave the death certificate."

Mike took his notebook frankly out of his pocket now.

"If you could tell me the dates—?"

"My uncle died at the end of June, the 21st, I think."

"And the business about the will?"

"That was some time during the winter or spring—perhaps about the end of

March. The will was dated March 31st. The dog had died about a fortnight before that."

"And between March and June there was no trouble?"

"None. At least I didn't notice any. I may say that I avoided my uncle, and Miss Keane too, during that time."

"And when did Mr. Burden come to live here?"

"At the end of September."

"Wasn't that very soon?"

"The will was quite straightforward. My uncle's solicitor, Mr. Farrell, was the executor, and he got probate after six weeks. Then it took about a month to find Mr. Burden. He came here quite soon after that."

Mike tapped his pencil gently on the cover of his notebook.

"You have done quite right in telling me all this," he said.

"You'll get another version from Miss Keane," said Mrs. Henry dryly.

"We get many versions of every story," said Mike. "We get good at estimating truth." He opened the book again. "Now if you can tell me how you spent the afternoon—?"

"I went to visit my dentist at three o'clock, by appointment. I did a little shopping afterwards, and came back here just after four."

"Were you alone?"

"One of the permanent residents, Mr. Heaslip, was with me all the time. He often comes into town with me."

"And when you came back?"

"I looked over cookery books in my room until it was time to dress for dinner. I had heard, of course, that Mr. Burden had been quarreling with the chef—I expect you've heard that story. He's a splendid chef, and I meant to soothe him down by suggesting a few experiments to him. He loves to be appreciated; and also I hoped that success in his own art would compensate for the injury he had suffered."

"You sound as if you had used that strategy before," said Mike with a smile.

"Yes. It's usually successful."

Mike reflected that not all women could command such ingenuity, nor be willing to use it even if they were able, when it was not directly to their own advantage. He could see that she was a clever woman, clear-sighted and direct. Throughout the interview he had been vaguely aware that she was somehow familiar to him. Studying her now as she gazed into the fire, he thought how rare a person she was, so calm and full of repose. The way her long hair was arranged, the fine slender lines of her face, her quiet intelligent eyes, all made a picture of man's classic ideal of woman at her most attractive. This was the face that launched a thousand ships. This was Penelope. This was Deirdre. And Mike thought he had discovered at last what it was that all these women shared with her. It was that they would never change. At eighty there would be still the calm eyes, the low sweet voice, the quiet hands, the stillness of contentment. He said:

"There is just one more question I must ask. Where is your son now?"

He saw her stiffen, and she seemed to be on her guard at once. She said. "I sent him away to boarding-school a fortnight ago."

"He's very young—only eight years old. I thought you had intended to send him to school in the town."

For the first time she showed signs of real agitation. Tears sprang into her eyes.

"I didn't want to send him away," she said. "But I had to. Mr. Burden—my cousin was interfering with him, teaching him to be rude to me, telling him that I was hoping he would own the hotel some day. Oh, it was terrible, terrible! A child of eight should never hear that sort of thing, never. I had to send him away."

Mike was really shocked. It was difficult to be enthusiastic in the pursuit of the remover of such a man. Mrs. Henry had regained control of herself and had risen to her feet. Suddenly Mike said:

"Have you ever had your photograph in the newspapers?"

"Frequently." She was smiling again. "Before I was married I was the women's golf champion of Ireland."

Now Mike remembered her. Barbara Murray, beautiful, tall, athletic, renowned for her straight, powerful drive, as straight and powerful as the force that had driven the knife into John Burden's heart.

When she had gone Mike settled down to make a few notes of what he had learned from her, and to try to assess its place in his problem. First of all, there was the story of the will. If it was true—and the manner of her telling it had been as clear as rock crystal—then it would be unlikely that she had murdered Burden in order to inherit. It would have been more economical to have murdered her uncle and been done with it. But then there would have been Miss Keane to contend with. With her suspicions aroused, it would have been extremely dangerous to have attacked Murray at all. Mike was convinced that at least part of her story was true—the visit of her uncle to her room late at night, for instance, had been a clear little picture. But the reason for that visit need not have been the one she gave. He had noticed that many of her statements were impossible to verify.

The strongest point against her was that when she found Mr. Burden even more unpleasant to live with than her uncle, she did not then leave Crane's Court with her son. Mike was quite sure that if she had wanted work in another hotel she would have had no difficulty in finding it. She breathed competence. In her years at Crane's Court she must surely have met some people who would help her. But instead of that she had endured Burden's insults, and had actually sent her small son away to boarding-school, much against her will. It was possible that she had known that this last was only a temporary necessity, since she had intended that her tormentor should not live much longer. He thought she had not meant to let him see that it had been her original intention to send the boy to school in the town. That had slipped out, he was certain, and he recalled her flushed face and sudden pause.

At this point, Mike decided that it was futile to speculate any further. There was no need to build up a case against Mrs. Henry before he had interviewed anyone else. He realized that the main reason why he had worked so hard on her was that he had found on other occasions that people are usually murdered by their nearest and dearest.

He sighed, and put his notebook away, and got up to leave the room. He made a face at the hearty, bloody books as he passed them by, and let himself out into the hall.

A young woman sat there in a glass cage, and Joe was gossiping cheerfully to her through the window. He jumped forward when Mike appeared and offered to conduct him wherever he listed.

"I'm your man, Inspector," he said. "You can trust me."

And his eyes popped out with excitement.

Mike said he would like to find Mr. Arrow's room.

"It's late," he said, "but I hope he won't mind my visiting him all the same."

"He will not, sir," said Joe. "Mr. Arrow is a fine decent man."

He started towards the back corridor, but Mike firmly hauled him back and obtained directions from him for finding George's room. Palpably disappointed, Joe returned to his gossip, and Mike went on his way.

As he turned the corner where George's room was, he stopped in astonishment. Coming towards him was a small familiar figure, grinning ingratiatingly from one large red ear to the other.

"Good evening, Martin," said Mike menacingly.

"Good evening, Mike. A very—a very good evening."

As he came closer an overpowering odor of rum became apparent. It was as if the little man's very clothes were soaked in it. Mike thought that if he put a match to him, he would probably glow with a blue flame, like an evil little plum-pudding. He said:

"How do you come to be here, Martin, so nice and handy? Who told you to come?"

"No one," said Martin, offended. "I have a citizen's rights to go for a walk and drop into the bar of a hotel to refresh myself before going home."

"You went for a walk!" Mike repeated derisively. "You never go for a walk."

"I do!" said Martin fiercely, and added, "now and then."

"You go for a walk," said Mike, "when there is a nice murder at the end of it. I have deep suspicions of you, Martin Hogan. I'm beginning to believe that when your racing tips go wrong, you commit a murder to divert the editor's attention from yourself."

"Ah, now, Mike, don't make unsuitable jokes," said Martin. "Murder is a nasty business."

"I have another theory," said Mike, "that you have a register of potential murderers, and that you watch them coming to the boil, so to speak. Otherwise, how in heaven's name do you *happen* to be here just when there is a bloody murder?"

"Please, Mike! Don't mention blood," said the little man, closing his eyes painfully.

"You little ghoul," said Mike. "Mention of it makes you thirsty for some, I suppose."

Mr. Hogan groaned, still with his eyes shut. He opened them wide, blue and watery and innocent, at Mike's next question.

"How did you happen to be in the neighborhood, then?"

"I've been spending my holidays in Salthill," he said. "Why shouldn't I?"

"And you were conveniently spending your holidays in Roundstone the time the Englishman murdered his aunt—in the depths of winter, too." Mike regarded Martin gloomily. "I hope you haven't been messing about here. If you've done any harm—"

"I haven't said a word," said Martin indignantly. "I'll admit I've been looking around to see if I could help, but I swear I haven't said a word."

"Just appeared here and there like a malignant ghost, upsetting my suspects' nerves, I suppose."

"Well, what would you expect? If a conscientious reporter hears that the boss of the very hotel he is drinking in has been done to death with a damned big saber, do you expect him to slip away quietly like a little gentleman, and say nothing about it? Think of his starving wife and children."

"Have you a starving wife and children?" asked Mike with interest.

"Good God, no! And I haven't even asked leading questions yet," said Martin mournfully.

"Well, please don't. I know your leading questions. 'Would you like to make a statement to the press as to why you committed the murder?' "

Martin grinned reminiscently.

"You'll admit that question produced results when I asked it," he said. "In spite of your ungracious attitude, Mike, I'm going to give you one piece of information. You have actually got a murderer under the roof."

"Isn't that why I'm here?"

"I mean a real known murderer, a convicted one," said Martin.

"Who is it?"

"Aha! I'm not going to tell you that. Surely you're not a detective inspector for nothing."

Mike made a grab at him, but he slipped past agilely and ran along the corridor to the hall. For a moment Mike considered pursuing him, and then he remembered Joe and the girl in the office, who would both be witnesses to his certain defeat. For he knew that even in the unlikely event of his catching Martin, he would never be able to extort information from him. With an exasperated shrug he continued on his way to George's room.

An invitation to come in answered his soft knock. He opened the door, and paused on the threshold with a slight sense of shock. Mr. Arrow was sitting huddled in an armchair before the fire. The face that he turned towards the door was gray, and again Mike saw the lurking spirit of fear in his eyes. There was nothing extraordinary in this, of course. It was almost certainly the reaction of a sensitive man against violence, and Mike had often encountered it before. It hurt him to have to probe a mind already raw. It was at moments like this that he positively hated the capacity implanted in him for discerning the wickedness of his fellow men, the capacity which had steadily pushed him forward on the road to promotion, almost without his consent.

He closed the door and walked across to the fireplace, where he stood looking down at Mr. Arrow, who was now trying to smile apologetically.

"Have you had a stiff drink?" Mike asked. "You may not realize it, but being pitchforked into a discovery such as you made can be a real physical shock."

"I know," said George wryly, visibly trying to control his twitching, bloodless lips. "At first I thought I had borne up very well, and then when I got back here I suddenly just curled up—"

"I can ring for Joe," said Mike, with his hand on the bell. "He'll bring you a whiskey and soda."

"Please don't," said George. "I'll just have a glass of water."

He went unsteadily to the washbasin and ran water into the tooth-glass. He half turned to Mike and said:

"Got a rocky heart, you know. I can't have large whiskeys at the rate I would like them."

A number of things fitted together for Mike, among them the ground-floor room and the oversized reaction to the death of Burden. And Mike could see now that it was an oversized reaction.

George returned to the fire with his glass of water and invited Mike to sit down. He was looking a little better now. Mike said:

"Do you feel up to answering a couple of questions? If you'd rather wait till tomorrow—"

"No. I'd rather go ahead now. You see, if I put you off till tomorrow I'll lose my night's sleep worrying about it."

A bit of a neurotic too, thought Mike. These chronic invalids often are. Always studying themselves and explaining themselves and their reactions with an unhealthy interest. And they are usually looking for comfort and assurance even when they would be afraid or ashamed to ask for it openly. Well, one reassurance could be given, though Mike had no intention of giving it. A man with a weak heart was an unlikely person to have succeeded in plunging a kitchen-knife into Mr. Burden.

Mike fidgeted with his notebook and asked:

"How long have you been staying here, Mr. Arrow?"

"Only four weeks," said George. "Since the middle of September."

"And had you intended to stay long?"

"I intended to live here—permanently," said George after a moment's hesitation. "My doctor advised it. One can live here very comfortably."

"I believe that. Did it strike you as odd that Joe should have summoned you to Mr. Burden's room, when you are not very long here, and since you have a weak heart?"

"No," said George. "You see, the person Joe summoned was really Professor Daly, who is an obvious person to deal with an emergency. I just happen to share his table in the dining room. As to the second part of your question, no one here knows about my heart. I particularly wished it that way. I don't want to become an invalid, never to be allowed to forget my disability. And I'll be obliged if you won't mention it to anyone."

Again Mike heard an undercurrent querulous tone in his voice.

"Of course I won't mention it," he said, "unless it is necessary. Well, since you have only lived here for a few weeks, I expect you were not very well acquainted with Mr. Burden?"

"I met him for the first time on the train," said George. "He was a man who readily conversed with strangers. In half an hour he gave me a good look into his mind."

"And what did you see?"

"Nothing very savory."

"You needn't answer my next question if you don't want to, Mr. Arrow. Have you any idea who killed Burden?"

"No," said George after a pause. He looked suddenly and sharply at Mike and said violently, "No!"

"That's all right," said Mike comfortably. "It's my own business to discover the facts. We sometimes get a helpful hint from an intelligent onlooker, but of course many people are afraid of creating an ineradicable prejudice against an innocent person by mentioning a name."

"I'm sorry I shouted at you," said George after a moment. "I find that I'm getting more intolerant every day."

"As long as you know what is happening you can stop it," said Mike, and then wondered if George would be offended.

But he was not. He sighed deeply and said:

"It's the inconvenient instinct of self-preservation, I suppose. As to who murdered Mr. Burden, I simply don't know. People who live here tend to become selfish and materialistic. It's too comfortable, perhaps. Or it could be that since none of us work our consciences keep telling us we're parasites. Even the people employed here have caught the feeling, though they work hard enough."

"Now perhaps you can tell me how you spent the afternoon," said Mike, as he got out his notebook.

George described his visit to Mrs. Fennell.

"Just before three o'clock, Mrs. Henry asked me to drive into the town with her, but I had accepted a formal invitation from Mrs. Fennell, so I had to visit her instead."

He did not say with what rage and despair he had watched Mrs. Henry drive off with Heaslip, though even now the very memory of it twisted his soul. He hurried on to tell of Mrs. Fennell's ghostly friend, Sir Rodney Crane, and after a moment's reflection he added the story of her belief that old Mr. Murray had been murdered.

"I'm fairly sure that she is not a dangerous lunatic," he said. "When you meet her I think you will agree with me. She seemed to me to be one of those people who get more than half of the truth right, and the rest of it all distorted and unreal."

Mike made a note of Mrs. Fennell, who sounded promising, before asking George to continue.

"I spent over an hour with her," said George. "When I came back to the hotel I found Professor Daly and Mr. Heaslip just setting out for a walk, so I went with them."

"It was rather late then, wasn't it?"

"About half-past five. It's still daylight until seven o'clock. We walked to the end of the strand together, and then Professor Daly and I turned home. Mr. Heaslip went on by himself. He watches birds. We walked back slowly and reached the hotel at about half-past six. I left Daly in the hall and came along here."

"And you were here until dinnertime, alone?"

"Maggie, the housemaid on this corridor, was here talking to me for the first ten minutes, but I was alone the rest of the time."

Mike wished Mr. Burden had chosen another time to be murdered. He was beginning to see that the hour of dressing for dinner might have been expressly designed for persons who need a quiet spell for the commission of crime.

He stood up to go and noticed how the weary, pinched lines had returned to George's mouth.

"You should have a sedative," he said.

"I haven't got one," said George shortly.

Though it was clear that the subject was unwelcome, Mike persisted.

"This Dr. Morgan who is staying here will surely be able to give you something."

"I prefer not to trouble him," said George stiffly.

"Doctors are used to being troubled," said Mike cheerfully.

With a word of thanks he let himself out into the corridor, leaving George standing on the hearthrug looking uncertainly after him.

6

Though lights still burned everywhere, there was no one in the hall when Mike reached it. The office was locked up for the night, with the heavy account-books neatly stacked on the desk. There was no sign of Joe.

He looked into the library, and saw a rather foppish man with tired white hair turning the pages of a book, and whistling through his teeth in an irritated way. He swung around when Mike appeared, and shot the book back into the shelf.

"You're the policeman," he said. "I thought you'd be wanting to see me. My name is Morgan."

Mike thanked him for the good order in which he had found things when he arrived.

"You have no idea what damage people can do if they are not stopped," he said. "They would have carried the body into the bedroom and laid it on the bed, taken out the knife, polished it up nicely and returned it to its owner, cleaned the carpet with the vacuum cleaner and dusted the furniture so as to have everything nice for the arrival of the police. That has happened to me before now."

"I don't think it would have happened this time," said Dr. Morgan. "There was an intelligent old buffer there who could be relied on to behave sensibly. Daly, I think, is his name. An ex-professor of English, they tell me."

"That's right," said Mike. "I'm well acquainted with him."

"Well, there was no doubt about the cause of death," said Dr. Morgan. "That knife was handled by a person of determination. Extraordinary how it penetrated the clothes so easily."

"They never seem to have trouble that way," said Mike. "I know a good deal about knives. They are quite popular in my district."

The doctor raised his eyebrows.

"As to the time of death," he said, "it would be difficult to say much with certainty. He was lying in front of a blazing fire, as you saw. It could have been any time between half-past four and seven, and I don't suppose that will be much use to you. Of course I didn't take his temperature or anything like that."

"Our own man will do all that," said Mike. "By the way, are you acquainted with Mr. Arrow?"

"Nervous, good-looking chap with fair hair? Yes, I met him over the body—he was with Daly. He seemed intelligent."

Dr. Morgan's tone left no doubt that this, in his opinion, was a rare quality.

"Well, this evening's activities have been a shock to him. I should say he's in for a bad night. Could you—would you mind giving him a sedative?"

"Can't he take an aspirin?" said Morgan impatiently.

"He says he hasn't got one; and he also says he has a bad heart. I'd be obliged if you'd just pay him a visit—he is in room forty-eight, on the ground floor."

Dr. Morgan looked sharply at Mike and said curtly, "All right. Hearts are my line, as it happens. I'll fix him up with something."

Mike felt some uneasiness now that he had achieved his object. "He didn't want to trouble you," he said. "It's entirely my idea."

"I'll treat him gently," said Morgan dryly, as he went out.

He almost collided with Professor Daly in the doorway. The old man stood looking after him.

" 'The keen unpassioned beauty of a great machine,' " he said, shaking his head. "I can't say I count him among my great loves."

"They get callous after a while, I suppose," said Mike. "It's a form of self-protection."

"Have you got callous?"

"Well, no. But that's different."

"The difference is in the degree of selfishness—"

"Come in and shut the door, Daly," Mike interrupted hastily.

"And cut the cackle," said the old man, doing as he was told.

They dropped into armchairs one on either side of the fire.

"Well, young Mike," said the old man, "how is your detection this evening?"

"It's not easy to say," said Mike cautiously. "It looks a rather complicated business. Burden seems to have been a most unpleasant young man."

"That is so. I never before saw a man make so many enemies in such a short space of time. In fact I think his murderer was a public benefactor. 'Where the offense is, let the great axe fall.' " He looked hopefully at Mike, and then said regretfully, "Of course you must not agree with me. An eye for an eye is your motto."

"Not mine exactly," said Mike uncomfortably, and then he realized that he was allowing himself to be drawn. He said firmly, "We're not going to argue the philosophy of the thing at this hour of the night, if you please. Joe gave me a list of people who threatened Burden, and I must go and question them all. *You* didn't threaten him, by any chance?"

"Good God, no! Though I will say that I thought—objectively—that it was time he was gathered to his fathers. But I didn't kill him, in fact."

"I'm very glad to hear it," said Mike gravely.

"Pity, in a way," said the old man. "I could make a fine speech from the dock."

"No doubt. Well, I'd better find Joe, to conduct me to these bloodthirsty people."

Mike got up and rang the bell.

"You won't be able to do it tonight," said the professor from the depths of his armchair. "A Crane's Court resident's bedroom is his castle. They won't let you in."

"But they'll have to let me in. I'm the Law."

"That won't weigh with them, I assure you. Take my advice and occupy the good bed that Mrs. Henry has provided for you and thank your stars that you're getting a night's sleep."

"But it's not proper," said Mike. "How will I be able to explain the delay?"

"You'll have to plead special circumstances," said Daly comfortably. "Surely no one would expect you to be sleuthing all through the night."

"You don't know the powers that be," said Mike gloomily. "But I suppose I'll have to wait till tomorrow morning. I don't want to force my way in."

"Do you know which room you're in?"

"Joe will show me. Poor Colm is going to sit up all night. But he says he doesn't mind. He has often done it in a currach on the bosom of the deep, he says, waiting for fish. Colm has a colorful turn of speech."

"Colorful, if obvious," Daly agreed. "By the way, O'Reilly's nerve is shattered. He says that, though you ushered him out with every appearance of trust and goodwill, he feels the shadow of cold steel hovering about his wrists."

"He didn't put it like that."

"No," Daly admitted, "but the idea was the same."

"He's quite right to be frightened," said Mike. "Knives are usually handled by their owners, and furthermore a chef would be a good carver. The only reason I let him go tonight was that something in the tone of his voice made me think he could be telling the truth. But either Colm or one of his minions will be breathing down his neck for the next few days. I'm taking a big risk in not locking him up at once."

"Am I right in assuming that this is your first visit to Crane's Court?" asked Daly.

"That's right."

"I hope you're not going to expect normality. 'Where were you at six o'clock on the night of the tenth?' 'Four yards east of the main gate of the hotel.' "

"That's not normality," said Mike decidedly.

"Well, all I can say is that whatever is normality, you won't get it."

"They're not all as mad as Mrs. Fennell?" asked Mike in sudden alarm.

"So you've heard of her? No. I shouldn't say they're *all* as mad as Mrs. Fennell."

"I think I'm going to need my night's sleep," said Mike gloomily.

The old man heaved himself to his feet.

"If you get into difficulties, you may call on me," he said heartily.

In the hall, Mike found that Joe was waiting to conduct him to his room. It was upstairs, to the front of the house, and it was furnished with an individuality and charm which he rightly ascribed to Mrs. Henry.

Left alone, he sat for a long time before the fire, turning over the things he had heard and speculating on the personalities he had encountered. And there would be more of them tomorrow. A man of lively imagination, he valued this opportunity of thinking himself into the mentality of the residents of Crane's Court. He believed that man's surroundings have a profound effect on his character and activities. There was an almost tangible aura about Crane's Court which seemed to encompass everyone who lived there in a greater or less degree. With Mrs. Fennell it had taken the form of the ghost of Sir Rodney Crane, with others perhaps it had been less extreme.

Reproving himself for these unpolicemanlike fancies, he went to bed.

At eight o'clock in the morning Joe brought him a cup of tea.

"Do you have any free time?" asked Mike.

"I'll be free this evening," said Joe, "and all day tomorrow. The mother will be expecting me at home to clean the range and do a bit of gardening, or anything else she can think up for me. She says I don't do any work at all in this place, only standing around. Could I send her a message that you said I was to stay here, sir?"

"She might go into the barracks in town and demand you back," Mike pointed out gravely, sipping his tea.

"She might," said Joe despondently. He brightened up to say, "I suppose you'll be asking questions off of the old jades today, sir? Old Ma Robinson's son is coming from Dublin this morning. He'll be here in time for lunch." He came close and hissed, "She sent for him!"

"Did she, indeed?"

Mike swung his legs out of bed.

"She did, so. She asked me to send him a telegram last night—the queerest telegram you ever saw. 'Come quickly. It has happened.' That was all. And he sent back a telephone message later on to say he'd be here for lunch."

"You sent that telegram without telling me?"

"I did, sir. I didn't mean any harm."

Joe backed towards the door.

"How much did she give you?"

"Nothing, sir. Honest."

"How much?"

Joe threw up his hands.

"All right, sir. Don't eat us. She gave me five bob not to tell you last night.

Little enough to risk my neck for, but sure, I didn't see any harm in sending a little telegram."

"I'm the judge of that." Mike was dressing rapidly. "Don't do any more jobs for anyone without telling me first."

"All right, sir," said Joe, very sobered. "But didn't I come and tell you first thing this morning? Now, didn't I?"

"Yes, that was something."

When the door had closed behind Joe, Mike grinned to himself. He was not sorry that the queer telegram had been sent, but it was well to curb Joe's helpfulness at an early stage. He wondered what had prompted the old woman to send for her son. If he had known about the telegram last night, he would have had an excuse for questioning her.

Before going into the dining room for breakfast, Mike found Colm and sent him home to sleep. The big fellow was quite unconcerned after his night's vigil, and only regretted that no one had tried to bolt during the night.

"I'll be back at six o'clock for certain sure," he said fiercely, as he climbed into the police car that had brought his substitute.

The dining room was almost empty when Mike went in. It seemed that most of the residents preferred to breakfast in bed. He saw that none of the people he had met yesterday were present, except Mrs. Henry, who came over to ask if he had been well looked after in the matter of his bedroom. She was pale, and she looked as if she had not slept at all.

The head waiter gave him a small table near the door, from which he could see down the length of the room. While his breakfast was being served he took the opportunity of quietly discovering from Fitzpatrick the names of the widely scattered people about him. Among them was Mr. Quinn, thin and fox-faced, dressed in jodhpurs and a stock. Mike found that he was surprised to hear him ask in human speech for fresh toast. It would have been less unexpected to discover that he conversed in short barks. A little away from Mr. Quinn there was Major Dunlea, who had the long wandering snout and dark-rimmed eyes of a badger, and whose hairy tweed coat continued the illusion. He was a small man, though his shoulders were broad. His scanty hair was snow-white, and his uneasy eyes looked upwards through black eyebrows. His chin was perpetually sunk on his chest. He ate in a hurried, nibbling fashion, as if he were afraid of watchers, and when he had finished he mopped up his plate with a piece of bread.

As Mike watched him, the Major shot him a sideways look. Then he got up hurriedly, almost upsetting his chair, scrobbled up his napkin and dropped it on the table, and scuttled out of the room. Mike raised his eyebrows and finished his breakfast, and a few minutes later he went out into the hall.

There were many people on his list to be interviewed, and of them all he wished to begin with Miss Keane. He sent Joe to find her, and went out on to the terrace to savor the fresh autumn morning. As he walked a few yards away from the house, he heard a step on the gravel behind him. He turned around and found the little tweed-coated figure of Major Dunlea at his elbow.

"Good morning, Major," said Mike. "My name is Kenny."

"Oh, yes, I know all about you," said the Major in a high querulous tone of voice. "Trying to find out about Burden, aren't you?"

"Yes," said Mike. "Do *you* know anything about it?"

"That's always the way," said the Major. "Catch a man out once and you never let him alone afterwards, always hounding him down, give him no chance to live—"

"Excuse me," Mike interrupted. "I'm afraid I don't know what you're talking about. Were you 'caught out' once?"

"Do you mean to say you don't know? I haven't changed my name or anything. And you were glaring at me suspiciously in there at breakfast."

"I often glare at breakfast," said Mike patiently, "but not necessarily suspiciously." Suddenly he remembered something. "Hadn't you better tell me the story yourself?" he said gently.

Again the wavering badger-like eye looked him over.

"I'm a murderer," said Major Dunlea simply.

"Someone mentioned last night that we had more than one on the premises," said Mike delicately.

"More than one? Then you don't think I killed Burden?"

"I have no reason to think that you did."

"I know who told you. It was that little rat of a reporter in the bar last night. I saw him watching me. You see, I once shot my cook."

"Indeed?" said Mike noncommittally.

"Yes. It happened this way." The little man looked down at his boots and cleared his throat apologetically, while still giving the impression that he was rather pleased with what he was about to say. He looked up through his eyebrows at Mike. "I used to be very particular in those days. It wore off me in jail."

"Ah, yes, I remember," Mike murmured. "You are not long—out?"

"Three months," said the Major. "I came straight here." He sighed. "I had a nice little place in the midlands"—he mentioned the name of the county— "and there was quite a good bunch of people like myself about. But though you'd think that would mean the servants would be efficient, it did not. They were abominable. And the county people didn't mind. They'd have eaten roast, stuffed fox without a protest. But I was a bit of a gourmet—I'm a good cook myself, though I say it. That's why I like it here—marvelous grub."

He licked his lips reminiscently while Mike waited patiently

"Oh, yes, I had lots of provocation. Nasty old slut she was that used to do my cooking. And had the gall to tell me that single gents can never afford to be particular! Well, one day I decided I'd had enough of it. I'm always determined to follow up a decision once I've made it—like a badger following up a scent, you know." He wagged his long muzzle while Mike gasped with suppressed laughter. "I read the Riot Act. I laid down the law. I delivered an ultimatum. I told her that if the Brussels sprouts were watery again, I'd shoot her. She didn't believe I meant it, of course. People never do when you say that sort of thing. Well, the next time the sprouts were watery, I told Callan, my man, to bring in my gun, and to send up the cook with the coffee."

"And she came?"

"She did," said the Major grimly. "She was afraid to disobey a direct order. So I shot her."

The little man shrugged.

"It was a short-sighted thing to do. I'd forgotten that Ireland has got so damned law-abiding. In France it would have been understood—it would have been a *crime passionel*. I probably would have got away with it. But not here. I got ten years."

"Yes, I remember hearing about it," said Mike gently.

"I never use a gun now," said the Major. "Can't get a license as a matter of fact. Still, I see their point of view."

"And you tell me you didn't—you hadn't anything to do with Burden's death?" Mike asked, prompted by something in the Major's choice of words.

"Certainly not!" said the little man indignantly. "If I can't use a gun, I certainly wouldn't use a knife, like a blasted native!"

"No offense meant," said Mike. "We have to ask these questions."

"Of course, of course." He looked up through his eyebrows again. "Then you're not following me about?"

"No, in point of fact I'm not."

"Good. Jail makes a fellow queer, you know. They were very nice to me there, though. I miss it sometimes. Do you think they'd like it if I went back to visit them?"

"I'm sure they would be delighted," said Mike gravely.

"Must do that, sometime. When this business is finished. I'd like to wait about to see you find out who done it. I take a professional interest, you know."

There was a gleam of amusement in his eye as he turned and ambled off up the terrace. Mike stood looking after him for a moment before he went back into the hotel. There had been an unmistakable ring of truth about Major Dunlea's contempt for the knife as a means of dispatching one's enemies, but for all that his activities would have to be investigated for any connection with Burden. It was possible that since his experience with his cook, he had learned that a little finesse in murder pays, and that it is worth while covering one's tracks. If he had nothing to do with the present problem, Mike thought irritably, he had certainly succeeded in clouding the issue.

In the hallway he found Joe smirking triumphantly, and a tall, flamboyant young woman whom he took to be Miss Keane standing a few paces behind him. She looked decidedly more angry than upset at the death of her friend. Mike guessed that Joe had been teasing her.

"That will do, Joe," he said curtly, and led Miss Keane into the library.

Under his kind and sympathetic care she soon dissolved into tears.

"All the better," thought Mike callously, for he disliked her type. "Tears often grease the tongue."

Soon she was informing him that Mrs. Henry was the murderer of both her uncle and her cousin.

"She wants the hotel for her son. Anyone with an eye in their head could see that. As soon as she saw I was getting great with Mr. Murray, she began to try to poison him. And she got away with it in the end, just when I got engaged to him."

"But there was a proper death certificate," said Mike. Miss Keane looked at him pityingly.

"That one is too clever," she said. "She knew how to make it look natural."

"Mr. Burden's death didn't look natural," Mike pointed out.

"That's her cleverness again. She knew she'd have to change her way of doing it this time. A young man of Mr. Burden's age doesn't die in his sleep. Oh, I can see you're on her side. That's always the way with her—she can wind all the men around her little finger."

"I'm not on anyone's side," said Mike patiently. "I'm simply trying to get at the truth."

He considered Miss Keane for a moment while he wondered how best to prod her into further accusations. He trusted himself not to be prejudiced by anything she would say, and he hoped she would supply him with a fuller picture of relations between the hotel residents. He said:

"You know a lot about Crane's Court. I notice a good many old people about."

She made a contemptuous gesture.

"They all died before the flood, but they don't know it. They have nothing to do all day but sit around running people down and criticizing. If I had my way I'd clear the whole lot out."

"I believe Mr. Burden shared your view."

"Yes. He agreed with me about a lot of things." A deep flush covered her face all at once. "Last night he was going to announce our engagement!"

"Indeed?" said Mike politely.

Suddenly she was on her feet blazing at him.

"Is that all you can say? 'Indeed!' Twice it's happened to me now, that the man I got engaged to was murdered, and you sit there and say 'Indeed!' If that's the best you can do, you should be out making the old women drive their donkey-carts on the left-hand side of the road, or asking the children what kept them from school, for you're not much good in the job you're at!" Suddenly her eyes opened wide. "I'm afeared, so I am! How do I know it won't be myself next?"

And she was really frightened, he could see. He decided that he had made a bad mistake with her, first of all in doubting the truth of her statement, but especially in letting her see his doubt. The reason why he had doubted her story was that each of her fiancés had been dead before the engagement was announced. Mike was long enough at his job to have noticed the number of people who lay claim to a special friendship with anyone who, being dead, cannot disclaim the relationship. This is especially likely, he knew, if any notoriety attaches to the circumstances of the death. He had seen casual acquaintances of the deceased wallowing in emotion, beating the ground and groaning that life held no more meaning for them, and then tidying themselves up briskly and getting on with their business obviously quite refreshed.

He made an effort to retrieve the situation.

"I'm sorry if I seemed to doubt your statement," he said. "You had come to an important point in your story, and I didn't want to interrupt."

"It didn't sound like that to me, then," she said sulkily.

But still he could see that she was pleased at having got an apology. He guessed that this did not happen to her very often. He waited for her to go on, and after a moment she said:

"It wasn't such a queer thing for me to get engaged to him. I was great with him from the day he came."

She had used the same curious local phrase in connection with Murray. Mike knew its exact connotation, which was that she had been on friendly, familiar terms with him, with the ultimate prospect, quite unexpressed, of marrying him some day.

"Indeed I think I was the only one in the place that was nice to him," Miss Keane went on. "I got sorry for him, walking around all by himself in the daytime and sitting in his room in the evenings, afraid to come out for fear those old ones would be turning up their noses at him. I used to go in to visit him in the evenings and we used to have a laugh at them all on the quiet. I told him about their goings-on of all sorts and he used to knock great fun out of teasing them afterwards." She laughed sourly. "He said that only for me he'd be driven daft. Then the night before last I told him how O'Reilly and Fitzpatrick were tormenting me. He said they were mad jealous, and he said he'd see O'Reilly in the morning."

She stopped and flushed again, and Mike said gently, "I've heard the next part of the story."

He could see that she was not anxious to describe how her champion had been pursued ignominiously up the stairs by his own chef.

"Well, I wasn't going to see him again until after dinner, but he telephoned to the office for me about five o'clock."

"And were you in the office?"

"Yes. I answered the telephone myself. I went around to his room at once."

"Try to tell me exactly what happened," said Mike. "Make a little picture of it in your mind and describe it to me."

"All right. You know the way Mr. Burden's rooms are, two doors opening on to the corridor, one from the bedroom and one from the sitting room, but inside there is a door between the two rooms."

"I've been through them. A very handy arrangement."

"Well, I knocked on the sitting room door and waited for him to tell me to come in. When he answered, I went in and saw him standing there on the hearthrug, sort of lifting himself up and down on his toes and heels. He looked very pleased, and I was glad of that, because he hadn't sounded pleased on the telephone."

"What had he said on the telephone?"

"He said, 'Miss Keane, can you come around to my room at once?' Quite rough. But I didn't think anything of it, because I thought there must have been someone in the room when he called me Miss Keane."

"Go on," said Mike.

"Well, he waited until I came over to him, and then he said, 'Eleanor, would you like to marry me?' I must have looked surprised, because—well, you don't expect a person to—to ask you like that. He said, 'I'm sorry I can't give more time to it. I never meant to ask you like this. But now I must find out quickly.' Well, I said yes, I would like to marry him, and then I hardly knew what to do next. He said something about us making a good partnership, and then he sort of laughed to himself and said, 'I'll announce it tonight after dinner, when all the old hags are together.' He said I was to wear my red dress and sit at his table in the dining room, to tease them a bit first. It was going to be a great joke. And he said it would learn—teach O'Reilly and Fitzpatrick not to be annoying me. It didn't turn out a bit like that," she finished dolefully.

"Did he mention his encounter with O'Reilly?"

"No, and I didn't ask him about it. I—I thought he wouldn't like it. But I saw O'Reilly's knife on the table."

"You did!" Mike shouted.

"Oh, my God, Mr. Kenny, you frightened the heart out of me! And my nerves are gone to hell since yesterday."

She burst into tears again, and it took all Mike's patience and tact, and ten minutes of valuable time, before she would consent to sit up and go on with her story. It was especially aggravating since he had noticed the pause while she realized the dramatic value of her last statement and regretted not having made more of it, then the watchful eye on him while she wept theatrically. He would have dearly loved to clump her head for her. He could have sworn she would understand that. But since this course was out of the question, he had to go through the business of soothing her down as if he meant every word of it. At last it was possible to say:

"Go on about the knife."

"I knew it was O'Reilly's knife. I've often seen it with him in the kitchen. I had heard how it got into Mr. Burden's room, too."

Very delicately put, thought Mike. He asked, "Which table was it on?"

"The small one, by the fire, where there was a bowl of chrysanthemums."

"Which way was the handle turned?"

"It was turned towards me. The point was to the wall."

"So that you could just grab it and plunge it into Mr. Burden. Very convenient."

She stared at him with her mouth open, while her face went quite white. When she spoke it was in a shaken whisper.

"Are you saying I did it, Mr. Kenny? Are you saying I did it?"

"No," said Mike comfortably. "I should have said, 'So that *one* could grab it.' Sorry if I upset you."

She drew a long shuddering breath and he wondered for a moment if she was going to faint. He would have been surprised if she had, because she seemed to be a person who never lost control of herself. She couldn't afford to, he supposed. It was interesting to see that when she was genuinely shocked and frightened, she did not fly into hysterics at all. He went on with his questions as if nothing had happened.

"You were saying that you got an impression that someone was with Mr. Burden when he telephoned to you," he said. "Did you think of this again when you went into his room?"

"Yes," she said. "And I know who it was, too."

"And who was it?"

He hoped it would not occur to her to revenge herself on him by withholding this vital information.

"It was old Mrs. Robinson."

"Did he mention that Mrs. Robinson had been with him?"

"No, but I smelt her," said Miss Keane simply.

There was a pause while Mike wondered how to put his next questions without an undignified giggle.

"Does she use scent?"

"No. But lots of old ladies have a sort of smell of their own, and I know Mrs. Robinson's."

Very nice, thought Mike, and had a nightmare vision of himself producing Miss Keane in court to testify that she had smelt Mrs. Robinson. The expression on the judge's face would almost make it worth while. He got her to tell him about Mrs. Robinson, and she was very willing to do so. She told him the story of the controversy about tea on the veranda, and said:

"I had told Mr. Burden that story, and yesterday he told Mr. Quinn he could bring all his friends in there if he liked. Next thing you know, Mrs. Robinson goes to visit him, and next thing after that—he's dead!"

"But he was alive after Mrs. Robinson visited him," Mike pointed out.

"Couldn't she have come back afterwards?"

It was interesting to see that Miss Keane now preferred Mrs. Robinson to Mrs. Henry as a murderer. Obviously, though she could have been right in either of her guesses, she hated them both equally. She was a queer, discontented girl, and he doubted if she would ever be happy now. She might have been happy with Burden, if he had lived. They were two of a kind, and they could have enjoyed being nasty together.

Miss Keane's frightened eyes were searching him.

"What are you thinking about, Mr. Kenny? What are you going to do now? I don't want to sleep in this place no more. I want to go down and sleep in my mother's place."

"Why? You'll be all right, I'll have a Guard here all the time. Anyway, why should anyone want to hurt you?"

She stood up by the fireplace, and he could see that she was shaking all over.

"Whoever killed Mr. Burden might kill me too. It's for the hotel they're doing it. I tell you." She gave a sort of sob, and said in a low voice, "He said he was leaving me the hotel in his will."

7

When Mike had once more succeeded in soothing down Miss Keane, he warned her to tell no one of Burden's intention to leave her the hotel in his will, at least until the contents of the will were known. She said he had made this promise about a week before his death. Miss Keane had regarded it as an important milestone on the way to her marriage with Burden. She did not necessarily believe that he would carry out his intention, but, as she said, it showed that he was beginning to take her more serious-like. An idea was beginning to take shape in Mike's mind, and he told her that as long as she kept her own counsel she would be safe. When she had accepted this she no longer wanted to retreat to the lodge.

"It's much nicer here," she said frankly. "There isn't much room for me at home and my father would be at me all the time."

Mike agreed that it would be more sensible to stay in the hotel.

"And I can be more help to Mrs. Henry," said Miss Keane virtuously, as she went out.

Mike mopped his brow when she had gone. He always felt exhausted after an interview with this unconscious type, which reeled off emotions, opinions and impressions with a complete disregard for their incompatibility. But he had often got valuable help from these impressions, if he did not make the mistake of accepting them as truth.

For example, Miss Keane was probably right when she sensed that Burden, and possibly Murray, had been murdered for possession of the hotel. It need not necessarily be legal possession. It could be that someone who wished to live at Crane's Court in peace had murdered Burden to secure that object. Some of the odd old people who inhabited the place might find this a reasonable course. And Miss Keane could be right when she sensed—or as she said, smelt—old Mrs. Robinson in Burden's room. And she could be right in connecting Mrs. Henry with the murder, or murders. He decided that he must find out more about Murray's death.

Another obvious thing was that Miss Keane would very much like to own Crane's Court herself. Could it not be that she herself had murdered both her fiancés in the belief that each had willed her the hotel before he died? He recalled the awful simplicity with which she had said that the hotel was much nicer than the lodge. He made a note to find out in what way her father would be "at her" all the time if she went home.

He went out into the hall, and immediately encountered Professor Daly, who was trying to look interested in a road-map of Ireland which hung on the wall. Mike suppressed a grin and wished him good morning seriously.

"Ah, good morning," said the old man eagerly. "You look sorter stuck up dis mawnin'."

"I've been having an amusing and instructive interview with Miss Keane, and now I want some information which I think you are likely to be able to supply. Or perhaps you are too busy?"

"Don't play that game with me, young Mike," said Daly. "You know quite well that my ears are flapping. Come out on the terrace and you can tell me all about it."

As they walked up and down in the sun, Mike described his interview with Miss Keane. When he had finished he said:

"Now, she is the second person who has told me that old Murray was murdered. And I also have information that he complained that someone was trying to poison him. It's a pity we were not told at the time. It's very late now to start finding out what he died of."

"Never end a sentence with a preposition," said Daly automatically. "Yes, at the time of Murray's death, Miss Keane said he had been murdered. But no one took much notice because she said we had *all* murdered him. I took that to mean that she believed we had shortened his life by causing him anxiety, and of course no one heeds that sort of statement. She never mentioned poison or blunt instruments or things of that sort. Then she was put out of her stride by the easy granting of the death certificate. After that she contented herself with saying, 'I know what I know,' until presently she fell silent for lack of an audience."

"Not much to go on," said Mike. "But still I'm disappointed in you, Professor. You could have told me privately."

"Nix," said the old man, shaking his head. "I've been bitten by that one before. Remember the time the nasty old woman disappeared, and everyone said she must have fallen into a bog hole, and my investigations proved her son-in-law had helped her in?"

Mike nodded.

"Well, I decided then to let these unnoticed murders pass in future. It's different in the case of Burden. The manner of his taking off left no choice. But on the whole, when I have a moral certainty that someone nasty has been done away with, I don't interfere."

"You sound as if the decision has to be made quite often," said Mike.

"Quite often? Well, no. But now and then."

"But what about justice?"

"I have no wish to judge my fellow men," said Daly. "And I see no need for the public to intervene when there is not much likelihood of the murderer plying his trade a second time. I leave him to his conscience."

"What of the death of Murray, then? If it was murder, we may take it that the same person is responsible for the death of Burden."

"Yes." The old man began to look worried. "I'm afraid it looks like that. But how was I to know? I assumed that Mrs. Henry would inherit the hotel, and then we would have peace."

"Did you think Mrs. Henry had murdered her uncle?" Mike asked softly.

"No. I won't deny that I speculated about it a good deal. I assumed that if Murray had been murdered it was for some personal enmity—perhaps connected with Miss Keane. I would as soon suspect Mrs. Henry as yourself. I didn't act in an altogether irresponsible way," said the old man, looking sideways at Mike's set face. "I suggested to Murray's doctor that he might have been poisoned."

"Did you, indeed? He should have informed me."

"Well, I didn't put it in such a way that he would feel it his duty to tell you. It was I who brought him into Murray's room as soon as he came that morning, and I said I was wondering if Murray could have eaten or drunk something that disagreed with him. I put it in such a way that he felt he had to reassure me. He said there was nothing surprising in the death of a man of seventy-eight, and that I mustn't worry my pretty head about it."

"And did you?"

"Not much. As soon as Miss Keane said she had been engaged to marry him, I dismissed her accusations as a yarn. Now I'm not so sure."

"Miss Keane confided in you?"

"She did, God help me. They all do."

"Then perhaps you can tell me some more about her. She says that if she goes to live at home her father will be 'at her' all the time. Did she tell you the reasons for this disagreement, or is it only mild family bickering?"

"I wouldn't exactly dismiss it like that," said Daly. "Her father is one of the gardeners here, known to everyone as 'The Slug.' Miss Keane doesn't like that, as you may imagine. She tries to dissociate herself from him as much as she can, with the inevitable result that she is usually known as 'The Slug's daughter.' But that is only the beginning of her troubles. When she came to work here first, she used to go home for a few hours every day, but gradually she went less and less often until at last she stopped going altogether. Then the Slug took to lying in wait for her when she went for a walk, and demanding money. She told him she was not so well paid that she could give him any. She has to buy herself good clothes and so on. Then—she says—he started inciting her to falsify the hotel books and pinch the money."

"And did she?"

"She says not," said the old man slowly. "And I'm rather disposed to believe her. On the whole I should call her the poor-but-honest type. It was probably her father's idea that she make the most of her chances by marrying the owner of the hotel. I need hardly add that if she had become the owner, and if her father and mother had begun to take an interest, the whole business would probably have been ruined in a matter of weeks."

"What is her mother like?"

"Noisy, righteous, inclined to explain herself too much. A good mother, as the saying is."

"Poor Miss Keane," murmured Mike.

He wondered if her father had indirectly incited her to murder. He knew that daily petty persecution, such as she had suffered, can drive people to extraordinary lengths. Their judgment goes awry, and they can think of nothing but how to escape from the nagging torment. Still he could not see Miss Keane actually killing anyone. She might plan it, she might even come to the very moment of it, but she was too sentimental to have carried it through. He thought she would be capable of slipping poison into a glass of milk, all right, and then dithering at a distance until her victim had swallowed it, but that would have been an easy way out.

Professor Daly's voice broke in on his thoughts.

"I have an unpleasant habit of examining all my acquaintances in the light of their capabilities as murderers," he said. "I have a cousin who is a doctor in an asylum, and she looks at everyone as if she were wondering in what way they would finally go mad. It's the same thing. May I offer you my opinion about Miss Keane?"

"Certainly. I should value it," said Mike gravely.

"She couldn't kill a wasp," said Professor Daly. "It would get away while she was chasing it."

"I had just come to the same conclusion," said Mike. "I thought she told me the truth, as she knows it, just now. She is convinced that the death of Burden has something to do with her."

Daly shrugged.

"What young woman does not think that anything exciting has something to do with her?"

"Perhaps."

As they reached the door of the hotel, the old man said:

"Will you sit at my table at lunch? Unless you have caught your man before then, of course."

Mike was glad of this invitation, for he hoped to create confidence in the innocent and lull the suspicions of the guilty by mixing with the guests. He had the delicate task of questioning Mrs. Robinson before him, but he intended to let her wait until her son arrived, and tackle both together. Mrs. Fennell was the next on his list.

Mr. Arrow and a man whom he had not met before came out of the hotel just as Mike turned away. Professor Daly introduced the stranger as Mr. Heaslip. So this was the bird-watcher, thought Mike with interest, noting the keen blue eyes and air of quiet patience. Mr. Arrow was looking better, he thought, and said so.

"Oh, yes," said George, smiling. "Dr. Morgan gave me something that made me sleep like a log. I'm afraid I was a bit ungracious to you last night. I'm not accustomed to murder."

"We were all very shocked," said Heaslip. "Dreadful thing to have happened."

Somehow he did not sound sincere, and Mike remembered that Professor Daly had described him as being entirely detached from everyday things. Scientific men are liable to become like this, Daly had said, and had added that it was not strange that when Heaslip had spent all day watching seagulls licking their feet, he should appear bemused by human company.

"I shall have to bother you all with questions," said Mike apologetically. "But there is no need to interrupt your ordinary routine. I'll try not to be a nuisance."

"Yes. I suppose you must try to find out who did it," said Heaslip with distaste. "I can't say I feel disposed to help you."

"Everyone seems to feel like that about Burden," said Daly. "But justice must be served. I'm sure we'll all do our best to help."

"Yes," said George doubtfully, and Mr. Heaslip shrugged.

Feeling like a cabdriver at a hunt ball, Mike slunk down the avenue. He could not blame them for not making him welcome, but each time this happened to him he found himself wondering why he had chosen to be a policeman. Only the presence of Professor Daly comforted him.

He recognized Mrs. Fennell's chalet from George's description, and picked his way among the exuberant flowers to the door. Bridget opened to his knock. They were old friends.

"You'll treat her gently, Mr. Kenny, won't you? She's not right in the head, you see, and I never know what she'll do next."

"Has she heard about Burden's death?"

"Oh, yes. Wasn't she up in the hotel for dinner last night? They all heard it then."

"Does she have all her meals in the hotel?"

"Except breakfast, and sometimes afternoon tea. It's a bit of fun for her to be trotting up and down, and besides we haven't much of a way of cooking here."

"I'll be careful," said Mike, and was about to ask about Mrs. Fennell's wanderings about the hotel when the door of the little sitting room opened and the old lady came out into the hall.

"Bridget! Don't stand there whispering on the doorstep. Bring the gentleman in."

"Yes, Madam," said Bridget, with a wink at Mike.

When she had seated him in an armchair by the fire Mike said, "Do you know why I'm here?"

"It's about Mr. Burden, isn't it?" she said. "They said at the hotel last night that he had been murdered. It was only to be expected, of course."

"You were not surprised, then?"

"Not at all. You see, his uncle was murdered only a little while ago. I had private information about that—from my dear friend, Sir Rodney Crane, you know."

"Ah, yes," said Mike. "Has he been to see you since Mr. Burden's death?"

"Not yet, but I'm sure he'll come in the evening. He often comes at dusk— just at dusk."

"Can you tell me about Mr. Murray's death?" Mike asked gently.

"Well, I haven't asked Rodney's permission," said Mrs. Fennell slowly. "Perhaps I should ask him first."

"I'm sure he won't mind your telling the Guards about it. Sir Rodney was distressed himself, wasn't he?"

"Oh, yes! Very distressed and worried. He didn't quite know what to do. He knew it was wicked and wrong, because Mr. Murray was a good old man. Rodney was very put out about it all."

"Then I'm sure he would be glad if you could help to catch the person that did it."

"Yes, he's afraid of that person. He would like him to be caught. I'll tell you."

She folded her hands on her knee and screwed up her face in a painful effort to concentrate, and then went on:

"Rodney was in the hotel. He often walks about the hotel. He was near Mr. Murray's rooms. No one saw him. He's not big. It was late at night. Yes, late and dark, and wet underfoot. His shoes got wet on the way home."

"What kind of shoes?" asked Mike softly.

"Pretty laced shoes, with a pattern of holes on top. The rain came through the holes. That was on the way home."

"He stood outside Murray's door," Mike prompted her, as she paused.

"Yes, he stood outside. He knew Mr. Murray was inside, because he could hear him talking about diamonds. You can hear through that door, always. Rodney hid behind a big flower-vase. It was so dark, so dark. Then Mrs. Keane's daughter came out. She's grown so I hardly know her. And pretty, too. She was smiling and her eyes shone like diamonds. Rodney waited. He was going to slip away. Then he heard voices inside Mr. Murray's room again, though no one had gone in."

The communicating door from the bedroom, said Mike to himself. Aloud he said, "What did Sir Rodney do?"

"He did a daring thing. He laughed and laughed when he told me, though he was frightened too. He looked through the big keyhole into Mr. Murray's room!"

"That was a daring thing," said Mike gravely. "What did he see?"

"He saw Mr. Murray in an armchair, saying how tired he was, he could not sleep. Rodney was interested, because often he does not sleep himself, and it's terrible, terrible! That other was bending over him, saying there was a thing to make him sleep. Mr. Murray looked up and said how grateful he was. That other showed him something, and it was a glass syringe, like they use in hospitals, but very big. Rodney saw it for a moment while that other stuck it in Mr. Murray's arm. Mr. Murray began to get sleepy almost at once. Rodney saw it."

Mike was afraid to prompt her when she paused again. He held his patience until she went on after a minute:

"Rodney didn't go away from the big keyhole at once. He watched Mr. Murray being helped into the bedroom, and he heard him being put to bed, so nice. Then he thought, perhaps Mr. Murray is sleeping now. Perhaps—that other—would give me some of the stuff out of the syringe. He waited and waited behind the flower-vase until that other came out. He asked for some of the stuff that put Mr. Murray to sleep."

Suddenly she was talking faster, breathing faster. Mike prayed she would not break down until she came to the end of the story.

"That other caught him and shook him and threatened to kill him, kill him, if he ever told. So then he knew that Mr. Murray had been murdered. Rodney swore he wouldn't tell, and he never did. But he didn't forget. Only yesterday I said something about it to that nice Mr. Arrow, but it was because I wanted to tell him how it used to be here long ago, so peaceful and nice."

Mike decided to put the question that was burning to his tongue.

"Who was that other?"

But she only gave him a long terrified stare, and then burst into tears and had to be led away by Bridget.

He let himself out mechanically, sick with disappointment. George Arrow's interview with Mrs. Fennell had ended just like this, at the same point. Who was it that she had seen actually killing Murray? For it was obviously herself and not the ghostly Sir Rodney Crane who had watched outside the door of Murray's room. The detail about the wet shoes had first led him to this conclusion, and later the remark about how Miss Keane had grown. If he found out that Murray died on a wet night, and if Mrs. Fennell owned a pair of shoes with a pattern of holes in the top, he would be morally certain that he was right. But as to legal proof, he would still have none, and there was no clue to the identity of the murderer. Mrs. Fennell had not even let fall whether it was a man or a woman. One thing had emerged if her story was true. It was not Miss Keane. He foresaw another interview with her, which, if he was not careful, might prove even more trying than the last.

There was another possibility which would have to be investigated, and that was whether Mrs. Fennell herself could have killed Burden. He knew that this ground would have to be cleared before a charge could be brought against anyone else. He could imagine the capital that any defending counsel would make of the presence in the hotel of a lunatic. Mrs. Fennell was undoubtedly a lunatic.

Back in the hotel, Mike sent Joe to fetch his sergeant, who was watching over the search of Burden's rooms.

"Mrs. Henry says you're to have the library, Mr. Kenny, sir, and I've put a notice on the door saying 'Reserved.' "

"Come and tell me if Mrs. Robinson's son arrives while I'm in there," said Mike.

"Oh, I will, sir. Indeed I will," said Joe, scuttling off with a red face.

Mike was gratified to observe that he could strike fear into someone's heart, even if it was only Joe's.

In the library, he read his notes moodily until Sergeant Mahon arrived.

"All quiet, sir," said Mahon as he dropped into a chair at one of the leather-topped tables. "Colm MacDonagh is an embittered man after last night. He spent the whole night sniffing outside O'Reilly's door like a cat at a mouse-hole, hoping O'Reilly would make a run for it. The young lad that was with him has the whole force told about it."

"O'Reilly is still with us, I hope?" said Mike.

"He's below in the kitchen, cooking like a demon. They're all afraid to speak to him, he's that cross and cranky. One young fellow—a kitchen porter he said he was—came up to ask me wouldn't we for God's sake arrest O'Reilly and take him away out of that, for they're afraid to breathe below. He says O'Reilly hasn't threatened a single one of them with a knife this morning, and that that's a sure sign he killed the boss!"

"You explained that we couldn't oblige, I hope?"

"I told him to tell them all to let O'Reilly alone and not be teasing him and inciting him to break the law. That shook him."

"A nasty situation could develop there," said Mike. "I wish people wouldn't make up their minds in advance of the police. I don't want them to injure O'Reilly."

"They won't," said the sergeant confidently. "I think I succeeded in frightening them off. I gave them the idea it was themselves we were suspecting. There's one or two of them, though, that's worried on their own account."

"Who?"

"There's the chauffeur, Ned, for one. Anyone with half an eye can see he has something on his mind. And there's a good-looking bit of a housemaid too, name of Maggie. And a waitress called Esther with dyed hair, as old as a field. She has something on her mind, I'll swear."

"We'll have to see them, and O'Reilly too," said Mike resignedly. "But before we do there are several other inquiries to be started. For instance, where did this Burden live before he came here?"

"Dublin," said Sergeant Mahon hopefully.

"Go on!" said Mike. "That's a great help."

"We can find out," said the sergeant meekly.

"Yes. You can see old Murray's solicitor, who tracked Burden down. Then we want to find out what he lived on before he came here."

"Blackmail, partly, I should think," said the sergeant, mildly.

"You can investigate that angle of him too," said Mike. "They often run true to type. Then we must find out if Burden made a will, and if so, who profits. Murray's lawyer may be able to help you there too. It's Johnny Farrell—do you know him?"

"Not to call Johnny, but I know him, all right."

"He's expecting you. I telephoned him this morning and told him you would be in. He should have plenty of time to dig up anything he knows. It's unlikely that Burden made a will before he came here, because he had not any property then. Ask Johnny if he knows who will inherit if Burden died without making a will."

Mike told Sergeant Mahon about his interview with Mrs. Fennell.

"Crazy as a coot, poor thing," he said. "She has given herself a second identity as Sir Rodney Crane, partly so that she can reconcile her conscience with walking around the hotel as if she owns it, I suppose. Lunatics often have very tender consciences, I'm told."

"That's what makes lunatics of them, maybe," said Mahon profoundly.

"You have been through Burden's rooms more thoroughly than I have," said Mike. "Mrs. Fennell said she looked through 'the big keyhole' and saw what was happening in the room. Would that be possible?"

"I think so," said Mahon, "if old Murray's chair was in line with the door. There's one of those big old brassbound locks on that door, with a big keyhole—the sort of thing you sometimes see on a hall door. It was probably put there for its looks—with the brass parts all polished up it looks very grand. And it's true that you can hear a good deal of what goes on in the room from outside. I had to warn my fellows not to give yelps of joy if they found anything interesting."

"Which all backs up her story," said Mike. "Not that it brings us to the name of our man. If only she were a normal witness—but then she would not have been there at all."

"We may be able to find a hypodermic," said Mahon.

"There's no harm in having a look. And we don't know what was in it, that wouldn't leave any signs and that could kill a man so quickly. Of course Mrs. Fennell could be wrong about the time it took him to die. I can imagine her remaining for several minutes glued to the keyhole with fright, and thinking later that it was only a short period."

"If I may make a suggestion, sir." Mahon coughed modestly. "A cousin of my own was done in by accident in a hospital in Dublin some years ago. The nurse was talking over her shoulder to another patient in the ward, and she must have forgotten she hadn't filled up the little glass part of the syringe. Anyway she stuck it into the cousin, careless like, and happened to strike an artery or a vein, I forget which, and shot a bubble of air into her bloodstream. The cousin was dead of heart failure like she'd been shot. There was a big row about it, and the nurse was fired out on her ear. Closing the stable door after the horse was gone, I thought, but I suppose they have to protect the public from the like of her."

"Maybe you have it," said Mike. "Damned clever, if that was it. And quite, quite impossible to prove at this stage." He got up dispiritedly and said, "I never in my life so much wanted to run away from a case. Martin Hogan can tell the people that read his rag that the Guards are baffled, and he'll be right, for once."

"There's always Burden's past life to work on," said Mahon.

"Yes. Off with you now, and see Johnny Farrell. You'll find me here when you come back, and don't keep me waiting for that information."

He marched out of the room.

"Baffled, now are you!" said Mahon aloud to himself.

Mike found his way unaided to the kitchens. These were to the back of the house, and were bright and well-fitted beyond what one would expect in a country hotel. There was no one in the main kitchen except the gloomy O'Reilly, stirring a saucepan. Mike paused inside the door and repressed a desire to say, "Eye of newt and toe of frog!"

He answered O'Reilly's glare by sniffing the air.

"Espagnole sauce?"

O'Reilly gave him a grudging smile.

"Thanks be to God there's someone in the house would know it from bacon and cabbage. I'm going to cook a dinner tonight that will surprise the pants offa that bunch upstairs."

He glowered into his saucepan again.

"What will it be?" asked Mike amiably.

"Mushroom soup—that'll give the old ones a pain in their gizzard, but that's all one to me. Kidney and ham patties and Espagnole. Lamb cutlets, sprouts, celery, creamed potatoes, Venetian cream. Gorgonzola and petit Suisse."

By the time he had come to the end of his litany he was much brighter. Mike said:

"I hope I'll live till tonight."

"Ay, that'll be a dinner to live for," said O'Reilly, "if I don't put a handful of p'ison into everything at the last minute." He stirred his sauce vehemently and then said, "Why are your fellows after me all the time? Didn't I tell you I didn't stick that knife in the boss?"

"Well, it was your knife," said Mike, "and you can see we can't agree that you had nothing to do with it just because you say so."

"I suppose you can't," said the chef grudgingly, "but why don't you get after some of the others? There's Ned had it in for Burden as well as me. And more to complain about too."

"All in good time," said Mike easily. "What had Ned against Burden?"

"Messing about with his girl," said O'Reilly. "You wouldn't get me so excited about a girl. 'Tis the way they're always chasing me, so that I has to carry a stick to bate them away! Wouldn't be bothered with any of them. But Ned is the kind that gets all worked up about things. I suppose you can't blame him, in a way, when he was going to marry the girl."

"What girl?"

"Maggie. Housemaid. Nice little bashte," said O'Reilly tolerantly.

"Where would I find Ned now?"

"Washing the car." O'Reilly jerked his head towards the back door, where sounds of running water could be heard. "Though what he does it so often for, I don't know."

"Thanks."

Mike went out the back door. The chef watched him go with a pleased look.

Mike found himself in a wilderness of outhouses and sheds. Again he was astonished at the ramifications of Crane's Court. A motor-generator for electricity ticked in a shed of its own on his left, and wood sheds, turf sheds, garages and stables were all around him. On a concrete slab in front of one of the garages, a tall, thin, middle-aged man in thigh boots was running a hose over a big car. He turned off the water as Mike approached and began to rub the windows with a cloth.

"You're Ned?" said Mike.

"That's right, sir. Ned Conway."

His voice was lifeless and his eyes, Mike noticed, were rimmed with red.

"Something on your mind, Ned?" Mike asked gently. "I'm Inspector Kenny, investigating Burden's death."

"I know," said Ned in a dead voice. "I was talking to Sergeant Mahon this morning." Mike waited, while Ned swallowed painfully. "Are you coming to arrest me?"

"Would I come alone?"

"No," said Ned slowly. "I suppose not. Why are you here, then?"

"Putting two and two together," said Mike. "You know something about Burden's death."

"How do you know?"

"You should be glad he's dead, and you're not, for one thing."

"I'd never be glad anyone was murdered," said Ned automatically, but Mike saw a gleam in his eye.

"You would be glad about Burden," Mike insisted, "if you thought you could afford to. But you're uneasy. Why not get it off your chest! You have nothing to fear, really."

"Haven't I?" said Ned, suddenly hysterical. "How can I be sure? I'm only a poor chap. I don't know what will happen to me—"

"Worse will happen if you withhold information," said Mike patiently. "You won't have peace of mind until you tell what you know."

"How do I know I'll have it then either? But it couldn't be worse than this," he said, half to himself. He turned suddenly to Mike and said savagely, "All right, then, here it is for you. I went to Mr. Burden's room yesterday afternoon to tell him I'd—I'd kill him if he didn't leave off annoying my girl, Maggie. He had his arm around her—the dirty little greasy rat!" There were tears in Ned's eyes. Mike waited while he gave a horrible long sob. "Burden was dead. Stretched on the carpet, dead. And Batt O'Reilly's knife stuck in him."

"What time was it?"

"Twenty-past five."

"Was he warm?"

"Oh, God! Do you think I touched him?"

"Pity. Did you think he was dead for long?"

"No. Not for long. His dirty little soul was still in the room."

"Feeling better now?" asked Mike.

"Not much. A bit. Aren't you going to arrest me?"

"Not likely. You're a valuable witness. Go and have a talk with Maggie."

Ned watched him walk away, his cloth hanging stupidly from his hand. Mike was jubilantly making a note in the timetable he was beginning to compose in the back of his notebook.

8

As Mike reached the hall he heard the gong boom out its summons to lunch. Professor Daly and Mr. Arrow were standing by the front door. Mike was very glad to see them, for he had not looked forward to entering the dining room alone.

"There you are!" Daly called out genially. "We've been waiting for you. Have you not finished yet?"

"You'll hear in good time when I have," said Mike.

They went into the dining room together. Professor Daly's table was now set for four, and sitting there, facing the door, was the small, smirking figure of Martin Hogan. He pulled out a chair with either hand and said ingratiatingly:

"I asked Fitzpatrick to put me here. I knew you wouldn't mind." He waited while his unwilling hosts looked at each other and shrugged. Then he said coaxingly, "Come along. It almost looks as if you don't want me."

"Don't cry, Martin," said Mike as he sat down resignedly. "We're really very glad to have you, though our feelings don't show on our faces."

"Yours do," said Martin. "I can be very useful to you. Introduce me to Mr. Arrow, please. Professor Daly and I are old friends."

"Mr. Hogan, Mr. Arrow," said Mike to the smiling George. "I can't imagine how you have escaped him up to now."

"Sir, you are a person!" said Martin, and fell on his soup.

Mike began to see the advantages of Martin's presence. If the little man had not been there, Professor Daly would have pressed for a full and free discussion of any theories which Mike might have formed. And Mike was not prepared to give away more information than suited his own purposes. He said, as he unfolded his napkin:

"Don't forget, Professor, that the press is listening to every word you say. Watch his ears twitch."

"They're not," said Martin indignantly. "Or if they are, it's the good soup. And I won't publish anything you don't want published. In fact I'll go farther. I'll say I can publish nothing because the Guards have no idea of how to begin to investigate a high-class murder like this one."

And he leered into his soup in a pleased way.

Mike sighed helplessly and decided to change the subject. He asked Professor Daly if the thing sitting with Mrs. Robinson was her son.

"The weak-kneed cobra," murmured George.

"That is Mrs. Robinson's son," said the old man with distaste. "You can see now how apt was my description, George."

Watching Mrs. Robinson's son, George recognized him as one of those creeping, ageless human beings, slack-mouthed, long-haired, dead-eyed and dangerous-looking in a mysterious way. They are not exactly snakes, he thought, and not quite monkeys. There is a streak of wolf in them, but of careful, work-by-night wolf. Their teeth are sharp, and protrude very slightly. Their complexion is scaly, their color a muddy gray. Their clothes, their hair, their eyes, their cigarettes, their hands, all droop thinly. They are a small but curiously uniform body. George's skin crawled a little as he watched him. He was eating his soup by a method which George had never seen before. He filled his spoon and then waited for a moment until, it seemed, he thought no one was watching, before flicking it between his snapping jaws with a single twitch of the wrist. His mother beamed on him with a softened eye, and he threw her an occasional sidelong leer.

Mike said, in a fascinated undertone:

"What does he live on? Has he a job?"

"An honorary job, I think," said Daly. "He has some sort of a flat in Dublin—one never hears exactly where. His mother sends him money—not very much, though she has plenty. She probably likes to keep him on a string. He writes articles about the decline of art, literature and the drama in Ireland, and sighs for the good old days before he was born. So, I imagine, do the editors whom he pesters with his stuff. He writes short stories, too, about dirty lodging-houses and smells and drains and so on. They never get published, I'm glad to say."

"Then how do you know?" asked Mike.

"He shows them all to me when he comes to stay. I can't say I welcome his visits. There's something odd about his present one. He's not due until Christmas. And though he's a good hour in the house, he has not yet approached me with a slim packet of what he rightly calls his Little Efforts. I wonder what he's up to?"

"So do I," said Mike. "I'd like an informal conversation with him, if I could be introduced."

"That will be easy," said Martin Hogan. "He'll be galloping up to me the moment dinner is over. He's always hoping I'll write a paragraph in the paper beginning, "Staying at Crane's Court this week is that brilliant young literary man, Horace Robinson—"

"Is his name Horace, really?" asked George in awe.

"That's right," said Martin. "Must we talk about him? It makes me feel ill."

"I see Miss Keane is back where she belongs, poor girl," said Professor Daly a moment later.

She was sitting silently, looking down into her lap, at her old place with the other office girls near the hotplate. George felt very sorry for her. Compared with the exuberant appearance last night in her red dress, she looked down-trodden and defeated now. He could see, too, that her colleagues were making her pay for her short-lived aspirations. They talked over her head, and laughed too loudly, and failed to pass her anything. George tried to excuse them on the ground that they were only displaying the instinctive, unconscious cruelty of the young, but he was none the less angry that she should have to suffer so much. Throughout the meal he could not forget her, though Martin Hogan and Professor Daly kept them all amused with their conversation.

While they ate, George covertly observed Inspector Kenny. He found himself wishing he could make friends with him, for Mike's strength of character was like a tonic. He would never forget his kindness to him the night before, when George had shown himself a querulous, self-centered invalid. He grew hot all over now, as he thought of the things he had said. He had completely spoiled his chance of Mike's respect, he was certain, and still Mike had sent him Dr. Morgan to see that he got a night's sleep.

Dr. Morgan had been very kind too. He had worked with Mick Moore, he said, and he knew Mick would not object to his examining George. Watching his face as he used his stethoscope, George had hoped to read something of his opinion, but Dr. Morgan had maintained a studiedly blank expression. He had gone away at last leaving some kind of sleeping pill, and with such reassuring remarks that if he had not held himself well in control, George might have burst into tears of gratitude. And he felt better today than he had done for a long time.

Mike had noticed earlier in the day that some of the look of strain had left Mr. Arrow's face. Now he wondered why, and since he was a born policeman, he made a mental note to draw out Dr. Morgan on the subject. He liked George, but thought he was facing his fate in rather cowardly fashion. Still, he reminded himself grimly, he had no guarantee that he himself would behave more nobly in parallel circumstances.

Suddenly, as he looked around the room, Mike noticed a curious thing. All the old people in the room were smiling, as if each had received a long-awaited present. Mrs. Robinson beamed at her son, Horace. Colonel and Mrs. Waters grinned frigidly at each other. Mrs. Ryan, Mrs. Mullery, Mrs. King and Major Dunlea, and all the other old people dotted around the room alone or in pairs, all were smiling toothless or china smiles of the purest satisfaction.

"Now, what are they so happy about?" Mike asked himself. "They are positively gloating. It is possible—is it possible—?"

His training and experience had taught him that everything is possible, but he was so taken aback at the idea that now flooded his mind, that he scraped away at his sweet-plate long after he had finished its contents. Professor Daly's voice recalled him to his senses.

"Young Mike, you are scraping the flowers off that plate. What is in your mind?"

"A thought," said Mike as he laid down his spoon.

They all looked at him hopefully, but he dared not say more. He was glad when the professor stood up and said:

"We have coffee in the drawing room. You can meet Horace there."

Mike had not been in the drawing room at Crane's Court before. It was a very large room, still with much of the original furniture. The immense fireplace held a proportionate fire, and the whole room was warm and inviting, and as little like a hotel room as one could hope to find.

Mrs. Robinson and her son were already settled in the choicest places by the fire. A Japanese screen with a flight of cranes in ivory sheltered the old lady from drafts. Horace sat forward on the sofa with his hands hanging loosely between his knees. He looked upwards and sideways when they came in the door, and then, sure enough, he came slipping and gliding across the carpet to catch Martin Hogan's hand in a limp tentacle. Martin shook himself loose and said:

"Hello, Horace."

"Good evening, Martin," said Horace in a husky voice, stiff with culture.

Absolutely perfect, thought George, who had been wondering how nature had got around the difficulty of fitting a voice to this specimen.

Within two minutes, Martin had introduced them to Horace and to his mother, and had retreated alone to the other side of the fireplace. Here he sat with a notebook on his knees, an absorbed expression on his face, but with an alert ear cocked towards Mrs. Robinson and her group.

George saw that his own role was to provide a background for Mike's conversation with the Robinsons. He was glad to remain silent for most of the time. Professor Daly had taken it on himself to bring the conversation at once to the subject in which they were all interested.

"Mr. Kenny is here to investigate Burden's death," he said. "I'm sure we are all willing to help him as much as possible."

"*I* am not," said Mrs. Robinson firmly. "And neither is my son, Horace. Horace! Remember, it is not our duty to assist the police in things which are no concern of ours."

There went his hope of an informal conversation about the murder, thought Mike in annoyance. He thought that Daly had shown even less tact than usual. Mrs. Robinson was smiling at him condescendingly.

"Of course, I quite understand that *you* must do your duty, young man. But

I can feel nothing but the keenest pleasure at the death of Mr. Burden. He was insufferable."

She settled herself comfortably against the sofa-back.

The other old people had come in now, and were sitting about the room. Esther served the coffee from a trolley driven by Joe, who was obviously nervous about the proximity to each other of Mike and Mrs. Robinson. He caught Mike's eye across the room and silently implored him not to mention the telegram until he had gone with his trolley. Mike had no intention of giving away his informant, and he tried to send him a reassuring glance.

Presently Mrs. Robinson took a sip of her coffee and said:

"Yes, Mr. Burden was insufferable. It was clear from the start that something would have to be done about him. He was persecuting everyone." She leaned towards Mike and lowered her voice. "He had actually arranged to have poor old Mrs. Fennell certified insane and put into a home! Well, we all know she's not quite herself, but there was no need to go to such lengths."

Mike looked across at Mrs. Fennell, who was sitting up perfectly straight holding her cup and saucer firmly. But for the fact that she was murmuring to herself continuously, she looked almost normal. He said:

"But Mr. Burden could not have had her certified without great difficulty."

"He said he could show good reason for it. He had arranged for the doctor from the mental hospital to come and examine her—without her knowledge, of course—next week."

It occurred to Mike that Mrs. Robinson must have obtained this information, if it was true, by devious methods. He decided not to question her statement, because it would be easy to ask the doctor if the appointment had been made. He hoped that Burden would have told the doctor the "good reason" why Mrs. Fennell should be certified. He was very pleased to have got this information now, for he guessed that soon Mrs. Robinson would be even less inclined to help than she was at present. For it was obvious that he would have to have a formal interview with her at once.

He put down his cup and got up, saying, with a glance at Martin Hogan:

"This is a rather public place for a discussion, Mrs. Robinson. I shall expect you in the library in five minutes."

He noted with amusement the look of disappointment on Martin's face, before he retreated as fast as he could, and with as much dignity as he could command in the circumstances. As he reached the door he heard Mrs. Robinson saying thunderously:

"What does he mean? What an impertinent young man!"

Professor Daly's voice reached him through the half-closed door.

"He means that he must ask you some questions. I should advise you to go to the library at once."

Though he spoke soothingly, his tone suggested that Mike was a man to be obeyed. Mike shut the door gently.

It was ten minutes before Mrs. Robinson appeared, glaring, in the library. Mike pulled forward a large chair to the fire and invited her to sit down. Behind her tottered Horace, who obviously did not know whether to smile ingratiatingly or to glare like his mother. He compromised by trying to look unconcerned as he let himself drop into the chair Mike offered him. Mrs. Robinson gave him a contemptuous glance as she towered on the hearthrug. She measured Mike and said:

"I have told you that I have no wish to assist you in finding the murderer of Mr. Burden. I can see no purpose in this interview."

"It's the duty of every law-abiding person to help in an investigation of this sort," said Mike warily.

Mrs. Robinson searched this statement for a moment before she said: "I don't agree."

"Then I can only say that I must question you about some of your own activities. Why did you word the telegram to your son as you did?"

She slid down, a mountainous jelly, into the chair. It occurred to him that she was rather old for this kind of shock treatment, and he wondered for one awful moment if she was going to have a stroke. It was wonderful to watch her pull herself back to her normal majestic state. As he watched, he imagined the thousands of little muscles tightening themselves up, forced by her invincible will. Presently he said, as if nothing had happened:

"You must admit the wording was rather odd. It almost made me think you had planned it yourself."

"How did you find out about the telegram?"

Her voice, husky at first, gained strength as she spoke.

"Oh, the police keep an eye on that sort of thing," said Mike easily, reflecting that if they did not always do so, they should.

"The telegram had nothing to do with the murder," said Mrs. Robinson tentatively. Then he could almost see how her mind observed that statement and approved of it as a line of defense. She said again, more firmly, "The telegram had nothing whatever to do with the murder, young man!"

"I'm afraid I can't accept that, Mrs. Robinson," said Mike. "If you will have patience with me, I'll tell you how I could read the whole situation."

She nodded offhandedly, but her watchful eye, and her tongue quickly licking her dry lips betrayed her avid interest. Horace raised his heavy eyelids to stare penetratingly—like a snake in a glass cage, Mike thought, which would dearly love to strike, but which knows it would be futile.

"Crane's Court was always a haven for old people," Mike said. "For many of those who live here, it is the last haven they are ever likely to find. Then came Mr. Burden, who set out to persecute the old people with the avowed object of forcing them to go. Now, I suggest that he drove them too far. I suggest that the old people banded together, as they had done on former occasions, to defend their rights. I have heard the story of the tea veranda, and of how it ended in a victory for the older residents once they stood together. Perhaps this incident gave them the idea that if they banded together again, they would be able to get rid of Mr. Burden altogether. I think it possible that they did this, and that they ended somehow by murdering Burden."

Mike paused, and watched Mrs. Robinson's face closely. She was frightened, certainly, but he thought that she seemed slightly relieved too. He concluded that the solution, as he had put it, must be incorrect, though he was convinced that there was a certain amount of truth in it.

They had both forgotten Horace. Suddenly he shrieked:

"You killed him! Mother! I knew you would do something stupid!"

Mrs. Robinson silenced him with one word.

"Horace!"

Her glare should have burned him to a crisp. He subsided with a hand over his face to shut it out. She turned back to Mike. Her attitude was not apologetic, though it was clear that she felt cornered. It was almost with contempt that she said:

"I don't know how you arrived at such a fantastic theory."

Instinct, thought Mike, and the smiling faces of people who looked as if they had not smiled for years.

"We had banded together, as you put it," Mrs. Robinson went on. "But we did not kill Mr. Burden. We never contemplated doing such a thing. We were very pleased when things turned out as they did, but it was not our doing. I can see you don't believe me," she said rather wearily. "Why should you?"

Mike said, "Can anyone corroborate what you say?"

"Perhaps Mr. Heaslip could. We did consult him."

Mike rang the bell, and when Joe appeared, asked for Mr. Heaslip to be found and sent in. They waited in silence until Joe announced Mr. Heaslip and scuttled away.

Mr. Heaslip stood inside the door looking from Mike to Mrs. Robinson, and then to the quivering Horace. Mike said:

"We thought you could help us, Mr. Heaslip. I have been asking Mrs. Robinson some questions."

The old lady glared at him, but this time she did not dare to answer back. Mike went on:

"I put forward a theory that the permanent residents here, when they failed to reach an understanding with Burden, banded together for the purpose of killing him."

He saw Mr. Heaslip start, and then thought he detected a gleam of amusement in his eye.

"Can you throw some light on this?" Mike asked.

"I told him we held meetings to decide what was to be done about Mr. Burden," said Mrs. Robinson, "but we never contemplated killing him. That would have been very wrong."

Mike had not heard about the meetings, of course. Mrs. Robinson said:

"You were at one of our meetings, Mr. Heaslip. I told Mr. Kenny that you would agree that we never thought of killing Mr. Burden—though I do remember saying how convenient it would be if he happened to have a bad heart."

Mike caught Mr. Heaslip's eye, and could not forbear a grin of appreciation. Mr. Heaslip said:

"Yes, I remember the meeting, of course. It was in your room, Mrs. Robinson. You asked me to come to advise you, because I had agreed with you that Burden was becoming quite intolerable."

There was a snap of real anger in his voice. Mike supposed that a good scientific man of any sort must have a fundamental thirst for justice. Mr. Heaslip turned to Mike.

"Some of the old people were making arrangements to leave Crane's Court. We all knew that this would be very bad for them, and possibly fatal in some cases. When I came to the meeting I was not surprised to find that they were all very angry. Mrs. Waters, I remember, suggested starting a counter-campaign of persecution, which she hoped would result in Burden's suicide."

"I thought it a good suggestion," said Mrs. Robinson, who had visibly recovered since the arrival of her companion.

Mr. Heaslip said hurriedly, addressing himself to Mike only:

"Of course I damped this suggestion. I pointed out that Burden was a tough specimen, and would be likely to come out on top in any rivalry of that sort. I said that they should get legal advice. The whole problem was beyond me, but I thought the threat of a legal action might impress Burden as no other argument could. They agreed to try this, but some of them were impatient at the delay, and they suggested another thing that could be tried in the meantime."

"And what was that?"

"We decided to ask for the dismissal of Miss Keane," said Mrs. Robinson.

In the pause that followed, Mike noticed that all three were watching him closely. Even Horace had lifted his head. It seemed that Miss Keane had returned to her position of importance, just when Mike thought he had her shelved for a while. He wondered wearily if he would ever pick the needle of truth out of this haystack of irrelevancies. He mentally hauled Miss Keane out of her retirement and asked:

"Why did you think her dismissal would help?"

"Because she was always carrying tales to Mr. Burden," said Mrs. Robinson. "She was a born troublemaker, and we thought that if she was gone, we would soon bring Mr. Burden to his senses."

Another piece of information fitted into place. Mike said:

"So you went to Mr. Burden *yesterday afternoon* and asked him to dismiss Miss Keane?"

"Did you know that all the time?" asked Mrs. Robinson, in a small voice.

Mike did not answer that question. He said:

"You should have told me long ago. Mr. Heaslip, you may go now, if you wish."

"Wait!" said Mrs. Robinson. "Mr. Heaslip had better hear the end of the story now." Her majesty was gone, and she looked like a tired old woman. She gestured towards her son, who seemed to have lost interest again. "Horace is no use to me. I do everything for him, and plan everything for him, but he does nothing for me. I wish I had a son like you, Mr. Heaslip."

"Just tell me what happened," said Mike gently, "and then you can go."

"I didn't kill Mr. Burden. I'm sure you would be very pleased if I had, young man," she said with a flash of her normal viciousness. "I went into his room after tea. He was standing with his back to the fire, with that horrid smirk on his face, as usual. He didn't ask me to sit down. His manners were dreadful. He was certainly not a gentleman. I went across to him and said I had come with a request on behalf of the older residents. I reminded him that we were the most valuable source of income to the hotel, that we had lived here for years and that we always praise the hotel to casual visitors. I said that in return for all this we were justified in expecting an occasional small favor. Then he began to shout. He said we never spend a penny more than our weekly bills for food and lodging. He said we never drink in the bar. He said we were keeping the business from expanding, and that we depressed intending visitors by our age. He was insufferable. I waited until he had finished, and then I reminded him that he had not yet heard what I wanted. His curiosity made him listen to me. I told him Miss Keane was causing trouble, and we were formally asking for her to be dismissed. I knew it was no use by then, of course, but I was determined to finish what I had come to say. He—he imitated what he imagined was my tone of voice, and said that he intended to marry Miss Keane, and then—and then I went away."

"I meant to see Burden last night," said Mr. Heaslip in a troubled tone, "to talk the whole thing over with him. But of course it was too late then."

Mike guessed that the interview with Burden had not ended as quietly as Mrs. Robinson implied. Burden was not the man to waste the violent possibilities of this scene. He imagined him pursuing her into the passageway with abuse and obscenities, and then returning to toast himself happily in front of his fire. It would not be worth the time and trouble it would take, to try to draw Burden's exact words from the old lady.

Greatly to their relief, he allowed the two Robinsons to go, and when he had thanked Mr. Heaslip for his help, he sat by the fire for a while taking notes of what he had learned.

It was fairly clear, on her own showing, that Mrs. Robinson had had the opportunity of killing Burden. But he thought she had not the necessary strength. Also, it would be incredible if in a woman of her age it had produced no violent reaction. Judging by the effect on her of his questions, he guessed he would have been completely prostrated if she had killed Burden. Still, she had been up to something shady, he thought, and he had a suspicion that she was still up to something. He had not failed to note, for example, that she had not answered his question about the curious wording of the telegram. Neither was it clear why Horace had come to Crane's Court at all. He had not been sent for to protect his aged, helpless mother, Mike thought grimly. He guessed that Horace's presence was a vital pointer, if only he knew how to interpret it.

The theory that the old people had formed an association for the purpose of murdering Burden was a fascinating one, though he thanked his stars that it now seemed unlikely. It would have been almost impossible to prove, but once proved it would have caused a world-shaking sensation. The beautiful simplicity of Mrs. Waters's plan to drive Burden to suicide left Mike gasping. He could see that he would soon have to make the closer acquaintance of the Waters family.

The motive behind the murder was still by no means clear, and now Mrs. Fennell had appeared in a further complication. If she had discovered that Burden was planning to have her certified insane, she might easily have decided to kill him. He knew that insane people often have physical strength far greater than one would expect, so presumably it was possible that she could have struck the blow. He would have to ask Bridget about the old lady's movements yesterday.

At this point in his meditations, Joe opened the door cautiously and nosed his way in with a tea tray. He was still painfully anxious to please.

"I brought your tea here, Mr. Kenny, because I thought you'd like to have it nice and quiet like," he said, and stood waiting hopefully for a sign of friendship.

"That was a good idea, Joe," said Mike. "I'm glad not to have it with Mrs. Robinson."

Joe took it that the hatchet was buried.

"I saw her coming out of here, sir, and she looked like someone had stood on her. Did she ask who told you about the telegram?"

"She doesn't know how I found out," said Mike.

"I'll never forget it for you, sir," said Joe earnestly. "I'm afraid of that one, so I am. It's a queer thing, sir, but a big, wicked woman like that is as bad as six men."

"You should get married, Joe," said Mike. "Then you wouldn't be so afraid of women."

"I'll always be afraid of them, sir," said Joe mournfully. "It's the way my mother brought me up. She'd tell you that herself." He brooded for a moment. "What kills me, sir, is when women fall out between themselves. That's the time when every decent man should get out of the way and leave them to it. There's Esther and Mrs. Robinson, now, after falling out with each other, and they have everyone heart-scalded, so they have."

"But I thought they were the best of friends," said Mike.

He did not remember who had told him this, but he was sure he had heard that Esther was the Queen-bee's devoted ally.

"They were the best of friends till this morning," said Joe. "No one knows what crossness came between them, but they're like tigers now. Mrs. Robinson asked Esther to do something, and Esther wouldn't—I think that's the way of it, anyway. Women are all the same, sir."

He arranged the tea tray on a small table by Mike's chair, and went out, still breathing devotion and loyalty.

Mike moodily drank the teapot dry. He was lifting the lid and looking hopefully into the pot, just as Sergeant Mahon came in the door.

"Late, I see," said Mahon. He reached for a sticky cake off the tray, and munched, while Mike said impatiently:

"Did you do any good?"

"Not bad. I heard a bit about Burden. He had a sort of hand-to-mouth existence until he came here. Farrell says he worked in an accountant's office for a short while, until he had learned the more crooked tricks of the trade. Then he did spells with business firms who wanted sets of books faked for audit. He made a regular trade of this. He used to get paid a lump sum for it—not very much. Farrell says it would have paid him better to be honest. He says he thinks Burden used to get after his customers again and try to blackmail another bit of money out of them, but he doesn't think he did so well out of that game. It nearly killed Farrell to tell me that," said Mahon appreciatively. "I could see him praying for guidance before he let it out. He has no proof, of course, but he knows someone that Burden tried it on."

"Where did Burden live in Dublin? How did Farrell find him?"

"He followed him from one shady job to another. The people were delighted to tell him what they knew about him when they heard it wasn't themselves that were wanted. Burden had a greasy bed-sitting room in Leeson Street. Farrell actually visited him there. He says Burden greeted him as if he was Santa Claus. He was down and out." Mahon looked around the library. "This must have been a great change for him."

Mike felt his first pang of pity for Burden. He had had so very little time to enjoy his unexpected luck. Mahon went on:

"Burden was never in trouble with the police, though they had their eye on him, and would have caught up with him sooner or later. Mr. Farrell says he didn't change much after he came here. He thought all businesses were conducted the way he had seen it done. Farrell thinks he wouldn't have paid the bills. He says too that Burden had already got a bit of a reputation for being a lad with the girls."

"Miss Keane would have stopped all that," said Mike.

He told Mahon about his interview with Mrs. Robinson, in the course of which it had emerged that Burden had intended to marry Miss Keane. Mahon said admiringly:

"There's no one can suck information out of the people like yourself, sir. But if you'll excuse me for saying it, you'd want to be careful with these old ones. We don't want another corpse on our hands."

"Quite right," said Mike dryly. "What about the will?"

"There is no will," said Mahon. "Though there almost was. Burden visited Farrell last week and said he wanted to make one."

"Did he, indeed?" said Mike softly. "Go on."

"Farrell never does anything in a hurry. I can't see him reaching out for a sheet of paper, and writing Burden's will on it so that he could sign it there and then. He asked him what he wanted to put into the will, and Burden said he was going to leave everything of which he died possessed to Miss Eleanor Keane."

"Ha!"

"Ha, indeed!" said Mahon. "Farrell showed me the will, all ready, but Burden never got a chance of coming in to sign it. He was to have come this morning. There goes Miss Keane's chance of owning this place," he added. "I wouldn't like to have her luck."

"Has Farrell any idea who will be the owner now?" Mike asked.

"There's no doubt about it," said the sergeant. "He says there's always a terrible long delay when there's no will, but he knows there is only one person who can inherit."

"And who is that?"

"Burden's first cousin, Mrs. Barbara Henry."

9

Although Mike had guessed that Mrs. Henry would inherit the hotel if Burden had made no will, this confirmation flooded his mind with latent ideas. He could not help observing how neatly she fitted in with all the essential attributes of the murderer. She was strong enough, and determined enough. She stood to gain lifelong security for herself and her son. She had no alibi, since she had said she was in her room looking at cookery books at the time of the murder. She was clever enough to have seen that the universal high feeling against Burden, which had grown up since his arrival, would go a long way towards protecting her from suspicion.

Of these, the fact that she would gain so much was easily the most convincing argument against her. Mike knew that many widows with children allow their protective instincts to lead them to extraordinary lengths. They literally do not see injustice in any action of their own which is designed for the so-called good of their children. He had not thought that Mrs. Henry was sufficiently unconscious for this role, but then even her air of dignified detachment could be assumed.

When Sergeant Mahon's voice broke in on his thoughts, it was obvious that he had been following the same line.

"Wasn't it a queer thing for Mrs. Henry to tell you that her uncle had suspected her of trying to poison him? Now, why did she do that?"

"She thought Miss Keane would tell me, and she wanted to get in first," said Mike. "That was the impression I got at the time, at least."

"Suppose she did it so that you'd say, 'No, no! A thousand times, no!' " said Mahon. "Then she might hope you would put her out of your head as a suspect."

"That could be," said Mike. "Or since she must have known she would be suspected anyway, she may have thought that if she told half of the truth, she could withhold the other half. She doesn't look like a liar to me, though."

"A good liar never looks it," Mahon reminded him.

Mike had to agree, and still he could not associate Mrs. Henry, as he knew her, with violence. He got up wearily.

"Well, now we must go into every move she made yesterday," he said. "The fact that she gets the hotel is enough reason for that. But there are other things to be done at the same time."

He told Mahon that Burden had been arranging to have Mrs. Fennell certified.

"That's Mrs. Robinson's story anyway," said Mike. "You had better go the Mental Hospital and see Dr. Bradley about it. If we're in luck, he went for the local man. If Dr. Bradley knows nothing about it you had better try all the other mental hospitals, beginning with Dublin, since Burden lived there so long. Then you'd better see Johnny Farrell again and find out if he can do anything to confirm Mrs. Henry's story about her uncle's will."

"Between ourselves, I'd be glad if it was Mrs. Fennell," said Mahon confidentially. "Mrs. Henry is a fine woman—"

"That's a most improper attitude for a Guard," said Mike severely. "It's fatal for a detective-officer to have likes and dislikes among his suspects."

Outside the door, Mahon rubbed his red ears and said to himself, "I walked into that. I wonder why he got so hot about it?"

Mike could have told him that it was because he was rebuking himself as much as the sergeant.

Mike went out into the hall. Tea in the veranda was over, and the old people were tottering away to their rooms for their afternoon naps. Through the glass doors, he could see out on to the terrace where Professor Daly, George Arrow and Mr. Heaslip were standing talking together. He went out and joined them. Daly said:

"What have you done to Mrs. Robinson? Since she came out of the library she hasn't spoken a word, and she's keeping Horace on such a short lead that no one can catch him and pump him."

"I only asked her a few questions," said Mike mildly. "Perhaps she's a very sensitive woman."

"Sensitive, my eye!" said Daly inelegantly. "I should miss the Queen-bee if you thought fit to arrest her, but there are many people whom we could spare less readily."

"She's in no danger of arrest at the moment," said Mike. "I was looking for Mrs. Henry just now. Have you seen her about?"

He saw Arrow's color rise a little, though his tone when he spoke was studiedly casual.

"I hope you're not going to treat her as you treated Mrs. Robinson. Our chivalry would force us to intervene."

Mike wondered again why Arrow had recovered his confidence so well. Yesterday he would have stammered. He said:

"No one would think of treating Mrs. Robinson and Mrs. Henry alike. One of the things I wanted to do was to break the news of her succession to her. I've just heard that Burden made no will, so now she will really own Crane's Court at last."

"Thank God for that," said Daly in heartfelt tones. "Peace after storm, and so on."

"The old ladies will be pleased," said Mr. Heaslip. "Do they know yet?"

"No," said Mike. "And I'm not sure that it would be a good thing to tell them all at once. I'd be obliged if you would not talk about it for the present—just let them simmer."

"Mrs. Henry was here a moment ago," said George. "She said she had some things to attend to before going into the town." Again his color rose as he said reverently, "She's asked me to go with her—to the dentist."

Professor Daly's quizzical eye was turned on George at once. Mr. Heaslip had obviously noticed too, and Mike was almost embarrassed for George's sake.

"Well, I'll find her before she goes, then," he said, and went back into the hotel.

While Joe went in search of Mrs. Henry, Mike thought he might usefully spend the minutes of waiting in interviewing Esther. She was on the glass veranda clearing away the remains of tea. She did not honor him by pausing in her work. Indeed she frequently turned her back on him and marched away bearing cups and plates, so that he had to follow her about in order to continue the conversation. He could plainly see that this was deliberately done to show him that he was an unwanted interloper.

Esther was all of fifty-five years old, Mike thought, but her back was as straight as a ramrod. Her hair was dyed a reddish orange, and was arranged to the best advantage under her white cap. He guessed that she was not clever, but she covered her deficiency with a contemptuous attitude towards anything that was beyond her understanding. She looked sour and domineering, and was probably given to conspiring in corners with her favorites. He had heard that she was an expert waitress.

"Of course I'm only a maid. I'm nobody," she said when Mike questioned her about her difference with Mrs. Robinson. "It's easy to understand why Mrs. Robinson doesn't feel *grateful* to me. But *I'm telling you, Mr. Kenny,*" she wagged a forefinger under his nose, "there's many a thing she couldn't have done without my help!"

She whisked a cloth off a table and shook it, and marched off, all to emphasize her words. Mike, who since his early youth had hated having fingers shaken at him, followed her meekly in the name of law and order. She folded the cloth with her back turned to him and slammed it on to a service table by the door. Mike tried again.

"When did you have this quarrel with Mrs. Robinson?"

"Ladies don't *quarrel* with maids," she rebuked him contemptuously.

He wished she did not get such a morbid satisfaction out of her low station in life. At the rate they were going it would take all day to get an answer out of her. While he wondered how to frame his question in a way that would please her, to his great relief she went on:

"I have done many and many a thing for Mrs. Robinson, things that she wanted me to do, but that I knew were not wrong. But this I would not do, not if she went on her bended knees. Mrs. Henry is a good woman, though she hasn't got the devotion to the hotel that you would like. Still, since it doesn't belong to her, I suppose one can't expect it."

Mike gathered, rightly, that she was conveying to him that her own devotion did not depend on ownership. He hoped she would go on with her explanation without further prodding from him, since everything he ventured seemed to be wrong. He reflected in anger against himself that he was far too diffident to be a policeman.

"And every mother thinks her own son is perfect," said Esther. "Though how Mrs. Robinson can look at that Horace I'll never understand. Never!"

Again she marched away. This time Mike waited until she came back for more cups and then said:

"What has Horace got to do with it?"

"Dear Horace!" said Esther with savage scorn. "For all his airs and his fine accent I'll say this about him—he's No Gentleman! No! Not if he went to school in Timbuktu, nothing would make a gentleman of him. *I* should know better than anyone."

"But what did Mrs. Robinson ask you to do?" asked poor Mike in despair.

Esther came close to him and gazed earnestly into his face.

"She asked me to do what I'd never do, and I told her so. Oh, I told her, all right. Never, I said—"

Mike decided to try to put an end to this. He said suddenly:

"Esther! Had *you* anything to do with the death of Mr. Burden?"

But he knew he had failed when she turned a pitying eye on him.

"I, sir?" she said delicately, and laughed a horrid little humorless laugh. "Oh no, sir!"

And she walked away again. What she meant was quite plain. A maid does not have anything to do with the murder of a gentleman, not even of a gentleman who is not a gentleman.

Mike moved towards the door, having decided that he was wasting his time. He knew that Mrs. Robinson's request had something to do with Horace and Mrs. Henry, and he supposed he should be pleased with even that much. If necessary he could bring the objectionable Esther into the barracks in town and let Colm MacDonagh have a go at her. Colm could make the stones talk.

But as he reached the door he heard Esther's voice, considerably softened now:

"Do you want to hear the rest of the story now, Mr. Kenny?"

So by accident he had discovered the way to make her talk. He turned and looked at her, with his hand on the doorknob, as if he were impatient of the delay. He said nothing. She sniffed hopefully once or twice, but when she saw that he was not going to ask any more questions she said:

"I suppose you have heard that Mrs. Robinson sent for her son Horace?"

Mike nodded. Esther looked at him with intense dislike, but he just waited. Presently she went on:

"She sent for her son as soon as she heard that Mr. Burden was dead. She told me that her son and Mrs. Henry had become attached to each other, but that, of course, I did not believe. Now, if she had said that her son had become attached to the *hotel,* I would have believed it. I was not supposed to know that she had sent for Mr. Horace, but I did know. She thinks that Mrs. Henry will own the hotel now, and she wants Mr. Horace to marry her!"

Still Mike waited. Esther said in a disappointed tone:

"That's all I know. She asked me to put Horace and Mrs. Henry at the same table in the dining room. She meant to have her meals in her own room, so that he'd have a chance of fixing things up. She thought that since Mrs. Henry is a widow, she'd be glad enough to marry anyone—she didn't tell me that but I knew. Then, as I said, I told her I wouldn't do it, and she's blackout with me now. Which saves me a lot of bother, I'm sure!"

"How could you arrange where Mrs. Henry and Mr. Robinson were to sit?" Mike asked.

"They're both in my section of the dining room," said Esther. "I could have fixed it, all right. Not that Mrs. Henry would have stood it for more than one meal. She'd have stayed out of politeness the first time, but after that I'm certain she would have insisted on making some other arrangement."

Mike thanked her gravely for her cooperation, without which, he said, his work would be seriously hampered. Then he went out of the veranda and crossed the hall to the library.

Esther's story was illuminating, in its way. Here was another mother conspiring for the advancement of her son. Mike thought that Mrs. Robinson's chance of success was very small indeed, but as Esther had remarked, no mother is likely to recognize the full repulsiveness of her son. Now he remembered Mrs. Robinson's complaint that though she planned for her son's future, he did nothing for her. She had not said that he had refused to fall in with her plan, however. Mike guessed that Horace would have cooperated with alacrity. He could imagine him queening it over Crane's Court, with other long-haired excrescences like himself for company. But he could not imagine Mrs. Henry ever allowing this to come about. It was clear that in this respect Mrs. Robinson was completely blinded by her devotion to her son.

And what an odd notion it was that Mrs. Henry should be glad of any offer of marriage! It was not the first time he had met this point of view, and he knew that many people regard a widow, however young, as completely *passée*.

He reflected appreciatively that Mrs. Robinson and Esther were well-matched. He wondered what the old lady would do next. She would surely not be foiled by this little setback. He guessed that she was keeping Horace in check for fear he would chatter about his hopes. With Esther against her, it was going to be difficult to throw Horace and Mrs. Henry together in a natural-seeming way.

At this point Mrs. Henry herself came into the room.

"Joe said you wanted to see me," she said quietly.

She looked very tired, and he guessed that she had reached the second stage of her reaction to Burden's death.

"You're going into town to see the dentist," he said. "Why didn't you put him off?"

"I'm getting some teeth filled," she said in a dead voice. "I wanted to get it over. I suppose there is no objection to my going?"

"No. Mrs. Henry, did you expect to inherit Crane's Court when your cousin died?"

"Certainly not," she said. "I think I told you his attitude towards me."

"Why did you not leave Crane's Court when you found him so unpleasant?"

She flushed to the roots of her hair.

"I cannot see what that could have to do with your investigation," she said stiffly. "I wished to stay here, and that is all."

"It could have something to do with it," said Mike. "In fact, John Burden made no will and his solicitor is quite certain that you will be the only heir."

She sat perfectly still for a moment, and her face was quite expressionless. Then she said:

"Is that the truth?"

"Yes," said Mike.

"Do you think I killed my cousin on the chance that he had made no will?" As Mike made no answer she said, "That was not a sensible question. If you thought I had killed him you would arrest me, wouldn't you?"

She stood up.

"Have you finished with me?"

"Yes," said Mike. "I just wanted to break the news to you that you are likely to be the *new* owner of the hotel."

She gave him a long questioning look, quite without anger, before going out of the room.

"That's a clever woman," said Mike to himself, and added disconsolately, "I hope she's not too clever for me."

He studied his notes for a few minutes before going out into the hall to find Joe, whom he asked to direct him to the Waters's rooms. To Joe's delight, he allowed him to escort him to their door on the second floor, and to announce him in a ringing voice.

Colonel and Mrs. Waters were both in their sitting room. The Colonel got up and bowed stiffly, while his wife nodded equally stiffly from her armchair by the fire. The room was comfortably furnished, and the long windows looked out on the well-kept gardens at the end of the hotel. Joe had told him that the arrangement of the rooms was the same as that of Mr. Burden's—a bedroom and a sitting room with a connecting door, and each room with another door leading to the corridor outside.

"The old fellow is as rich as Damer," Joe had said, "but he's nearly too mean to feed himself and the wife, not to mind offering hospitality to anyone else."

Colonel Waters offered Mike a seat at the fire with what passed with him for affability. His wife wore the fixed expression of a perfect lady who regrets the necessity for politeness. Mike looked at her with particular interest, as the author of the plan to drive Burden to suicide. Her eye was the hardest he had ever encountered, which was saying a great deal. Her white hair lay in perfectly flat waves on her small thin head. Not very clever, was Mike's conclusion. He usually found that a small head held a small brain, though there were exceptions, and the converse was not always true.

The Colonel was an impressive enough figure, though he was not a big man. Under the mask of a gentleman, Mike thought he spotted a gamey eye. He rather thought that this side of the Colonel got small encouragement from his wife.

Gradually he got them to talk about Burden. At the mention of his horrid end, Mrs. Waters broke into the same cold satisfied smile that Mike had noticed in the dining room. She said:

"It was quite the best thing that could have happened, Mr. Kenny. Quite the best thing."

"I'm sure you'll understand that I can't take that attitude," said Mike.

She shrugged, while an uneasy look flitted across her husband's face. Mike said:

"I just want to ask you if you can throw any light on the affair. Perhaps there was something you noticed that was not as usual—"

"Nothing," said Mrs. Waters firmly, not troubling to conceal her satisfaction. "Nothing whatever."

"And you, Colonel?"

"Well—"

"Edmund!" said the old lady warningly.

"Yes, my dear?"

"Remember!"

"Yes, yes, of course."

The old man looked quite flustered, and Mike said soothingly:

"It would be far better for you to tell me if there is anything."

But the Colonel was shaking his head and his wife was looking pleased again. Mike found himself surmising that left to himself the Colonel would be neither as mean nor as stiff as his reputation made him. Living with a woman of his wife's caliber would sap the initiative of a stronger man. Mike addressed himself to Mrs. Waters.

"I understand that Mr. Burden had made himself unpleasant to nearly all of the permanent residents, and that meetings were called to discuss how best to circumvent him."

She looked uneasy for a moment and then she said firmly:

"That is so. I was at the meetings. I thought it all very silly. Mrs. Robinson was simply using the situation to make herself important." She looked him blandly in the eye. "I told her that things would work themselves out, and that there was no need for all the fuss."

So that's her line, said Mike to himself. Aloud he said:

"You were not at all concerned about the future, then?"

"No. Mr. Burden was a most unpleasant person, most unpleasant. But I felt quite sure that something would happen to rid us of him soon. I just felt that things would be all right."

Mike was struck dumb. She obviously did not care whether he believed this statement or not. She must know that if he had heard about the meetings he would have been told about her suggestion for dealing with Burden. How, then, could she now pretend to have been unconcerned about the whole business? Mike had difficulty in restraining himself from tearing his hair.

One thing was certain. It was no use asking this woman any more questions. If her object had been to get rid of him, she had a notable triumph, for he talked himself out of the room within two minutes. He had promised to come back, to be sure, but he fervently hoped that the necessity would not arise.

Before he had time to reach the head of the stairs, however, he heard heavy steps running, like a trotting bear, and a voice calling in a penetrating whisper:

"Inspector Kenny! Wait for me!"

It was Colonel Waters, and his heated look was not due merely to his exertions. He gripped Mike by the arm.

"I want to talk to you," he said, still in a hoarse whisper, and with a backward, fearful look over his shoulder. "Where can we go?"

"Down to the library," Mike suggested.

When they were seated there, the Colonel looked longingly at the bell-push. He cocked an eye at Mike.

"Do you know, Kenny, I think I'll just have a quick nip while I have the chance. What about you?"

The question was asked apprehensively.

Mike shook his head.

"Not during working hours, thanks."

The Colonel brightened at this and rang for his drink. He paid for it, Mike noticed, from an assortment of coppers, sixpences and threepenny pieces which he had pulled, loose, out of his pocket. Then he looked towards the door.

"I'm afraid you'll think it very odd," he said, "but I'd like to feel we're safe from—from interruption. Would it be possible to lock the door?"

Mike got up obligingly and did so, transferring the key from the outside to the inside of the door for this purpose. Colonel Waters said, heavily casual:

"No one in the hall, I suppose?"

"No one," said Mike and returned to his chair.

The Colonel cleared his throat and took a long drink.

"I expect you're wondering why I'm here," he said. As Mike made no answer he went on: "I thought I'd better explain my wife's attitude. She's a very nervous woman, you know. Nervous and highly strung. She's not like other women."

He looked hopefully at Mike and then went on resignedly:

"Well, I'm married to her for thirty-five years, and I know she's like that, but you wouldn't be expected to believe it."

"Of course I do," said Mike. "Please go on."

"She doesn't know I'm here," said the Colonel unnecessarily since Mike had guessed that Mrs. Waters was the expected interrupter. "I told her I was going out to the bathroom, and when I get back now I'll tell her I went for a stroll on the terrace." He looked up from under his eyebrows. "I often spin yarns to her to save her from worry. She takes things very hard."

"She seems to have been quite philosophical about Burden," said Mike.

"That's what I want to explain," said Colonel Waters. "You must have heard that she was far from philosophical about him. I wasn't at that wretched meeting, or I might have been able to soothe her down. But it was no sooner over than one of those silly old hens—Mrs. Devlin, I think—came prattling to me about Mildred's wonderful plan. Heaslip seems to have been there, and he did what he could to damp the idea. But I was not at all sure that he had succeeded, and when I heard that Burden was dead, I was damned glad to hear that it could not have been suicide."

"It was not suicide," said Mike.

"I'm putting my cards on the table," said the Colonel. "I don't like this hole-and-corner stuff. The reason the ladies were so keen on Mildred's idea was that they had been so successful in the matter of the veranda. That convinced them that the gods were on their side—gave them a nice satisfied feeling. I know all about that feeling because I experienced it myself in connection with a bathroom. You may have heard about it? The ladies themselves were the victims on that occasion. I must say I enjoyed that."

He took another swallow of his drink.

"Great stuff, Dutch courage," he said. "I don't get half enough of it." He paused to consider. "The bathroom, yes. Burden got the better of me there, though. Decided to charge two guineas a week extra for it, and of course Mildred wouldn't—I wouldn't pay that. I was furious about it at the time but—no, I didn't kill him on account of it, in case that's what you're thinking."

"The thought had occurred to me," said Mike gently.

"Well, put it out of your head, young man. It wouldn't have paid, you see."

Mike wondered if Colonel Waters was really as reasonable as he sounded. He had heard the story of the bath from Professor Daly, and the description of the Colonel's fury had been impressive. Now the Colonel seemed to want him to believe that a gentlemanly shrug of the shoulders had been his only reaction. Mike was certain that the threats as repeated to him had been very real, at least at the time.

"You must have noticed how pleased my wife looked just now," the Colonel went on. "I wouldn't like you to take too much notice of that. It's just that she likes to have her own way, and she feels that it was only right that Burden should have been removed since she didn't approve of him." He waved a hand helplessly. "Women are extraordinary creatures."

Not for the first time it crossed Mike's mind that the Colonel himself might have been directed by his wife to remove Burden. He thought it just possible. The old man was obviously under her thumb. He had let slip the fact that she controlled the money, and his pitiable collection of small coins showed that his own pocket-money was very restricted. Then it seemed that he had to provide an excuse for leaving her, even for a few minutes. Would it be very strange, then, if on the promise of a reward—freedom, money, perhaps—she had induced him to kill Burden? And if this idea was too farfetched, there was another that was not. If Mrs. Waters had done the job herself, her husband would never give her away. Mike could imagine her as she was thirty-five years ago, a cold beauty. Probably in the Colonel's eyes she had never changed. He had met this phenomenon among married people before. And Colonel Waters was now so accustomed to protecting her that it had become automatic.

But somehow this theory did not please him. The amount to be gained by her was too nebulous—unless she was insane. He did not think she was. She was criminally selfish and vain, but that is not insanity.

Colonel Waters finished his drink and looked regretfully into his glass. Mike said:

"Why did your wife warn you to be careful what you said?"

"I was coming to that," said the Colonel. "I was foolish to tell her about it, but she saw I had something on my mind and she—well, she got it out of me." He fiddled with his glass. "You see, I went to see Burden on the afternoon that he died."

Mike suppressed a groan. Here was another of them! Was it a conspiracy? And they all tried to look so innocent as they told him about it. He got out his notebook and made an entry as he asked:

"At what time did you visit him?"

"At about a quarter to five."

"Was he alive?" asked Mike ironically.

"Of course he was."

"Was there anyone else in the room when you arrived?"

"No one. But I thought someone had been there. Burden was standing on the hearthrug, grinning like a man who has just won a battle."

The battle with Mrs. Robinson, thought Mike. The Colonel had lost his uneasiness now that he had begun this part of his story, and he went on animatedly:

"I went to see Burden to talk to him man to man. Perhaps you heard about my wife's garden? Well, it wasn't her garden, really, but she called it hers, and no one ever interfered with it. When Burden took that garden from her, her life became unbearable. You see, Kenny, my wife never reads. I do, and she gets very impatient with me. She doesn't care for sewing or knitting or any of those other things that ladies amuse themselves with. She hasn't made many friends here, either, though we have lived here so long. The only thing she did was to look after that garden. I really thought Burden behaved very badly about that. She wasn't doing any harm, and the piece of ground wasn't much good for anything else. Do you know it?" Mike nodded. "Well, you saw the tall trees in the middle, and the roots of trees sticking out of the ground all over it. She had really made it quite pretty—like a child's garden—primroses and bluebells and daffodils and stocks and so on." He paused. "Burden said it was the notice that irritated him. And he was determined not to let anyone bully him. He wouldn't listen to me at all, at first, until I came to my own view of the affair. He appreciated that. He actually said that there was something in it, and that he'd think it over. I believe he would have promised to give back the garden there and then only that he was always so afraid of losing face."

"How did you convince him?" Mike asked curiously.

"Nothing would make me disloyal to my wife," said Colonel Waters. "Nothing. But I put it to Burden that it was a great strain on me to be with her all the time, as I had to be since her garden was gone. It was not that I didn't want to be with her," he explained painfully, "but it was just that if I went off by myself for a while I seemed to come back refreshed. It was never for long, an hour or so at most. I used to go to the garden when I'd come back, and admire what she had done and take her in."

Mike looked at him with astonishment and pity. He wondered what special grace from heaven had stopped the Colonel from wringing Mildred's thin, blue neck years ago. The life he described was grim. She didn't read. She liked to talk—nastily, no doubt. And then the Colonel's only free time had been swept away by a decree of Burden's. Mike wondered again if the Colonel was as ingenuous as he sounded. Perhaps Burden had not been so reasonable. Perhaps, elated by his victory over Mrs. Robinson, he had laid down the law about Mrs. Waters's garden, and had said that as long as he lived she would never have it back. Then perhaps O'Reilly's tempting knife had been too near the Colonel's hand, and in a surge of fury he had thrust it into Burden. Mike could see the scene. Colonel Waters was capable of it, mentally and physically. His long devotion to his Mildred could prove a superhuman strength of mind, in Mike's view, as easily as it could prove the opposite. It could be the same strength that makes a mother devote her life to the protection of a weak-minded child. And Burden, in attacking the Colonel's charge, had asked for trouble.

"How did your interview with Burden end?" Mike asked.

"He was quite friendly. He said he liked me as well as he liked George Arrow and Heaslip and Daly, and that it was good to have friends. He said he would lend me books. I wouldn't have thought him a bookish chap."

Neither was he, thought Mike, remembering the cache of brown-paper-covered pornography that had been found in one of his suitcases.

"You do believe me, don't you?" Colonel Waters asked anxiously.

"Can you prove any of it?"

"Of course not. I told you we were quite alone. It's not likely that anyone was eavesdropping. If it's any help to you, Burden picked up the house telephone and asked Miss Keane to come to his room just as I was going out. If she remembers that, it might go some way to prove that he was alive when I left."

"Thank you. Did you tell your wife that Burden had promised to restore her garden?"

"No. You see, he had not definitely said that he would. I did not tell her I had been to him at all until after we heard that he was dead. But even then I didn't tell her that he had promised anything, for fear his successor would not agree. I thought it would be foolish to raise her hopes."

This was very plausible, though Mike would have been glad of confirmation of the whole story. Still, even if Mrs. Waters had said that the Colonel had come straight from his interview with Burden and told her all about it, he could not have believed it. She was a woman who simply had no use for truth.

Colonel Waters got up with a sigh and said:

"Well, I must be getting back. That was really all I wanted to tell you. You won't want to question Mildred again, I hope?"

"No," said Mike with feeling. "I hope not. Just one more question, Colonel, before you go. Did you see the chef's knife while you were in Burden's room?"

"Yes. I didn't know whose it was, though. It looked like one of those big paper-knives one sometimes sees."

"Where was it?"

"On a small table by the fire."

Mike unlocked the door, peeped into the empty hall and then nodded to the Colonel that it was safe to go.

He came back into the library and looked out on to the terrace through the long windows. George Arrow and Mrs. Henry were getting into a station wagon, which had "Crane's Court" painted in small gold letters on its front panels. They were absorbed in each other. Mrs. Henry got into the driver's seat. As Mike watched George climb briskly in at the other side, he took out his pencil and tapped his teeth with it. Then he bit the pencil methodically in a pattern all around the top. It tasted sweet, and the shiny paint was delightfully slippery under his tongue.

He was remembering a phrase he had used to Martin Hogan—something about potential murders coming to the boil. This one had come to the boil on the day of Burden's death, he was sure. It had not been a sudden impulse, though it may have lain dormant for a long time in the mind of the perpetrator. It was no coincidence that at least three people had visited Burden in the last hour of his life, all angry with him, all wanting something that only he could grant. If their stories were true, the murderer was a fourth visitor. At some time, Burden had condemned himself to death, either by one of his outrageous interferences with his subjects, or by his very existence.

Mike's success as a policeman had arisen because he had not got a mathematical mind. He hated sums, and he never put two and two together if he could avoid it. This was one reason why he shied away from the easy solution that Ned had killed Burden for annoying his girl. It was not because this was an obvious solution that he did not accept it. It was that he felt that all Burden's unpopularity had been used by the real murderer to cover his own long plans.

"But of course that's all theory," said Mike to himself, as he looked with annoyance at his ruined pencil.

10

As the station-wagon moved up the long driveway through the trees, George felt a little tinge of pure happiness run through him. He did not care now if ten Burdens lay draped on hearthrugs at Crane's Court. He had Barbara to himself, and nothing else mattered. This was not the first time, of course. They had gone for several walks—after he had watched for hours at his window for her to come out on the terrace, and had raced around through the hall to appear casually at her elbow. Curiously enough, the exertion had done him no harm, though he made a point of walking slowly afterwards.

Conversation had been difficult on these occasions. They had often walked as much as a mile without exchanging a word. George was floating in a bog-hole of uncertainty from which he saw no hope of rescue. He had no idea what was in her mind, but he was pleased that she was content to be with him. They must make an odd pair as they rambled along, he thought, each looking so abstracted.

But it was different today. George almost felt grateful to Burden for getting himself murdered, since it had at last created a subject of conversation between himself and Barbara. He wondered if people in love always felt such tension between them. He had understood that there was never any conversational difficulty, and in his search for signs and portents, he took this to mean that Barbara was not in love with him. Which was just as well, he thought sadly, for he could not envisage himself explaining about his infirmity and, as it were, apologizing for having misled her.

"What do you think of Kenny?" Barbara asked suddenly, her eyes on the road ahead.

"He doesn't go about measuring footprints," said George. "But he's clever. He measures one's mind instead."

"I wish he would hurry up and catch his murderer, so that we could all begin to forget about John Burden." She paused. "The inspector says that Crane's Court will be mine now."

"Yes, he told me too. Will you be glad?"

"I don't know," she said slowly. "I haven't been very happy there. Still, I should be glad."

"You could sell it," said George.

"No!" She laughed suddenly. "Well, that answers the question. I suppose I am glad to own it. There are so many things I can do. And all those old people can settle down again—oh, there are lots of things."

"Who do you think killed Burden?" George asked quietly.

She gave him a quick sideways look before she answered.

"I have no idea. It couldn't be anyone we know." She frowned. "I told the inspector that I thought someone must have followed him here from Dublin. I'm sure he had lots of shady associates there. Perhaps one of his old friends was jealous of him, even."

"That would hardly be enough reason for killing him," said George. "Of course it would be very convenient if it turned out to be some complete outsider. But after all, how well do you know any of the people in the hotel?"

"I know most of them very well," she said. "After six years—"

"Yes, but how much do you really know about them?" George insisted. "People in hotels have no background, except what they fill in themselves, and you snatch at that eagerly because you are so anxious for the gap to be filled. Then you are satisfied because the person is complete in your mind, though half of the picture may be quite false."

"Of course that is true," she admitted. "I suppose they only show as much of themselves as they want you to see. Still, I can't imagine any of them being a murderer."

"Take Professor Daly, for example," said George, "though we know he didn't do it. He looks a genial, affable extrovert. How do we know what he may not be hiding? Why did he joke and laugh over the body, instead of feeling ill, as I did?"

"He's always like that in the face of tragedy," said Mrs. Henry. "When my uncle died it was the same. His attitude then did more to make me feel better than all the condolences of the others. Then when Miss Keane began to make a scene he handled her quite calmly and efficiently, hustled her off where she would not be overheard and explained away what she had said so that no one took much notice."

"You didn't think he was too good at it?" George suggested.

"No. It was the very same spirit in which he came down and helped to cook dinner when the chef was ill." The recollection amused her. "He brought that queer little Major Dunlea along with him, and they found O'Reilly's private recipe book and cooked a dinner that no one will ever forget. Of course the other kitchen staff could have cooked a perfectly good meal, but Professor Daly insisted that it would be unfit for human food, and he turned them all out. He and the Major used every cup and plate and spoon in the kitchen, and they covered the floor with scraps of food, but it was a first-rate dinner. I'd be sorry to find that Professor Daly was the murderer," she finished. "Crane's Court would never be the same without him."

"Of course it's not Daly," said George, alarmed at what he might have started. "I was only using him as an illustration."

He could not imagine life without the old man either, at least until he had learned to keep his own spirits up as effectively as Daly could do it for him. Mrs. Henry was saying:

"Yes, they are all shadowy. I know nothing about them except what they have told me. Perhaps that is why a maid from Connemara who stays with us for a few months on her way to America is more real than any of them."

They had reached Galway by now. In all his weeks at Crane's Court, this was George's first visit to the town. He had almost enjoyed the mental slackness that had prevented him from making even such a mild excursion. He had badly wanted some new books, and still he had kept putting off from day to day the little decision that would have been necessary. Mrs. Henry had asked him to go with her several times, and he had actually refused, like a fool. Then on the very day when he had decided to go, he had had to visit Mrs. Fennell instead. That was a judgment on him, he felt.

They stopped in front of a small gate leading into a long passageway between tall houses. In front of them was the tumbling river, plunging under a broad bridge. From where he stood at the car door, George could see the dripping brown mill-wheels of three factories.

"I'm afraid I brought you here under false pretenses." Barbara was laughing now. "Do you mind coming right in with me?"

"Of course."

"I mean right into the surgery to watch the whole business, of my teeth being filled?"

"Of course I will!"

"It's the dentist, you see." She reddened a little, though her eyes were full of amusement. "I can't go in alone. He has—amorous intentions!"

"Has he, indeed?" said George angrily.

She laid a hand on his sleeve.

"Oh, I don't mind that. He's rather sweet, really. But he's not very articulate except when he's showing me his favourite instruments. Then he gets quite lyrical. He'll glare at you, but please don't take any notice. He always glares at poor Mr. Heaslip." She blushed again. "I should go to another dentist, of course, but I don't want to hurt his feelings by changing before he is finished."

George's soul was flooded with admiration for her. She turned her eyes down suddenly and said:

"Well, shall we go in?"

They went down the passageway, which widened out at the end in front of a small house that seemed to peep pertly up at its tall neighbors. Its door shone with brass and there were window-boxes full of geraniums on the sills. Presently they were being ushered into the surgery.

The dentist was an immense black-haired man with a soft apologetic voice. His name was Cooney. He glared at George, as Barbara had predicted, and jerked his head to indicate a particularly hard chair for him to sit on. Then he turned large brown eyes full of devotion on Barbara.

"I heard your bad news," he said in a low voice. "You needn't have come. I was very sorry."

He helped her into the dentist's chair. George sat in agony while he put his arm around her shoulders and picked an instrument off his little shelf. No one spoke. The only sound was Mr. Cooney's heavy breathing. Once Barbara gave a little gasp. George leaped to his feet. Mr. Cooney crawled apologetically. Looking at him, George was overcome with embarrassment. He felt sure that Mr. Heaslip, if he were here, would have strolled over genially and forced his own conversation on the dentist, for Barbara's sake. But George was too angry to do anything of the sort. His embarrassment for Mr. Cooney had turned into fury, and by the time Barbara was released and he was holding her coat for her, he could almost have bitten the dentist's hand outstretched to help. He stalked out of the house, herding her before him, slamming the door on the staring maid. He marched after her up the path to the gate. Suddenly he noticed that her shoulders were shaking and her head bent. Panic seized him. Had he gone too far? He touched her, and she turned around. She was laughing! She was laughing helplessly, while her eyes filled with enormous tears. The sight of her amusement increased his rage, though he had not thought this was possible. He gripped her arm and shook her. She gasped:

"The two of you—in there—!"

And she was off again.

"There's only one way to stop you," he said between his teeth.

It stopped her, all right. Fortunately they were out of sight of the house, or Mr. Cooney might have expired of jealousy at his own surgery window. The little gate on to the street was fitted with a sheet of metal to prevent passersby from looking in. Still, Barbara looked nervously at it as if expecting to see a crowd of grinning faces, when he released her. Then she looked down at the toes of her shoes.

"I'm sorry for bringing you in there," she said in a low voice. "I didn't know—"

"Mr. Heaslip would have been more useful," said George bitterly. "I'm sorry."

"Oh, don't spoil it all by saying that!"

They were silent while they went outside and got into the car. Sitting there, at last he told her his miserable story. As he talked, the last spark of his anger went cold.

"So you see," he finished, "I have no right to interfere with anything you do, because I'm not really alive any more."

There was a pause before he went on:

"It's queer that until now I had no special reason for wanting to live."

There was nothing for her to say. But the silence now was more companionable, and George's pity for himself had quite given place to pity for her.

After a few minutes, by common consent they moved on to continue their planned series of commissions in the town. She brought him to a bookshop at last, where he found many of the books he wanted. The shop was a series of isolated bays, well-lit and somehow so hospitable-looking that it was no surprise to find that one had to edge carefully around reading customers everywhere. Suddenly Barbara said:

"Look!"

He followed her gesture and saw, seated in front of a large fire at the back of the shop, in an armchair provided by the management, the tweedy, shabby figure of Major Dunlea. He had on a pair of very black-rimmed glasses, which accentuated his resemblance to a badger. He had a large book high in front of him, and seemed, by the continual little twitching of his hands and his lips, to be nibbling rather than reading it. While they watched he laid the book down on his knees, turned a page while his tongue protruded hungrily, and then lifted the book to go on with his nibbling.

They walked over to him, and George touched him on the shoulder with a friendly, "Good evening."

All movement stopped dead for a moment while he looked up sideways to identify them. Then he said, as he stood up: "Ah, good evening. Yes. You surprised me. Didn't know you were in town. Fine book, this." He showed it to them lovingly. "Too expensive for me, though. They let me come in here and read it. Must be the only bookshop in Ireland where they'd do that."

He held up the book for them to read the title. It was a translation of a French cookery book.

"I'm interested in cooking, you know. Got me into trouble once," he added reminiscently. "But I'm not so rash now. No."

"Would you like to come home with us?" Barbara asked. "We have the car outside."

He looked up at her gratefully, and then longingly back to his book.

"Thank you. I walked in, you know. But perhaps after all I'll wait for another little while. They don't close here until six."

"We won't be going until six," she said quickly. "George hasn't seen the town yet. We've been shopping all the time. We'll call for you at six."

"Thanks," said Major Dunlea. "I'll just get on with this until then."

And he waved his book.

"Do you think it would be useful to us at the hotel?" she asked innocently.

A look of bliss overspread his face.

"Just to read it is a joy," he said. "Just to read it!"

"I wonder if you would do me a favor? If I buy it, would you be so kind as to experiment from it? I'm sure Mr. O'Reilly won't mind. I'll fix it with him. Would you do that for me?"

Two large tears came into his big badger's eyes. He was too overcome to speak. He stretched out a claw, his left one, since his right one held the book to his breast, and took her hand for a moment reverently. She said:

"That's settled, then."

While they stood at the counter waiting for change, they heard him pattering towards them. He said:

"If you're going to show Mr. Arrow the town, you mustn't forget the jail. Very interesting place, though it's being knocked down now to build a cathedral instead. A young Connemara man was hanged there once, for a murder he never committed. He understood no language but Irish, and he was tried and condemned to death in English, so he never even knew what he was accused of. They'll show you the remains of his cell, if you tell them I sent you. I'm interested in jails, you know. Very interested."

They did not visit the jail, however, though they drove past its high limestone wall. They hung over the bridge by the salmon weir, where, she told him, in summer thousands of salmon lie lazily in the shallow water, which tickles their backs so that they sway from side to side with pleasure. Then they went by back streets through the town, past limestone warehouses with mysterious, flat-arched doorways, out on to the fish market and through the Spanish Arch to the docks. There were black tarred fishing boats there, with soft-voiced Connemara men shouting from one to the other in Irish. A wild-haired young giant in gray tweed trousers and a blue fisherman's jersey commented that if Barbara were cut in two at the waistline, she would make a fine figurehead for his boat. George called out to him, in Irish too, that it would be a fair exchange if he were beheaded to provide a figurehead for the station wagon.

There was a howl of delighted laughter from the others. This was what they loved. They jeered and called to the young man to prod him to another remark, but he had never expected his first one to be understood, and he had crawled, blushing, into the hold of his boat and refused to come out.

They walked around to where the *Dun Aengus,* the little steamer that visited the Aran Islands several times a week, lay against the wall. She looked a character, even leashed as she was. George had never been to the Aran Islands, and Barbara said:

"It's not too late in the year yet. We can go together—"

She stopped as she remembered how the *Dun Aengus* butted drunkenly at every wave, as if it were saying: "I'll get there, you see if I won't!"

It was not a journey for a man with a weak heart.

As they turned back, she said with a sigh:

"It has been wonderful, this few hours off. Though I have a lot to be thankful for, really. People staying in the hotel have been very kind—only one of them is anxious to go away at once. The rest have all behaved as if nothing has happened. But I do wish Miss Keane wouldn't glare at me!"

"It's really not surprising," said George. "She may not have anything against you personally. I'm more inclined to think she is jealous of your position, in some way."

"Surely no one would be jealous of a widow with a small son to bring up!"

"She wouldn't mind being a widow," said George. "I fancy she thinks she would find it rather interesting."

"She seems determined to stop being Miss Keane at the earliest possible moment," said Barbara thoughtfully. "Did you know that she was going to marry my uncle?" George nodded. "He would have been good to her, though of course he was old enough to have been her grandfather. John Burden might have been more uncertain. She's had a very narrow escape, though she can't be expected to appreciate that. It almost seems a pity that he didn't have time to make a will in her favor."

"Rubbish!" said George. "It would have been disastrous."

"I'm sure it would be a good thing for everyone if she got over the idea that she would like to own the hotel," said Barbara wearily. "We're all quite worn out with the strain."

"Perhaps she will leave when all the fuss about Burden is over."

"I don't think so. I couldn't ask her to go, of course, and I don't think she's sensitive enough to think of it herself."

Back at the bookshop, Major Dunlea was waiting, with his precious cookery book clutched under his arm. He got into the back of the station wagon, and sat up very straight all the way home. No one spoke much, though George felt an almost tangible peace all about him, as if each of the three of them had a separate reason for being content. It was easy to understand Major Dunlea's pleasure in his cookery book, but why should Barbara be smiling to herself and looking eagerly at the road ahead as if she were looking at a long happy future? And his own mood of optimism, which had evaporated when he had made his confession to Barbara, was back again. Clutching at a straw, he thought, and tried to feel bitter, but it was no use.

It was almost dusk when they slid down the drive to the hotel. They passed Mr. Heaslip on the way and waved to him. At the front door, Professor Daly and Joe were conversing. As they got out of the car, Joe's loud young voice floated across to them.

"Ah, she'd turn a horse from his oats, that one! Always trying to look as if she has the plans of the castle in her buzzom—"

He became aware of the group within easy hearing, and emitted a low: "Oh, my God!"

He shot into the hotel.

Professor Daly was grinning wickedly from ear to ear. He said suavely:

"Ah, good evening. I wondered where you were all gone. I've been chatting with Joe, here, while I waited for you."

"So I heard," said Barbara dryly.

"Poor Joe. He's easily embarrassed. He was referring, of course, to Miss Keane, who is going about looking knowingly mysterious. She is quite obviously hoping that someone will ask her what it is that she knows, so that she will have the pleasure of refusing to part with her information."

"Has Inspector Kenny questioned her?" George asked.

"Not since the morning."

It occurred to George that it might not be safe to look knowingly mysterious immediately after an as yet unsolved murder. He determined to find Miss Keane at the earliest opportunity and advise her to tell the inspector whatever she knew.

"What is that you're clutching, Major?" Daly asked.

"It's the Book. You remember, I was telling you about it. Mrs. Henry has just bought it for the library." He lowered his voice reverently. "I'm going to try some of the things in it."

"I've often thought," said Daly, "that cookery books are really the finest literature in the world. They show you life in the raw. They employ an economy of phrase almost amounting to terseness. They teach you the composition of life, the blood and the bones of reality. Every time you open one, you find something new and stark. They give an intellectual as well as a physical pleasure to the analytical palate. They flavor one's outlook; they can create an optimistic view of life or the reverse, at will. They have a greater influence for good and evil than any other art form. I would say without fear of contradiction," he declaimed, "that thrones have fallen and dynasties have been founded on their inspiration!"

In the middle of this piece of nonsense, Horace Robinson had sidled out of the hotel. When he became aware of the subject of the old man's discourse, he assumed a slightly contemptuous, knowing expression, designed to show that he knew literature from its seamy inside, that he was, in fact, one of the gifted Olympians who provide the material for the literature professors of the world.

Daly looked at him with an academic dislike.

"Our friend here," he said, "scrabbles on his hands and knees in the dust at the great men's feet. He belongs to the school that, instead of washing the world's dirty linen, just takes it in and mixes it around a little and sends it out again as dirty as ever. Some day I shall write a monograph on the subject of dirt in literature. One could analyze Flaubert's description of the beggar who lay in wait for the carriages going up the hill, for instance. And there is a whole generation of aromatic moderns to be investigated."

Horace leered, but seemed not to be offended. He had looked a little put out at first, but had brightened at the mention of Flaubert in connection with himself. It was possible that he would not realize the full implications of Daly's remarks for a while, George thought. He had noticed the snakes' eyes resting on Barbara, speculatively, and he felt a twitch of anger run through him. Now Horace slunk up to Barbara and began to talk about Crane's Court, and the pleasure it was for him to return to it. He leered again, intimately, and George longed to punch his flat nose. Barbara, of course, was the soul of politeness, and George hated the way she smiled and, it seemed to him, encouraged Horace to further odious familiarities. He was overjoyed when Professor Daly looked at his watch and said:

"Time to dress for dinner. In fact it's a little late. Have you noticed a great silence within during the last few minutes? Ah, here comes Heaslip."

Mr. Heaslip was walking slowly down the drive towards them.

"It's a shame to go in," he said. "This would be a wonderful evening for a walk on the shore."

As they all turned to look down at the panorama of sea and mountain, Inspector Kenny came quietly out on to the steps of the hotel behind them. He had had a nerve-searing day, and he drank in the peaceful scene with intense and healing pleasure. In a moment he was jarred by the sight of Horace Robinson becoming playful, pulling Mrs. Henry by the sleeve, urging her to come and walk with him along fairy paths across the seas to Tír na nóg, to forget about dinner and everyday responsibilities in the joy of his company. There was a great deal more. Mike's inside curled up with disgust as he listened. Daly was grinning with wicked delight. Mr. Heaslip was expressionless. Mrs. Henry was embarrassed, but smiling in a sick-looking way. And George Arrow was getting redder and redder while his rage increased, until at last it boiled over.

"Stop it!" he shouted. He stammered and fumbled. "I mean, don't do that. I—I must explain. Barbara—!" He looked at her imploringly. "Mr. Robinson, I d-didn't mean to be rude. I should have explained—that is to say—oh, damn it! Barbara and I are engaged to be married!"

Time stood still while they all looked at him. He blushed still further, and moved his head as if it hurt him. Barbara said quietly:

"Thank you, George dear," and touched his hand as she passed him on her way into the hotel.

No one else spoke. Horace stood with his mouth open, and the dangerous eye of a petty man insulted. Professor Daly was not smiling now. George looked across at Horace and said uncomfortably:

"Sorry, Robinson. You should never forgive me."

He brushed past Mike through the front door.

When he was gone, the remaining people came to life again. Horace began to swear in an ugly tone. Mike moved out on to the terrace and joined the group. Professor Daly was saying:

"That won't help things now, Horace, old man. It wasn't your fault. Just one of those nasty accidents." His tone was slightly doubtful. "You couldn't possibly have known about their engagement. I imagine they arranged it only this afternoon."

Horace's brow was still black with fury. One could almost hear his scales rattle, Mike thought. Professor Daly regarded him critically for a moment and then chose his words carefully.

"For Barbara's sake, the only gentlemanly thing you can do now is to forget the whole thing."

At the magic word "gentleman" Horace's face cleared, and he assumed the wooden expression proper to the designation. He obviously saw that this was his opportunity for recovering face. The others, anxiously watching, all gave a little sigh of relief. Mike reflected that the sight of a man who has lost control of himself sufficiently to reveal his true character is most unnerving. He had often noticed how onlookers hold their breath until he has recovered himself, as if they were watching the death-dance of their own carefully built up exteriors. It is part of the mysterious brotherhood of man, and he quoted to himself the line he always remembered when he observed how a crime of violence touches one after another of the people present with a leprous finger: "Therefore send not to find for whom the bell tolls; it tolls for thee."

"Damned philosophizing policeman," said Professor Daly's voice in his ear, as Horace marched stiffly into the hotel. "Your thoughts are written on your face."

"They shouldn't be," said Mike amiably. "Did you know that Mr. Arrow and Mrs. Henry were engaged to be married?"

"No. Did you, Heaslip?"

"I can't say I did," said Mr. Heaslip, "though I suppose we should all have noticed that things were heading that way. But then, I don't know Mr. Arrow very well." He looked at his watch and said, "Will you excuse me, please?"

"Of course."

When Mr. Heaslip had gone into the hotel, Daly said:

"George's announcement surprised me, I must say. You know, of course, that he has a bad heart?" Mike nodded. "He has been in love with Mrs. Henry since the day he came, but he told me that he could never get married. I don't know what to make of this business."

"I don't think he would have said anything only for Horace's little show," said Mike. "It was a disgusting exhibition. It would have taken a stronger character than Mr. Arrow's to stand it. I felt a great urge to twist Horace's head off myself."

"You're not in the same case as George, I trust?" Daly asked anxiously.

"By no means. I'm on duty."

"Of course very few people know about George's heart. He told me in strict confidence, and I haven't told anyone until now. He was very depressed about it—broke up his whole life in Dublin on the advice of his doctor and came to live here. I must say I didn't think that was psychologically sound, but then I'm not a doctor. Of course you won't have to make his story public?"

"No," said Mike.

"All this fuss must be very bad for him," said Daly. "He's not supposed to have shocks. I think I'll just drop into his room on my way in and see that he's all right. You'll dine at our table, of course?"

"Thanks, but I think I'll just have a tray in the library," said Mike. "I'd like to finish up here and leave you all in peace as soon as I can."

"Are you talking about finishing already?" the old man asked eagerly. "Do you know who the murderer is? Did you find fingerprints on the handle of the knife?"

"Aged ones of O'Reilly's, some of Burden's own—he carried it upstairs, you remember—and blurred marks of the fingers of gloves."

"Gloves! Then the murder was not a sudden impulse. No one pauses and asks the victim to wait while he puts on gloves. It also shows our murderer as something of an expert in his craft."

"I had reached those conclusions unaided," said Mike dryly.

"Women are more ruthless than men," said Daly after a pause. "You have a crop of them there who would stop at nothing. Mrs. Robinson? Mrs. Fennell? Miss Keane? And plenty more. Just take your choice."

"As easy as that," said Mike wearily, and followed the old man into the hotel.

Joe was coming down the stairs.

"You have only seven minutes left, sir," he said. "You'll have to gallop."

"Give me an extra five minutes, Joe," Daly pleaded. "You needn't strike the gong exactly on time tonight."

"Tonight of all nights it must be on time, sir," said Joe. "O'Reilly said that if I don't have everyone in the dining room sharp on time, he'll throw the whole dinner out the window. He will, too," said Joe hopefully, "if he gets into a worse wax than he's in now."

Professor Daly waited for no more. As he hurried past George's door he paused uncertainly and then saw Maggie coming towards him. He stopped her with a question.

"Have you been in Mr. Arrow's room? Is he all right?"

"He is," said Maggie. "He looked a bit shook when he came in first, but he's dressing now."

"Good," said Daly, bounding up the stairs.

George was dressing slowly and mechanically, fumbling with blind fingers at his tie and struggling desperately to maintain his self-control. In five minutes he would have to appear in the public dining room, looking unconcerned, and eat a meal to the accompaniment of Daly's conversation. If he rang the bell, he could have dinner in his room, but he knew that for Barbara's sake he must not hide. He still shied away from the contemplation of what he had done. He knew he should feel remorse, and in a sense he did, but at the same time he could not repress a feeling of pure delight in the sound of the words he had used. They had sounded so right and inevitable, though they were, in fact, the wildest folly. They seemed not to have injured his relationship with Barbara, but he was beginning dimly to realize the difficulties into which he had plunged her.

At the first stroke of the gong, he examined himself curiously in the glass to see if he was fit to appear. He saw a pair of frightened eyes staring back at him, and he felt a surge of futile anger against himself.

Going towards the dining room, he saw the competent figure of Dr. Morgan walking ahead with his wife. His very appearance gave George a little confidence, and he longed to rush up to him like a puppy looking for comfort.

"Pretty soon I'm going to be more in need of a psychiatrist than a heart specialist," he thought grimly, as he remembered the variety of emotional waves on which he had ridden during the day.

In the dining room, Martin Hogan was sitting at the table, but Professor Daly had not yet arrived. He came, looking rather pinker than usual, just as the soup was served.

"That was a near thing," he said, "but I made it, all right."

He waved across to O'Reilly, who was glooming over the hotplate, and got a sour nod for acknowledgment.

"Try to look happier," he whispered to George. "This is a special night for O'Reilly, and we must all visibly enjoy his cooking."

The chef stayed by the hotplate throughout the meal, watching wickedly for signs of insubordination on the part of the guests. George noticed how each dish was greeted with elaborate cries of surprise and pleasure, and how even the aged dyspeptics managed to clear their plates, with a conciliatory look towards the artist. At last O'Reilly snorted and stamped out, and a sigh of pure relief went up.

"Well, that's over," said Daly, "at least for this time. We have it every three months or so. O'Reilly cooks a test dinner to find out if we appreciate him. Every one of us old-timers will write him a letter of congratulation this evening, referring specially to the dish we most enjoyed. But oh, the bellyaches there will be in this house tonight! The mind boggles at the thought. Thank God I've always had a good digestion."

Barbara joined them in the drawing room for coffee. Horace was there, and his stiff bow was designed to be that of a perfect gentleman whose finer feelings have been lacerated. His mother glared uninhibitedly, however, and was easier to endure. The conversation was general, but it was obvious that there were furious undercurrents flowing in all directions. Martin Hogan and Daly kept a flicker of conversation going, but one could see the little journalist's eyes darting eagerly from face to face, as if he knew the murderer was present and expected to identify him by a black mark on his forehead. The Waterses sat together on a sofa, without a word, and stared vacantly. Mrs. Fennell whispered busily to herself and drank her coffee. George began to feel that it was all a macabre ballet, in which the main theme was repeated at intervals, with each time a different shade of meaning. He drank in the pleasure of his proximity to Barbara and shut his mind resolutely against intruding thoughts of the future.

As he placed his cup on Esther's trolley, he noticed that Joe was talking to someone at the door. A moment later Joe was at his elbow saying:

"Inspector Kenny wants to speak to you in the library, sir."

"I'll come at once," said George, surprised.

"What is it, George?" asked Barbara.

"I don't know. Kenny wants to see me."

He tried not to sound querulous. She paused for a moment and then said:

"I'll come with you. Mr. Kenny won't mind."

They found Sergeant Mahon standing outside, and he led them silently to the library door, opened it and followed them in. Mike was sitting in a straight chair at the table. He raised his eyebrows at Barbara, but made no objection to her coming in. Dr. Morgan was standing with one foot on the fender and his arm resting on the mantel, looking into the fire. George crossed the room uncertainly and stood looking down at Mike, with Barbara just behind him. Sergeant Mahon had taken up a position with his back to the door. Suddenly George said:

"You wanted to see me. What is it?"

Mike turned a straight gaze into George's eyes and said:

"Mr. Arrow, can you tell me why I should not arrest you for the murder of John Burden?"

11

There was a long pause, after Barbara's first gasp. George stood like an alabaster statue, quite white and still. Mike continued to hold him in his gaze. Mahon shifted from one foot to the other. Dr. Morgan looked across at the group in the middle of the room with professional detachment. At last Mike said:

"You heard my question, Mr. Arrow."

George opened his stiff lips and said:

"Is this a joke, or a trick?"

"No." Suddenly the pencil Mike held between his hands was cracked in two. Both he and George looked down at the pieces. Then Mike said:

"I will repeat my question. Can you tell me why I should not arrest you on a charge of murdering John Burden?"

"Because I didn't," George burst out angrily. "I had no reason to. Besides, I couldn't have. I have a bad heart. The effort would have killed me."

"Dr. Morgan," said Mike quietly.

Dr. Morgan straightened up and looked at George.

"Mr. Arrow," he said carefully, "your heart is as sound as mine. There is nothing whatever wrong with it."

"But—I was told—"

He stopped and looked at Barbara wildly. Confused thoughts stumbled through his mind. Hysteria gripped him, so that he had to struggle for control. For a terrible moment he wondered if he had gone mad, and was creating illusions for himself. He closed his eyes and shut out Mike's hostile look. Suddenly he felt very weak.

"Do you mind if I sit down?" he asked.

Mike got him a chair. Sitting there, George began to recover his wits. He was going to need them, it seemed. He looked up at Inspector Kenny who was still staring at him as if he wished to see into his brain. George said:

"It's nonsense to doubt my word. Dr. Moore, the doctor I visited in Dublin will confirm it."

"I was hoping you would suggest that," said Mike. "No one but yourself has the right to ask him. There would be a question of professional secrecy."

"Dr. Morgan was not so particular about professional secrecy," said George bitterly.

"I told you I don't like this, Inspector," said Dr. Morgan, who had got very red at George's last remark.

Mike said quickly:

"I got it out of him almost without his knowing it, Mr. Arrow. He was worrying about how to tell you—"

"Why do you believe him? Perhaps Dr. Moore was right. If he was, you may find yourself responsible for my murder."

But Mike asked Morgan to recite a list of his qualifications and experience which made it clear to George that it would be ridiculous to doubt his authority. Besides, George began to have a deep physical conviction that Morgan was right. He had experienced several severe shocks in the last twenty-four hours, and their effect had been stimulant rather than the reverse. That extraordinary depression from which he had suffered, too, could easily have been the protest of a healthy body against unnecessary pampering. If he had been really ill, he would have expected soon to have achieved the necessary resignation to his fate which his body would have recognized as inevitable. But now he could understand, since he must believe such an eminent man as Dr. Morgan, that he had been like a healthy man condemned to death for a crime which he had not committed—bewildered, angry, frightened, lost and resentful by turns.

As these thoughts rushed through his mind, his main feeling was one of exultation in his release. But then he suddenly remembered Inspector Kenny's opening question, and decided that this nonsensical suspicion must be disposed of at once.

"I'll telephone to Dr. Moore," he said. "He will be at home now. He'll tell you I thought I had a very bad heart."

He sent Barbara a glance of quiet assurance. She had not spoken a word, but he had felt that her trust in him had not wavered. He said as he got up:

"We can telephone from the office. You can all come with me and listen."

Mike nodded to the wooden-faced Sergeant Mahon, who opened the door, and they all moved towards the office in the hall. Mike walked in front beside George, with Dr. Morgan behind, uncomfortably escorting Barbara. At the office door, Morgan tried to make his escape, mumbling:

"You don't need me any more."

But Mike asked him smoothly to accompany them in.

They were all silent while George booked his call, but a tension crept about them when he was put through almost at once. The listeners could hear a faint, distant, barking sound, which was Mick Moore's voice. George said:

"Dr. Moore? . . . Hello, Mick. This is George Arrow. . . . Oh, I'm very well, thank you. . . . Mick, can you get me out of a spot of trouble? . . . I have an inspector of the Guards at my elbow, who thinks I murdered a man whom I never saw till I came here. . . . What's that? . . . Yes, I said 'murdered.' . . . With a damned carving-knife. And that's important, because I told him I couldn't have, that I have a rocky heart. And what does he do then but produce a bird called Morgan," George cocked a contemptuous eye at him, "who says my heart is as sound as a bell. . . . Yes, Morgan, Dr. Morgan. . . . It doesn't matter what or who he is, Mick, nor whether he's right or wrong. All I want you to do is to tell the inspector here that *you* told me I have a rocky heart. . . . Yes, that's all. . . . It doesn't matter that you were wrong, I tell you. . . . That's neither here nor there. . . . Mick! What are you saying? Mick?" George's face went dead white. "You won't do it, then. . . . Very well. . . . No, there's no need to tell the inspector. I'll tell him myself."

They heard the receiver click at the other end, and George hung up. He turned slowly to the little group watching him and said huskily:

"I think you gathered what has happened. I put my question stupidly and frightened him. He's gone all stuffy with fear for his own thick neck. As soon as he heard the name of Morgan he went to ground. I owe you an apology, Morgan. I didn't know you were such an eminent man."

He came to a stop jerkily. Dr. Morgan turned away. Suddenly he whirled around and burst out savagely:

"I'm sick and tired of cleaning up after Mick Moore! Mr. Arrow, as soon as you told me he was your doctor, I knew I could expect bungling stupidity. That's why I examined you at all. Perhaps I shouldn't have interfered. Oh, damn it all!"

He made for the door. Mike signaled to the sergeant to let him go. Then he turned back to George.

"I don't usually explain my methods, but I'm going to do so now." He paused for a moment before he went on. "I'm going to find it difficult to make you understand why I took this rather unorthodox line. Look at it from my point of view. A man is found dead. No one has an alibi except you, with your weak heart. Then it is borne in on me that you may be shamming, and that if you have not got a weak heart, you must be suspected at once. When Dr. Morgan went to visit you, at my request, on the night of the murder he saw that you had nothing wrong with your heart. He knew the physical signs. He said that indigestion could have caused your fainting fit, and he blamed Dr. Moore severely for building so much on this one incident. He mentioned it to me, as I said, because he was worried about how to tell you."

George listened expressionlessly. Mike went on:

"In your favor it must be said that you offered with great alacrity to telephone to Dr. Moore. On the other hand, this might be because you had arranged with Dr. Moore beforehand that he would corroborate your statements. You could not foresee that he would become frightened and let you down.

Next we come to the question of motive. It seems to us possible that your motive was the common one of gain—"

"But I don't need money," George interrupted. "I have house property in Dublin which pays me very well."

"Well enough for a single man, perhaps, but not well enough for one who contemplates marriage and who has acquired expensive tastes."

"But I didn't contemplate marriage."

"That brings us back to the same point again. You announced your engagement in my hearing only a few minutes ago. There was no reason why you should not contemplate marriage if you were, as in fact you are, a normally healthy man." George was silent, and Mike went on: "Ever since the day you came, it has been obvious to various residents here that you were—attached to Mrs. Henry. Admittedly most of the people here are idle, and perhaps not too much to be relied on, but on the other hand, idle people have time for observation. They all agree that they daily expected the announcement of your engagement."

Barbara, who had not seemed to be listening to Mike's exposition, now intervened.

"Mr. Kenny," she said earnestly, "will you believe me when I tell you that until today there was not the smallest hint or talk of marriage between George and me?" Her voice shook a little as she added, half to herself, "This is a nightmare."

"I have not said that you knew anything about it, Mrs. Henry," said Mike, "though I must consider that too." He turned back to George. "We can easily see that if you disposed of Burden and married Mrs. Henry, you would be a very wealthy man. It also appears that you may have known Burden before you came here. The staff agrees that you were on familiar terms with him when you arrived—"

"I met him on the train!"

"So you say. Well, perhaps you did. But perhaps you knew about him and his inheritance and his widowed cousin before you decided to come here at all. You had time to kill Burden, by the way, in the interval between leaving Mrs. Fennell and meeting Daly and Heaslip at the front door. You say you were walking up and down the drive, but no one saw you."

"This is fantastic," said George. "Are you basing *all* this on the fact that I said I had a bad heart?"

Mike did not answer, though he looked troubled.

"And of course you must have heard the story that Mr. Murray was murdered. Why don't you pick on one of the older inhabitants?"

Mike got up wearily.

"I must ask you not to leave the hotel for the present, Mr. Arrow. If you attempt to do so, you will be stopped. I won't detain you any longer."

Silently, George went out of the little office and walked mechanically towards his own room. He was aware that Barbara had not come with him, and that the cautious boots of Colm MacDonagh were padding after him at a discreet distance. With more curiosity than fear he noticed how everything had changed for him in the last few minutes. It was as if the familiar things had all shifted awry, so that he could not trust anything or anyone. Except Barbara, of course. It would have been hard to blame her if she had believed that he had deceived her, but she had shown only pure joy at Dr. Morgan's revelation. He flushed hotly as he remembered Kenny's vile suggestion—made in her hearing too—that her inheritance had attracted him more than herself. He longed now for her company, and hoped that she would soon find it possible to come to him. He repudiated the idea of going to find her, ignobly followed by a watching Guard. He resolved to stay in his room and wait for her all evening, if necessary.

He pulled an armchair close to the fire and settled down to think out the problem of how to impress Inspector Kenny with his innocence. The question was so fantastic that it was difficult to concentrate on it, and he found endless excuses for putting off the beginning of it. He smiled grimly to himself as he heard Colm MacDonagh move about outside the door, and at last lean his large back against the panels with a heavy sigh. It gave him some satisfaction to shoot the bolt on the inside of the door, after which he returned to the fire.

Back in the library, Mike was saying to Sergeant Mahon:

"It's a risky business. I could see no other way of making him telephone that doctor in Dublin. He played into our hands by putting his question as he did, poor chap."

"Is he being watched?"

"Colm is on the job. You may be sure nothing will happen." He pulled his notebook towards him. "Now, we had some other points to clear up. There's Mrs. Fennell first. I feel certain she has a vital part in the business. Did you see Dr. Bradley?"

"Yes. He was to come here at the end of the week to see Mrs. Fennell. He says Burden told him she was a dangerous lunatic. Of course Bradley is always having people in telling him that sort of thing, sometimes just to get rid of a relation they're tired of, so he said he would come and see her himself."

"What was Burden's evidence?"

"It seems she keeps dozens of cats and lets them breed regardless, and then she bumps them off and uses the corpses to manure the flower-beds."

"Indeed," said Mike.

"Yes, indeed," said Mahon, almost daring to mimic Mike's well-known comment on any surprising news. He went on hurriedly as Mike cocked an eye at him, "Now if she killed Burden herself, you'd nearly expect her to bring him down and bury him in the front garden, wouldn't you?"

"Not necessarily. If she did it would imply a complete absence of the power to distinguish between right and wrong. I don't think she's mad enough not to know that it's better to be quiet about a murder. Did you find the shoes?"

"Here they are, sir."

He drew a parcel out of the pocket of his greatcoat and laid it on the table. Mike opened it and picked up the shoes. They were pathetically small and old-fashioned, and they had a pattern of holes on the uppers.

"It's nothing like conclusive," he said, "but it helps us to believe that she really saw Murray being murdered, with something—or nothing—out of a hypodermic. And if that is so, in future we must assume that she and the ghost of Sir Rodney Crane are one. I'll have to see Bridget again. And Mrs. Fennell too. I think she could tell us a lot if we only knew how to persuade her."

"Dr. Bradley says she may go off her old rocker altogether if we frighten her," said Mahon. "There's another piece of news about Burden, too. I found it waiting below in the barracks for me. Do you know, those Dublin fellows are very quick," he said grudgingly.

"What was the news?"

"That Burden did a lot of blackmailing on the side in Dublin—apart from trying to blackmail his ordinary clients, of course. He had a list of girls with small jobs—typists and shop-assistants and the like—and he used to collect five bob a week off them not to tell their mothers where they spent their spare time. Oh, he was a rat of the deepest dye," said Mahon feelingly. "He had bigger game too, from time to time, men who could afford to pay him in pounds instead of bobs. They were smarter than the girls, though. They've all gone underground. I'd say Burden used to lose them after a bit. He wasn't the kind for real efficient villainy. I'd say he was a bit of a softie behind it all."

"They often are," said Mike dryly. "So nothing is known about these people?"

"Mighty little. They've all disappeared, you see. I have a list of them here, if it's any use to you."

Mike put out his hand and took the list. He glanced through it.

"The names mean nothing to me," said Mahon. "I'd say a lot of people will breathe easier when they read Burden's death notice."

"You can see, of course, that this may broaden our problem considerably. Mrs. Henry suggested once that someone had followed Burden here and killed him. But if all his blackmailers have escaped him, why should one of them do that? Besides, since Burden had come into money he was not likely to continue his blackmailing. Unless—"

"Unless what?"

"We must see Bridget at once," said Mike. "Send Joe down for her, Mahon."

He studied his notes moodily until she arrived. When Joe announced her he looked up and said at once, gently:

"Bridget, why did you not tell me about Mrs. Fennell's cats?"

The effect of the question was instantaneous. She burst into tears and collapsed into the chair that Sergeant Mahon held for her. Over her head, Mike and the sergeant exchanged glances, and by common consent allowed her time to recover herself. After a few minutes Mike said:

"You had better tell us all about it now, Bridget."

She mopped her tears away and looked up hopelessly.

"I suppose you won't understand how I feel about it, Mr. Kenny. It's always the same. I've had these patients one after the other for years, and I get as fond of them as if they were my own children, yes, although they were all old when I got them. That will sound like rubbish to you."

"Of course not," said Mike. "It shows you're good at your job, that's all."

"I don't know about that," said Bridget dejectedly, though she was obviously pleased too. "Anyway, that's the way I feel about them. No matter how cross they are, or how queer or trying, I never lose my patience, and I always feel that my main business is to protect them from people that wouldn't understand their ways. That's why I didn't tell you about the cats."

She drew a long breath and went on:

"This kind of patient always has some special peculiarity. One would be a kleptomaniac, and another would have to be coaxed to eat, and another would stand in a crowded street, maybe, and scream at the top of her voice. I've had all these things, and they're all hard to deal with. But Mrs. Fennell never gave me any trouble at all. She's a perfect lady, always. As long as she has her garden in the daytime and her cats in the evening she's all right. And I quite like cats. Not so many of them, of course, but I'm not one of those people that get the creeps if a cat comes in the room."

She had regained possession of herself now, and was able to smile apologetically at Mike.

"I'm sorry I made a fool of myself," she went on. "I've had those cats on my mind for a long time now. You see, I wasn't supposed to notice anything, but of course I began to miss an odd one of them from time to time, and when I'd tell Mrs. Fennell she'd just grin to herself and say nothing. I knew she had a name on every cat of them, so it wasn't that she didn't miss them."

"How long has all this been going on?" Mike asked.

"Nearly a year. When the poor old thing needed someone to look after her, she moved out of the hotel down to the chalet with me. She had lived in the hotel for years, of course. She has a nephew in Africa who is supposed to take an interest in her, but he's so far away that he can't do much for her. Her solicitor looks after her money and comes to see her now and then."

"And when did she get the cats?"

"Well, she had a lot of them in the hotel. That was one way they knew she wasn't right in the head. She was collecting cats everywhere, advertising for them in the papers, even, and at last old Mr. Murray said she'd have to go. He wouldn't put her in a home, though. He was a good-hearted enough sort of a man. He fixed up the chalet for her and she's been quite happy there ever since. Of course it paid him to keep her there."

"And she brought the cats with her?"

"Yes. She said that now she could have as many as she liked, and she kept all the kittens and got more big ones—it was getting to be a nightmare. She was getting a bit upset too, because she couldn't see where it would all end. Then one day I came home from my free afternoon out, and found them all gone except for a dozen.

"She was exhausted that day. I had to put her to bed and send up to the hotel for her dinner. She had been gardening all afternoon, she said, and sure enough, every plant in the garden looked as if it had been lifted. She kept on talking about the cats, and how she'd keep only twelve in the future, and call them after the twelve Apostles. She was very happy about it all. I needn't tell you I was puzzled, and the next day, when I got a chance, I lifted one of the plants and found the remains of a cat underneath. I got an awful shock, you may be sure. I rooted around and found a few more, and I didn't know what to do. I pictured her doing them all in one after another and I said to myself, she's gone over the edge at last. I didn't know how she did it. There wasn't a mark on a cat of them. I watched her very closely for the next week, but she was as sweet and as gentle as ever. So I let the whole thing slide. Every now and then I'd come home and find an Apostle gone and a big kitten promoted to its place, but I shut my eyes to it, as long as she was not getting any worse, God forgive me. It always happened on my day out, you see. She was well able to look after herself for an afternoon. I once offered to stay in with her, but she got so agitated that I didn't suggest it again. I thought of making an excuse to come back some day and find out what was going on, but the fear of upsetting her stopped me. You have to be very careful with people like Mrs. Fennell, you see."

"You should have told me all this yesterday," said Mike.

"I suppose I should," said Bridget. "But sure, I got too fond of her, as I said, and I couldn't bring myself to do it. This very afternoon, when I was out—she insisted on my going out—I came back to find another cat gone the voyage."

Mike sat up straight and said softly:

"Did you, indeed?"

Bridget said, with a sigh:

"Well, I suppose this is the end of her. She'll have to be put away now. Anyone can see it's not a very far jump from killing cats to killing Christians, though I never would have thought her capable of sticking a knife in anyone. Never. She's so gentle and quiet——"

Bridget was on the verge of tears again. Mike said:

"What kind of a cat went missing today?"

"It was a big Siamese called Peter—a lovely cat."

"Mahon! Get the boys to dig out that garden until they find the body."

"It's going to be a bit of a job in the dark," said Mahon.

"Nonsense," said Mike. "It's a fine moonlit night."

"There's no need to dig it all out," said Bridget. "A new rose tree came today—one that she wasn't expecting till next week. You'll probably find the cat's body buried under it."

"Will you go down, then, and show it to Sergeant Mahon?" She nodded. "You can bring back the body here. I don't suppose we'll learn very much from it that we don't know already, but I want it anyway. Don't meet your troubles halfway," he advised Bridget, as he held the door open for her. "Just keep an eye on the old lady. One of my men will be close by, and you can yell for help if you need it."

"She'll never attack *me*," said Bridget. "I'm quite sure of that."

When they had gone Mike sat for a few minutes, thinking deeply. The proof was the stumbling block. He was able to make a good guess at the motive and, in Murray's case, at the method, but there was no obvious connection between the murderer and the victim. He knew that he would never get a confession. The motive, as it appeared at present, was not likely to impress a jury, even of twelve romantic Irishmen. He was relying too much on the long chance he had taken, he thought. There was one other thing he could do. He put his papers into his pocket and left the library. He walked through the hall to the office, where he put through a trunk call to Dublin.

Meanwhile, from the front window of Mrs. Fennell's chalet, two pairs of eyes watched the approach of Bridget and Sergeant Mahon, and another Guard who was armed with a spade. Mrs. Fennell gave a little giggle and said softly:

"I always love standing in a dark room looking out. See how bright the moon looks, like a polished tray, or a cat's eye."

"Ssh!" said the other softly. "We'll just watch."

A soft hand held her arm, and she shivered happily. She was not silent for long, however.

"I wonder why they're coming here?" she whispered. "Perhaps we should go out and let them in."

"Wouldn't it be more fun to let them ring, and just not answer? We could be looking out at them and they wouldn't know we're here."

"Yes, yes. We'll do that!"

"And then if they don't go away, you can let them in while I slip out the window. You know I don't like to be seen here. Did you lock the back door?"

"Yes, of course. I always do. Oh, I feel so *wicked!*"

"Bridget is out there. Has she a key?"

"No. I took it from her when you told me to. Now I leave the back door open and she comes in that way. But she can't come in now, because it's locked."

"So there's no one in the house but us two."

"Us *three,*" she corrected.

"Three? Who is the third?"

The voice was urgent now.

"Rodney, of course!" She gave a little tinkling laugh. "You are always forgetting Rodney."

"Ssh! They'll hear us."

They watched in silence for a moment. Then Mrs. Fennell said:

"Do you know, I think they're digging up my new rose tree?"

"Are you sure?"

"Not quite sure. But I think they are. It will be very bad for it. I should run out and stop them."

But the hand held her arm firmly and the soft voice said:

"Why are they digging it up? Why?"

"I don't know. Perhaps they're going to steal it. I must stop them."

"No. If they steal it I'll get you another one."

"But Peter is buried under it. It would have come on so well with a fresh cat buried under it."

"Peter! You told me you'd wait till tomorrow!"

"I couldn't bear to wait. It was such a lovely day, and I thought it might rain tomorrow. There he was, all ready to be buried, so I just went out and did it while Bridget was out."

The hand tightened on her arm.

"Then why is Bridget there now? Did you tell her that I killed the cats for you?"

"No, no! You're hurting me!" She whimpered a little, but did not raise her voice. "Of course I didn't tell Bridget. You said not to. And besides, she's only a servant."

The hand which had fumbled for and found the hypodermic syringe relaxed. Still the other one gripped her arm.

"Inspector Kenny came here and talked to you?"

"Yes, but I didn't tell him anything. Really I didn't. And I didn't tell that nice Mr. Arrow either. I only told him about using the cats for manure. That was Rodney's idea, of course, not yours, so I knew it would be all right."

"You told Mr. Arrow!"

The fingers clutched the syringe again.

"Yes. He asked me how I killed the cats, but I just laughed and said that was my secret. I didn't even tell him that I don't kill them myself, that I have a kind friend who does it for me."

The other sighed.

"Then Mr. Arrow must have told the Guards. You really shouldn't have mentioned it to him at all."

"Well, it was Rodney's idea in the first place, and he didn't mind. I'm sure Mr. Arrow is the only person who knows about it. But then why are the Guards here?"

"Bridget—"

"I tell you, Bridget is stupid. She hardly noticed that the cats were gone. Look! They're finished."

They could see that the man had stopped digging, and had uncovered the cat, which they now wrapped in a sheet of paper. Bridget, who had remained apart from them all the time, made a move towards the chalet. Sergeant Mahon spoke to her and she paused to answer. The voices came dimly through the window, but the words were indistinguishable. The silver moonlight glittered on the little group in the garden so that the watchers could see them plainly. The soft voice said:

"It looks as if Bridget is coming in here, and the Guards are going back to the hotel. When they're on their way, I'll get out of the window. Don't let her in until I'm gone."

"Won't you stay and have supper with me? I can explain to Bridget that you just dropped in."

"No. She'd want to know why she saw no lights."

The fingers fumbled longingly with the syringe. Was it safe to let her live, even for an hour? That was the question. But it was too late now. The Guards were on the drive already, and Bridget had rung the back-door bell once.

"I have a little job to do at the hotel, but I'll come back later. Leave the window open for me."

"Yes, yes. I'll be waiting for you. We'll have a chat, and I'll make some tea. I get so lonely sometimes—I don't know what I would do without you and Rodney."

She opened the widow, and her visitor climbed over the low sill and slipped out into the garden without a sound. The back-door bell rang again, and she went to open it.

"I was just having a little doze before the sitting room fire," she said, as Bridget came in.

She rubbed her eyes elaborately and then giggled to herself. She allowed Bridget to help her into her nightdress and dressing gown, and then she sat by the fire drinking a glass of hot milk. Presently Bridget conducted her into her room and she got docilely into bed. She waited and waited with the light off until she was sure Bridget must be asleep. At last she got up softly and slipped on her dressing gown again, and crept out to the sitting room. She poked up the fire, ever so gently, and then she went over and unlatched the window. Back at the fire, she settled down to wait for her visitor's return.

George had actually fallen into an uneasy sleep in his armchair when the first tap came at the window. The little sound wove itself into his dream, so that he was not properly awake until it came again. He started up, feeling heavy-headed and slow-witted, and turned towards the door. Then he heard it for the third time, and now he identified it joyfully as the sound of a fingernail on glass. Barbara! She must have seen Colm at the door, and decided to circumvent him by using the window instead. He hurried to pull back the heavy curtains and unlatch the window. But the figure outside was not Barbara's. He hid his disappointment as best he could, and said:

"Oh, good evening. Won't you come in?"

The visitor climbed easily into the room saying:

"Thank you. This is an odd way to come in, but I saw a large Guard prowling at your door, and I did not wish to arouse his interest. By the way, why is he there?"

"Hadn't you heard? His superior officer thinks that I murdered Burden. It makes no difference to him that I never saw Burden in my life until I came here."

Leaving the window open, George pulled across the curtains again. He laughed bitterly as he came back to the fire.

"That Guard is watching to see that I don't go off and murder someone else."

"Why do they think you did it?"

George hesitated for a moment and then decided that there was no point in trying to keep it secret.

"In order to marry Mrs. Henry and own the hotel. Oh, it's damnable! In my blackest nightmare I never thought of this. I pleaded my weak heart, but he brushed that aside. He said it was all an elaborate blind."

As George turned away wearily he did not see the look of triumph in the other's eyes. He went on, half to himself:

"The trouble is that I don't know what to do next. I suppose I must get a lawyer at once. I was trying to think it all out just now, and I actually fell asleep over the fire. I never would have thought that at the biggest crisis of my life I would fall asleep."

"The human mind is always springing surprises," said the other. "Probably what you need is a good night's sleep. In the morning your brain will be clearer and you will have no difficulty in deciding what is best to be done."

"Perhaps," said George. "But at the moment I don't feel that I am likely to sleep well. By the way, did you want to see me about something in particular?"

"Not exactly. I was wondering if you have any idea of what Miss Keane is up to. That girl gives me great uneasiness. She's the cause of all the trouble, really. If she hadn't been so anxious to marry successive owners of Crane's Court, I suppose neither of these murders would have happened."

"Oh, you believe that Murray was murdered too, then? Old Mrs. Fennell told me he was murdered, but I thought she was vaporing."

"She told you that too, did she?"

All movement had ceased suddenly, and fear and hatred showed for a second. George said, looking into the fire:

"Yes, she said Murray was murdered, but in the next breath she said that Sir Rodney Crane had told her so, and since he's dead at least a hundred years, her word can't be taken too seriously. As for Miss Keane, when I heard today that she was hinting that she knew something important I resolved to advise her to tell the Guards at once, for her own protection. She might actually endanger her life by keeping an important piece of information to herself."

"She might, indeed!"

"Later, of course," said George with a sigh, "I forgot all about her, on account of my own dilemma. Perhaps you could see her tonight? It's not too late, I'm sure, and it might be important. It's no use my trying to see her, because I don't believe I will be allowed to leave this room."

"That is true. Yes, of course. I'll go straight to her from here."

George did not notice the purposeful, menacing tone.

"I'm very glad you came," he said. "I'm feeling more optimistic already." He smiled shyly. "Perhaps you would do another thing for me too. I had rather expected Barbara—Mrs. Henry—to come here to see me. She may have been frightened away by seeing the Guard outside my door. Would you just tell her I'd like to see her? Tell her how you came in the window, and that I'll wait for her. She needn't come in, of course, but if she stands outside for a minute, so that I can talk to her, I won't find the night so long."

"I'll tell her. But you should have something to make you sleep."

"Dr. Morgan gave me something last night, but I don't want to see him again."

"As a matter of fact, I have something here with me that I take myself from time to time. I can give you some of it."

"No, thanks," said George firmly. "If I start taking drugs now, I'll be an addict in no time. I don't believe in Dutch courage."

"But this is not a drug. It's quite harmless. It will make you sleep like the dead."

"No. It's very kind of you, but I'd rather not."

Drops of sweat appeared on the other's forehead.

"You could just take it there as you sit in your chair. It's quite easy. It's an injection, but I can give it to you myself. You needn't be afraid it will work too soon, before you have time for a word with Mrs. Henry—"

Suddenly George looked up and saw the agitated face, and the shaking hands in which the syringe had mysteriously appeared.

"Why are you so anxious that I should have this injection?" he asked sharply. "My no is no. I'm not a persuadable person." He had been leaning back, but now he sat up straight. "And now that I come to think of it, why are you not afraid of me? When I told you I was suspected of murder, the normal thing for you would have been to back away and get yourself out of my presence as quickly as possible. But you stayed to chat with me. That could be because you are a kindhearted charitable person, or it could be because you knew you had nothing to fear. And the only way you could know that would be that you are the murderer yourself!"

The visitor laughed uneasily.

"You're upset. I'll take no notice of your insults, because I know you don't mean them. Now just let me give you a shot of this stuff, and you'll feel miles better in no time."

"No!" George leaped to his feet.

The other jabbed wildly at him, and almost succeeded in knocking him back into the chair. But George slipped over the arm and succeeded in getting the chair between himself and his now snarling opponent. They faced each other warily, and again the visitor made a sudden dart forward, but George side-stepped and got across the room behind the bed. He could hear Colm MacDonagh now, pounding on the door, which was bolted against him, and saying:

"Open that door! Open up, I say!"

"Break it down, you fool!" yelled George.

There was a second's silence, and then the crash of Colm's bulk against the door. One of the panels splintered. While Colm drew back for a second attack, George's assailant darted across to the window. Just then the curtains were hurled back and Sergeant Mahon shot into the room, followed by three others. They had no difficulty in securing their prisoner. George pulled back the bolt of the shattered door, and Colm, looking disheveled, mopped his forehead with a large red paw as he came into the room. Lastly came Mike, white with anger.

"Mahon!" he snapped. "Why did you wait so long? You should have broken up that party five minutes ago."

"Sorry, sir," said Mahon, looking down at his boots.

"It's no use apologizing, Arrow," said Mike to George. "The whole affair is a disgrace to us."

"That's all right, Mike," said George jauntily. "I can stand a bit of rough-and-tumble!"

Mike shot him a glance of delighted gratitude before turning to look at the now dazed prisoner. His voice had softened with pity when he said: "Take him away, Mahon, and charge him. You had better address him as Aeneas Walsh, alias Jerome Heaslip."

12

At one o'clock in the morning. George Arrow, Professor Daly, Mrs. Henry and Martin Hogan were sitting in the library before a blazing fire. At the old man's elbow was a bottle of whiskey and a siphon of soda. Mr. Hogan had a private bottle of rum, which he drank neat from a tumbler. He smirked to himself and seemed very content. Professor Daly had just finished pouring drinks for the other two when Inspector Kenny came wearily into the room. Daly hurried to fill the remaining glass. Mike took it and dropped into an armchair by the fire. Daly occupied another armchair, and George and Barbara sat together on the sofa. Martin Hogan, for reasons of his own, chose to occupy a straight chair within reach of the door. Mike said to him:

"Have you managed that job for me, Martin?"

"It's all fixed." said Martin. "She's prepared to tell you the whole story now."

"You're a genius," said Mike fervently. "I've said hard things about you from time to time, but I'll withdraw them all now."

"You may not like my methods, Mike," said Martin uneasily.

"I don't care what your methods are, as long as they have produced results," said Mike. "If you have really done the job, you have sealed up the whole case for me."

"I've done it, all right, but there will have to be a little quid pro quo," said Martin. "Not for me, of course, but for her."

"Anything, even to half of my kingdom," said Mike heartily. He turned to the others, who were listening with fascinated but uncomprehending interest. "Is it too late to talk over the whole affair? I owe you an explanation, George, if you would like to have it."

"It's not too late for me," said George. "This is my first whiskey for months, and already I feel as if I could stay up all night."

"If I don't hear how you arrived at your conclusion that Heaslip was the murderer," said Daly, "I think I shall expire of curiosity. I have lost a dear friend," he added, half to himself.

"So have I," said Barbara softly.

There was a short pause before Mike said:

"The part of him that was your friend was really no more than a myth. He had put on such a cloak of scholarly detachment that he deceived everyone. I've just had a long conversation with him. Would you have believed, for instance, that when he sat alone on the veranda or in the dining room, with a large book in his hand, that he never read a word? He tells me now that all his faculties were concentrated then on picking up useful gossip."

"But I often saw him turning the pages," Daly protested.

"That didn't prove that he was reading," said Mike, and added quizzically, "I'm surprised at you, Daly. I thought you were a better detective than that."

"A hit, a palpable hit," said Daly. "But I could have sworn he was lost in his book. I've often tiptoed by without speaking to him, for fear of disturbing him. And if he was not reading then, when did he acquire his knowledge of birds?"

"He read in his room in the evenings, when the public rooms were deserted. He had always been a bird-watcher, but he learned a great deal more after he came here. It's a most innocuous-looking hobby. Incidentally, birdwatching requires the same patience that Heaslip exhibited in carrying out his long-laid plan."

"Then it was a plan," said Barbara. "I thought he had killed my cousin on the spur of the moment, and then panicked and attempted to kill George."

Her voice trailed off, and she laid her hand on George's sleeve. Mike said, with a sigh:

"Yes, it was all a plan. It began a long time ago, but it showed itself first in the murder of Murray. Heaslip has now got to the stage of boasting of his cleverness. We often find that criminals do this—trying to bolster up their courage, I suppose. Well, it's useful to us, because it fills in the gaps in the story."

They were silent while he took out his pipe and filled it, pressing down the tobacco with precise movements of his long, fine fingers. Then he went on:

"When I had questioned everyone, I asked myself, 'What do we know about the murderer?' We knew very little. It seemed likely that the motive was possession of the hotel, since Burden, and possibly Murray, were the victims. This brought us to the person who benefited by Burden's death—you, Mrs. Henry."

She wriggled her shoulders a little, but said nothing.

"It was logical for us to suspect you, Mrs. Henry," Mike said apologetically. "You were not wealthy. You should have inherited the hotel from your uncle. You'll forgive me for pointing out that many women feel justified in making sure of their rights by devious means. You were strong enough to have stabbed Burden, and, in common with everyone else, you had no alibi for the time of the murder. There was another thing that made me suspicious about you. Your story was that you had advised your uncle to leave his property to Burden. Presumably you expected to be able to stay on here, as you had done with

Murray, and send your little boy to school in the town. But Burden, as we know, turned out to be an impossible bounder, and still you did not leave Crane's Court. You sent your son away to school, which you had never intended to do, and you stayed here allowing Burden to insult you and overwork you. I asked myself why you did this, and the easiest answer was that you did not intend to suffer it for long, that you planned to murder Burden.

"There were several unsatisfactory things about this theory. The first one was that you were clever enough to have seen that if Burden was murdered, you would be the first to be suspected. The next thing was that you had really advised Mr. Murray to leave Crane's Court to Burden in his will. Murray's solicitor, Johnny Farrell, confirmed this. He thought you were mad, by the way, but Murray was very impressed with the idea, and told Johnny that he would have peace of mind for the rest of his life. Unfortunately, he told you to tell no one the details of his will—I think this was on account of Miss Keane. He was shrewd and hardheaded enough, and he and no intention of mentioning wills to Miss Keane until after they were married. We have an unreliable witness who overheard him promising her diamonds on the evening of his death, but he did not promise her the hotel. I fancy, however, that Murray never meant Burden to have the hotel. Burden was only a convenient name to use until he would substitute the name of his wife. Perhaps he even meant to name you, Mrs. Henry, as a part legatee, at some future date. We have no way now of discovering these things. Johnny Farrell was so pleased that Murray was making a will at all, that he did not protest too much for fear of frightening him off altogether.

"After I had watched you for half a day, of course I knew why you had stayed at Crane's Court. It was because on the day that the objectionable Burden arrived, George Arrow arrived too."

She blushed to the roots of her hair. George turned to her wonderingly and said:

"Me?"

"Of course," she said, and laughed at his astonishment.

"We guessed that the murderer was probably in financial difficulties," Mike went on hurriedly. "But the gentlemanly atmosphere of Crane's Court was hard to penetrate. We still do not know much about the assets of the various guests, because we have had no time to investigate them. So we left the murderer for a time and concentrated on the character of Burden himself. For the only clues were there. Sergeant Mahon said casually that he looked like a blackmailer, and though it was only a half-joking remark, I thought it would be worth while investigating his life in Dublin from this aspect. Meanwhile we considered the other possible motives, and we found such a nest of them as I hope never to encounter again. Crane's Court is stiff with neuroses. Murderers are usually less clever than other people, not more so. In investigating a murder, the difficulty is usually in understanding the kind of mind that sees in murder a solution of its problem, and then in observing which of the people concerned has the necessary kink in his point of view. There are so many kinks at Crane's Court that if I followed my usual line, I should have concluded that a number of people were capable of murdering Burden, and that it was only by chance that they were not all creeping up on him together. This was a night-mare prospect, I need hardly say. Let me take them in turn.

"First of all, there was Mrs. Robinson. She brought suspicion on herself by summoning her son, Horace, by means of a strangely worded telegram. I was thankful to her later, because she pointed out the real motive of the crime. Mrs. Robinson had a grievance against Burden because he had insulted her, and robbed her of her self-assumed authority. He had humiliated her, and had even threatened to force her to leave. Now, Mrs. Robinson is a wealthy woman, but she had her son, Horace, to think of. She knows he is a poor specimen, and that he will never be able to look after himself or earn his living. The fact that this is largely her own fault is beside the point. She thought of a plan that would ensure that Horace would have a roof over his head and a keeper for life." Mike hesitated. "You must have guessed by now what it was. Horace was to marry Mrs. Henry."

"Oh!" she gasped.

"Yes," said Mike rapidly, "that was her idea. It was devised, of course, be-fore Murray's death, when she thought you would inherit. She was a bit put out at Miss Keane's attention to Mr. Murray, but she didn't feel any real fear of her. Mrs. Robinson thought she had a certain amount of influence over you— I expect you were too deferential in your manner to her—and she thought you would be happy to marry Horace if she suggested it to you. Like any other person, she thought a widow should be glad to marry anyone."

"Idiot," muttered George.

"Yes, it was crude," said Mike, not choosing to discover whether George's remark was directed at himself or at Mrs. Robinson. "Well, it occurred to me when I got to this stage that Mrs. Robinson must have been annoyed when a young and healthy Burden turned up, and Mrs. Henry was no longer eligible for Horace. But I already thought she might have helped Providence in the disposal of Murray, and it seemed that she could have done the same with Burden. Her telegram hinted at a prearranged plan. 'It has happened.' What had happened? Burden's death, to be sure. I had the truth from Horace this evening. He came and wept on my shoulder, after dinner. He was attached to you, Mrs. Henry, undoubtedly."

"Poor old Horace," she murmured.

"Rubbish," said George. "He's a snake."

"But a simple-hearted snake," Mike interposed. "His mother reads the cards, that's all. She's awfully good at it, he says, and has foretold most extraordinary things. He asked me if I am psychic. I rather put him off his stride by telling him that I believe in God. Well, she read the cards over Burden, if one can say such a thing, and she foresaw that he was going to die. So she wrote joyfully to Horace and told him that he was to keep a bag packed, so that when it happened he could light out for Crane's Court without delay and support Mrs. Henry in her distress, thereby winning her affections. Horace liked the idea. He thinks his mother is very clever." Mike shrugged. "By the time I heard this story, I had other ideas about Burden's murderer, or I should certainly have considered arresting Mrs. Robinson. It would not have been the first time that someone has foretold a death, and then made certain that it occurred. I think that if Heaslip had not killed Burden, Mrs. Robinson might actually have done it herself, at some later stage. I had part of this story from Esther, who was expected to cooperate with the plan. But she has taken a stand against Mr. Robinson, and there is open war between them."

"Oh, dear!" said Barbara. "Esther is really becoming impossible."

"I had the temerity to suggest that she was in some way responsible for Burden's death. She curled me up. 'I, sir? Oh, no, sir!' That was enough for me. But there was Maggie, who had a grievance against Burden, and her fiancé, Ned, who had a worse one. I was very uneasy about those two, especially because Ned acted as if he was guilty. But I came to the conclusion that Ned was one of those people who are shattered by any psychological problem, because the workings of the human brain are a mystery to them. On the other hand, it is well established that murder is usually the prerogative of the uneducated classes.

"Next we come to Major Dunlea, whom we all know to be not quite normal. Naturally, we devoted considerable attention to him because he was convicted of murder before." Mike stopped suddenly. "I shouldn't have told you that. It's too late at night. My tongue is slipping."

"That's all right, Mike, old man," said Daly. "We won't tell anyone. Give us the rest of the story now that you've gone so far. Who did he murder?"

"His cook. She gave him watery sprouts, so he shot her."

"Did he, indeed! Good man!" Professor Daly chuckled with delight. "I've often wanted to do the same myself. I must congratulate him."

"If you breathe a word about it," said Mike, "I'll tell everyone about Rosemary Downes."

"You wouldn't do that!" Daly wailed.

"You wait and see," said Mike complacently. "You didn't think I knew about her, did you?"

Mrs. Henry was looking from one to the other of them.

"Who is Rosemary Downes?" she asked.

"She's Professor Daly's guilty secret," said Mike. "I thought at one time that he might have killed Burden to stop him from spreading the news about her!"

"Mike!"

"Yes, I did. Burden had a nose for the one thing that everyone wants to hide, and I was certain that he would not have overlooked Rosemary. I had nothing to go on except Daly's obvious pleasure in Burden's death. Without exaggeration, Daly, I can say that you acted like a circus ringmaster. You positively pranced about with joy. Usually when I arrive on the scene of a murder, I am met by hushed voices, people step back quietly and let me find my way over to the body as best I can. But you met me at the door of the room with open arms, introduced me to everyone with a flourish, and ended up by exhibiting the body as if you had arranged it yourself. Yes, that was the thought that crossed my mind. Then I remembered Rosemary. I've known about her for a long time, and so, no doubt, have other people. But you don't talk about her yourself, and I thought that perhaps you imagined she was a deadly secret. Burden was not the man to keep such a secret. At best he would tell everyone about it. At worst he would try to blackmail you."

"He did try to blackmail me," said Professor Daly. "It was rather funny, really, though I was very angry about it at the time. You see, Burden thought that Rosemary Downes was a real person, a kept woman, to use an old-fashioned phrase—excuse me, Barbara. He suggested that I might pay him to keep quiet about her, but I soon put an end to that idea. I actually went to see him on the afternoon he was murdered, at about four o'clock."

"You did! Why didn't you tell me this before?"

"I didn't want to be led off in chains," Daly explained mildly. "For all I knew, I was the last person to see him alive."

"At four o'clock? Plenty of people saw him after that." Mike took his notebook out of his pocket and turned the pages. He made a note and then read aloud, "Professor Daly, four o'clock. Mrs. Robinson, quarter-past four. Colonel Waters, quarter to five. Miss Keane, five o'clock. Heaslip, ten-past five, killing Burden. Ned, twenty-past five. So you see, you were by no means the last person to see him alive."

"So I see. Still, it could be of no interest to you to know that I went to see him—"

"For all you knew, you might have been able to establish the time of his death."

"If you believed me."

"Stop arguing about it," said Martin Hogan. "Tell us about your visit to Burden."

"Well, I just told him that Rosemary Downes was not such a guilty secret as he seemed to think. I told him she was only a pseudonym under which I wrote trashy novels in my younger days, and to prove that I did not really care if people knew about her, I told him that I had confided her existence to George, here, on the very day he arrived. I don't do that to everyone, of course, but I was out to amuse George, because he seemed upset and worried."

George nodded to Mike's inquiring eye.

"I further said," Daly went on, "that I would inform the police of his threats and that he would probably be prosecuted for attempted blackmail. Of course he nearly went on his knees to me then. I let him haver for a bit, and then I said that I would let the matter rest this time. But I advised him to drop his old habits now that he had no further need of them. He didn't like that, but he was afraid to be uncivil to me."

"This may explain his ferocity to Mrs. Robinson," said Mike. "When she had gone he slipped out and got Mr. Quinn to bring his friends on to the veranda. Then his satisfaction in having ousted Mrs. Robinson made him comparatively pleasant to Colonel Waters."

"Waters was concerned with his bathroom, I suppose," said Daly.

"No. It was really about his wife, he says. Her grievance had overshadowed his own. I rather favored Waters for a time, but not for long. His motive was not really strong enough, and he didn't impress me as being an unbalanced man. If he was going to murder anyone, he should have begun with his wife. Now, she's the type to have killed someone, if she had the energy, or the determination, or the decisive faculty, or whatever you like to call it. But she's the passive type. She likes to work from her armchair. She controls the Colonel from that position with great success. We learned that she had suggested starting a counter-campaign against Burden, in the pious hope of driving him to suicide. That sort of thing is more in Mrs. Waters' line. She is one of those excessively stupid women who are as bad as they know how. The only fortunate thing is that they don't know how to be very bad. Mrs. Waters hated Burden with a sinful hatred, far worse than any of the other old people. As to them, I dismissed them quite early as a pack of silly hens, and you know what becomes of hens when the fox comes along. At one time I had an idea that they might all have collaborated to kill Burden, but I never set much store by it. I used it to frighten Mrs. Robinson into talking, though. Heaslip came along very kindly and defended her, and hoped to lull my suspicions of himself by his well-known frank and engaging manner. He succeeded too, to a certain extent.

"The only one of these old people that I had to consider seriously now was Mrs. Fennell. Compared with her motive, the others were quite insignificant. Mrs. Robinson had found out somehow that Burden had planned to have her certified insane, and it occurred to me that she might have told Mrs. Fennell herself.

"Mrs. Fennell's attendant, Bridget, says that she is always slipping up to the hotel and wandering about there. Bridget had got her to lie down after Mr. Arrow had gone, but Mrs. Fennell would have had time to get out of the window and go up to the hotel, kill Burden and come back again before Bridget visited her again. Mrs. Fennell had never shown violent tendencies, but she had talked about murder both to Mr. Arrow and to myself, and this from an insane person could be a danger signal. However, when Mahon told me about the cats, I guessed that someone had been killing them for her. Mrs. Fennell obviously did not know how Murray was killed. She was quite vague about the whole business, and even said she had thought the injection was to make Mr. Murray sleep. I dug up the last cat's body and found no sign of how it had been killed, and then I guessed that the same method had been used for the cats as for Murray. This was the first time I was really sure she was not the murderer. She has the sort of lunatic cuteness necessary for keeping a secret, but if she had known all about how to use a hypodermic syringe, I did not think she would have spoken about it in the way she did. She had told me that she had actually seen Murray being murdered, by the old-fashioned method of looking through the keyhole, but she had been so thoroughly frightened and warned to keep her mouth shut that nothing would induce her to name the person she had seen do it. This was the job I gave Martin Hogan, here, to persuade her to tell me, in the presence of witnesses, all about her association with Heaslip. She will do it, Martin?"

"She will, for a price," said Martin. "I found her in her sitting room, in the dark, with the window unlatched. I asked her would she be glad if her friend didn't come back any more, and she said she would, that she's really afraid of him. She liked the excitement of that for a while, but lately she has got almost too afraid of him to enjoy his company."

"She was right," said Mike grimly. "Heaslip told me that he was glad to be arrested now, because he had intended to go down and kill Mrs. Fennell. He had arranged for her to leave the window open for him. But he wasn't going to like doing it, he says, because she reminds him of his mother."

"Well, well," said Professor Daly.

"Yes, and there was Heaslip's mistake. Without Mrs. Fennell—though we might have known he was the murderer of Murray—we might have been unable to prove it. It would have been more prudent of Heaslip to have killed her as soon as he found her outside Murray's door, but instead of that he attempted to frighten her into silence. The cat business was an unfortunate one for Heaslip. And he really began it out of kindness, though he may have thought that he was also safeguarding himself.

"It was Heaslip who suggested to Mrs. Fennell that she should keep her cats down to a permanent dozen. He told her he knew of a painless method of getting rid of them. This was quite true and at the time he may have had no second thought in his mind. She herself thought of using the bodies for manure, and Heaslip was delighted, because their disposal might have created difficulties. So he came down one afternoon when Bridget was out and polished off a whole lot of them—I don't know how many, but that doesn't matter. Then he used to come again, always on Bridget's afternoons out, and kill off one or two more, to keep the numbers down. It may even have put the thought of killing Murray into his mind. All this began early in the spring, so that he was quite well in practice by the time it came to Mr. Murray. He had made one stupid attempt to poison Murray, but it had gone wrong on him.

"That brings me to the next point. How was Mr. Murray killed? Mrs. Fennell, who was watching, said it was very quick and painless, and that a big hypodermic syringe was used. At first I thought of an injection of air. But later I wondered if this would be reliable enough. Surely Heaslip would not take the risk of the thing not working. And to be sure of creating an air embolism, the air would have to be injected into a large vein in the upper body, in the arm, for instance. Even then it might not work. But a very large hypodermic would have to be used to make reasonably sure of success and this fitted in with what I knew. I have my information from Dr. Morgan. Now, Murray liked and trusted Heaslip, but I could not imagine his allowing him to inject air into him from a large syringe. Finally I thought of the surest and safest way that it could have been done, and Heaslip tells me now that I was right.

"He gave the cats—and Murray too—an injection of insulin.

"This had to be injected into a vein too, but its effect was certain. Death did not result at once, as Mrs. Fennell imagined, but the victim becomes drowsy very soon, falls into a coma and presently dies. Heaslip helped Murray into bed and went away. He had no difficulty in getting the insulin, by the way. It can be bought at any chemist's without a doctor's prescription. The chemist who supplied it says that he knew him very well, and was quite sympathetic about his having got diabetes!

"Heaslip kept his syringe in the little kitchen of Mrs. Fennell's chalet, where he used to kill the cats. He never let her watch him, of course, and he hid the syringe under a loose tile in the corner of the floor. He thought that if it was found she would be blamed. She would naturally be suspect if the story of the cats leaked out. So you see that though she reminded him of his mother he was not prepared to sacrifice much for her."

"Why did Murray allow Heaslip to give him an injection at all?" asked Daly. "I'm sure I would decline the offer of one from even my dearest friend—unless he was a doctor, of course."

"Heaslip told him that he had been a male nurse," said Mike. "It's astonishing how many people allow nurses of all kinds to prescribe for them—and how many nurses are short-sighted enough to do it. Heaslip has a bedside manner that would be the envy of many a doctor, and he speaks with great assurance. But Burden would not have been so gullible. For Burden and Heaslip were old acquaintances."

"I would never have believed it!" said Daly. "No one would have guessed that they knew each other before."

"Neither of them wished to let it be seen," said Mike. "Now, if Heaslip has advanced on Burden with a hypodermic, he would have had difficulty in using it. But O'Reilly's knife was providentially there, and according to Miss Keane, the handle was towards his hand."

"Just like Macbeth," said Daly. "Did it ever occur to you that Miss Keane might have done the fell deed?"

"Only momentarily. She was right when she said that the reason for it all was to make sure that she would not have the hotel, though her part in it all was only a subsidiary one. She hastened Burden's death by agreeing to marry him. Heaslip was in Burden's bedroom listening. He had followed Mrs. Robinson there, to hear if she succeeded in her aim, and he heard Burden chase her away with loud cries. He had stayed for Colonel Waters's interview, he had then heard Burden summon Miss Keane and ask her to marry him. He had heard her accept and go away with her silly head in the clouds, and then he came out of the bedroom to talk to Burden. He had determined by now to kill him, but he had not decided how. O'Reilly's knife was like a sign from heaven. He seized it without a word and plunged it into Burden. He was wearing his gloves, because he was all ready to go for a walk with Professor Daly.

"Then he went away quietly. Burden lay on the hearthrug, as you saw, and we might never have succeeded in establishing the time of death but for Ned's visit to Burden ten minutes later.

"Now I come to the curious relationship that existed between Burden and Heaslip. Heaslip had been various things, including a male nurse, in the course of his life. He ended by being a buyer of ladies' underclothing at one of the big Dublin drapers. He was well paid, and good at his job. He likes things smooth and neat and pastel-colored, like seabirds' plumage, no doubt! He was efficient too, and that is still one of his characteristics, though he overrates himself a bit there. By contrast, Burden was strikingly inefficient and inept. He sought out Heaslip, or Aeneas Walsh, as he was then, and told him that he had evidence of a former crime of his. Aeneas Walsh agreed to pay him to be silent. Burden used to call at the shop every week to collect his money, a pound or so at first, and later about two pounds a time.

"Burden was really an odd blackmailer. He was not the stuff of a criminal at all. He used to get fond of his victims, and confide in them, and want to make friends with them. When they rejected him, as of course they did, he used to feel hurt and go away brooding on the hardness of the world.

"But Heaslip let him talk away, and beyond a mild protest by way of routine, he paid up like a lamb. So he very soon learned, as George learned on the train, about Burden's uncle who owned a hotel in Galway and who would probably leave it to his widowed niece when he died. He thought of himself as being young and attractive, so that any woman should be glad to get him, particularly a housekeeping widowed niece. This is the same queer idea we have come across before, that a widow should be so delighted to get a chance of marrying again that she will take anyone who offers. People go on thinking this although they see women getting married three or four times—it's quite common. Heaslip might never have done anything about it but for the fact that he came into a little money. It was not much—about a thousand pounds—but it was enough to keep him in moderate comfort for a year or two until his plan would have matured.

"So he gave up his job and left Dublin, without telling Burden, changed his name, and came here to live at Crane's Court. Burden was furious when he found he had gone. He was always losing his victims, and every time it happened he felt injured and misused. He explained this to Heaslip when he came here.

"I don't think Heaslip ever meant to murder Murray. He would have preferred to wait until Murray died naturally—provided he didn't take too long about it. But he overheard Murray talking to Miss Keane one night, asking her to marry him and promising her diamonds. So, in the crazy manner of such people, he decided that there was no time to be lost, and he went in and gave him the injection that killed him. Afterwards he was quietly attentive to Mrs. Henry; he was not going to risk frightening her off by appearing to be in too much of a hurry."

"I never even thought of marrying him," said Barbara. "He was like a reliable, benevolent uncle."

"He overdid it, it seems," said Mike. "The whole plan seemed to him quite likely to work. He had eliminated personal feeling from it altogether, except that he was glad, he says, that you turned out to be so attractive. He hastens to add that even if you had looked like the Hag of the Mill, he would not have been put off. I only repeat all this," said Mike uncomfortably, "so that the whole case will be finished in your minds, and you won't waste time on painful speculation."

"Thank you, Mike," said Barbara quietly.

It was the first time she had addressed him by his Christian name, and he found himself glowing with pleasure. He went on with his story.

"When he found that Burden had inherited the hotel, Heaslip was astonished. He never discovered how this came about, because he was afraid to show any interest by asking questions. He considered leaving Crane's Court then, but he had set his heart on owning it. It was then that he decided to kill Burden.

"He visited Burden in his rooms on the day that he arrived, and, as he had expected, Burden greeted him like a long-lost friend. Burden was a simple soul. He suggested that he might blackmail Heaslip again, but Heaslip pointed out that since Burden no longer needed the money, this would not be sensible. Burden thought he was buying Heaslip's friendship by keeping the secret of his changed name and by ceasing to blackmail him.

"Presently Heaslip saw, to his horror, that Miss Keane had gone to work on Burden and showed distinct signs of success. He would have enjoyed killing her, he says, but he knew it would be more economical to kill Burden. He hates Miss Keane for having made the murder of Burden suddenly necessary. He thinks that if he had had more time to plan it, he would never have been found out. As he went on, of course, it became easier to kill, and as soon as George announced that he was going to marry Mrs. Henry, he decided to put him out of the way too. He had no intention, now that Mrs. Henry had at last become the owner of Crane's Court, of allowing it to slip through his fingers.

"Your death, George, was going to be made to look like heart failure—the insulin again, of course. It had gone about that you had a weak heart, but Heaslip did not realize that this had made you determined never to marry. You had not really taken serious steps to ensure that no one heard about your heart?"

"I guessed it would become known gradually," said George. "I just tried to postpone the day."

"Morgan told me very early that your heart was sound. He'll never forgive me for using him. He's going to complain to everyone about it."

"I'll see him," said George. "I have no complaint!"

"I'm glad to hear that. I made shameless use of you to force Heaslip to convict himself. The only justification is that it worked. You see, by a process of elimination, and by watching Heaslip, I had to come to the conclusion that he was our man. His anger against Burden seemed more personal than one would expect from a scientific, detached man. And still he was said to be on good terms with Burden. Again, when I told him I suspected that Mrs. Robinson had a hand in Burden's death, he looked at me with pitying amusement. I did not think this was a normal reaction. It was all very nebulous, but I was sure I was right. Have you ever played the game of 'Twenty Questions'? You know how it happens that after you have collected a certain amount of information, the answer suddenly presents itself. You know you are right. You ask more questions and still you are no nearer to proof. The only way to be sure is to announce your solution and ask for confirmation.

"So it was in this case. I could not prove anything. Technically speaking, George could have been the murderer, as I showed him, but psychologically he did not fit in at all. I had let Heaslip know that George was in his way, and George had obligingly confirmed that in Heaslip's hearing, by announcing his engagement. I hoped that Heaslip would now attack George but this time I wanted him to feel that he was going to get away with it. So I dug up the latest cat, and then I planted Colm outside George's door, where Heaslip saw him, and guessed that George was now the favourite suspect. George was to be found dead of heart failure, as I've said. Then the police were to close up their case, with George in the role of murderer, and go away satisfied. George played up beautifully, and it all worked out so that we got our evidence. I did *not* intend that Mahon should wait while Heaslip chased you around the room," Mike finished angrily. "He could have interfered long before he did."

"Don't blame Mahon," said George happily. "You have no idea how much I enjoyed that run around."

"Earlier in the evening I had telephoned the Guards in Dublin, and asked them if any of Burden's blackmailees had been a bird-watcher. They gave me the name of Aeneas Walsh, and the description fitted Heaslip. That was the only tangible piece of evidence we had. I prayed for a dropped glove, or a waistcoat button, or even a cigarette end, but Heaslip was too clever to make any of these obvious mistakes. He should have changed his hobby to stamp-collecting when he came here."

"What am I going to do with Mrs. Fennell?" said Barbara. "It would be a pity to put her into a home just for her chance share in all this."

"What does Martin think?" asked Mike. "Has she got any worse under the strain?"

"No, I don't think so. I should say she will be the same as usual." Martin stood up and went over to the door. He watched Mike uneasily as he went on, "She's very happy about the future. She's looking forward to meeting you tomorrow, Mike, because I managed to persuade her that you are really the ghost of Sir Rodney Crane. That's why she's going to tell you about Heaslip." Martin opened the door as he saw Mike's expression and said rapidly, over his shoulder, "I told her you'll come and kill her cats for her in future, and visit her twice a week as well. That's the little quid pro quo I was talking about. You *said* you didn't care what I offered her. You said—"

With a low roar, Mike leaped out of his chair and shot across the room. But Martin was off long before he reached the door, and they could hear his little shoes skipping away down the hall.

"It's no use," said Mike. "I should be thankful he's got away. I'd have wrung his neck if I caught him. But he'll turn up grinning at my next case as if nothing had happened."

He dropped despondently into his chair.

"It will be interesting to be a ghost," said Daly mischievously. "I'd rather like the job myself."

"Do you think she'd allow me to transfer it to you?" asked Mike hopefully.

"Not a chance," said the old man, shaking his head. "She knows me too well."

"She's a very nice old lady," said George consolingly. "You'll get quite fond of visiting her. And when you have finished you can come up to the hotel and have dinner with us."

Mike looked better pleased at this, but he was already planning to make

Colm MacDonagh his deputy ghost. He had been informed that Colm had great charm.

"Then there is Eleanor Keane," said Barbara. "I don't know what to do about her either."

"She has made her own arrangements," said Daly. "She confided in me this evening that she is going to get great with Joe and marry him in due course."

"Marry Joe! But I thought—"

"Yes, she has at last decided against bettering herself. She's convinced now that Fate is against her. And she's right. She had just decided to confer her affections on Heaslip! She had come to the conclusion that he was the most eligible person remaining—and the next thing is that he's arrested for murder. So she says she's finished with the so-called upper classes now, and that the only people you can trust are the people you can understand. She says that Joe's mother runs a lodging-house, and that she and Joe will take it over and make a small hotel of it."

"But how does Joe like this?" asked Barbara wonderingly. "She and Joe are always quarreling."

"Joe has had his eye on her for years," said Daly. "It's his idea that they run the lodging-house together. But he says he wouldn't have anything to do with her till she dropped her high notions. She dropped them this evening at the moment of Heaslip's arrest, and tomorrow she's going to make the acquaintance of Joe's mother."

"In these parts," said Mike, "they say that it is a sure sign that a boy and a girl are falling in love when they throw stones at each other."

"That is known as 'The way they court in Glann,'" said Daly. He got up and yawned luxuriously. The clock in the hall struck two in its habitual whisper. "And now, to bed, if you please."

As they got up to go, Barbara said:

"There is one thing I want to know, George. Who is this Dr. Moore, and why did you choose him at all?"

"I knew him in college," said George tolerantly. "He was a big gom from the country then. I remember that almost the only remark he was ever known to make was, 'Arrah, go on, now!'"

"And you picked him as your doctor! You let him change your whole life, and never asked for a consultation!"

"Let no one ever say a word against Mick Moore," said George firmly. "Tomorrow morning I'm going to write him a letter of thanks."

THE END